MU[illegible] IN THE PARK

A completely unputdownable cozy mystery

VERONICA HELEY

The Ellie Quicke Mysteries Book 9

JOFFE
Ostara
CLASSICS

Revised edition 2024
Joffe Books, London
www.joffebooks.com

First published by Severn House in Great Britain in 2007

This paperback edition was first published
in Great Britain in 2024

Cover art by Dee Dee Book Covers

ISBN: 978-1-83526-374-7

CHAPTER ONE

Ellie Quicke was no longer a woebegone widow. Sometimes she even felt like a merry widow. Fiftyish and prematurely silver-haired, she'd discovered the pleasures of independence, made some good friends, and once or twice even stood up to her dreadful daughter Diana.

On that fine summer's day Ellie was thinking how pleasant life would be if only she could be left in peace to work in her garden, to babysit for her grandson once or twice a week and to have the occasional coffee and chat with her friends. However, she was realistic enough to know that life is not always a bed of roses . . . as she found to her cost when a dangerous dog was let loose in the park nearby.

* * *

Baby-faced Mick had been warned not to let Toby off his chain in public, but it was safe enough to set him free in the park, wasn't it? There was hardly anyone about. It was a hot summer's afternoon and he wished he'd a baseball cap to cover his shaven head. He also wished someone would come along using a mobile. Someone easily scared. He needed some cash. The aunt had given him some, but not enough.

He spotted a couple of young black boys larking about on a mountain bike. He could get a good whack for that bike in a car-boot sale. There were a couple of women pushing baby buggies some distance away, but down here under the trees by the river it was quiet and shady.

'Let us have a ride then,' Mick said to the boys. They stared at him, uneasy. Were they stupid or were they stupid! The younger boy clung to the bike but the other looked round for . . . who? Mother? Father? A strongly built black woman was sitting on a bench some way off, attending to a child whose shoe had come off.

'Give us!' said Mick, laying hands on the bike.

'Mu-um!' The older boy started to run back to the woman on the bench, who looked up, startled. The younger brother clung to the bike till Mick backhanded him and he sprawled on the ground, hiccupping.

Mick straddled the bike, laughing, calling Toby to his side. His baggy jeans hampered him, and he took a couple of seconds to pull them up. The woman began to lumber over to him, shouting, 'Clear off, you!'

The dog Toby growled, heavy head swinging to face the woman, who raised her arm to swipe at him. Toby knew a threat when he saw one, and so did Mick. Panicking, he gave the fatal command.

'Kill, Toby! Kill!'

Toby launched himself at the woman. He didn't knock her to the ground but got her upper arm in his powerful jaws. Blood spurted everywhere. She tried to shake him off, but Toby had been bred for fighting and knew how to hang on. Her boys screamed. One ran away, the other jumped from one foot to the other, helpless, not knowing what to do. The little girl stood by the bench where the woman had left her, finger in mouth, eyes wide in shock, mute.

The dog shook the woman's arm to and fro, worrying it. Gasping, she sank to the ground. The dog lost interest when she no longer moved.

Satisfied that she was no longer a threat, Mick mounted the bike and with the dog loping along behind him, cycled out of the park.

* * *

Some problems are insoluble, thought Ellie, contemplating the disastrous effect of rain on Albertine. Last week her favourite rambling rose had been covered with clusters of pale pink buds promising a spectacle to gladden her heart, but two days of rain had blackened the buds. Years of gardening experience had taught Ellie that there was nothing to be done about it, for Albertine would not flower properly this year. Oh a few buds might struggle through. The plant might even go on producing the odd flower till well into the autumn, but there would be no spectacular shower of pink blossom covering the fence as happened in drier seasons.

A couple of schoolboys passed along the alley at the bottom of her garden; she waved to them and they waved back. Nice lads. School was out and they were carrying plastic bags with them, so it must be their day to visit the local swimming pool.

Back to the garden. Well, what can't be mended must be endured, as her mother used to say. Ellie fetched her secateurs from the garden shed and bent down to dead-head some love-in-the-mist, which had seeded itself around the sundial in the middle of the lawn. She had no idea where the original plant or seed had come from and rather liked the flowers, but knew that if the seed heads were left on the plants there would be not ten, but a hundred, plants next year.

Bother — was that her phone? She'd left the doors and windows open at the back of the house, and could hear it even halfway down the garden. She'd promised herself a whole afternoon in the garden and was half inclined to ignore it. Let the caller leave a message. It couldn't be anything important, could it?

Well, she supposed it could. She ditched the seed heads in the compost bin and made her way up the slope to her house, through the kitchen and into the hall. Just as she got there, the answerphone clicked in. Someone in trouble, gasping, crying. 'Ellie, are you there? Oh, please God, be there!'

Ellie dropped her secateurs to snatch up the phone. 'Felicity? Is that you? I was in the garden and—'

'Can you come, Ellie? Please! I can't . . . I don't know what to do!'

An emergency of some sort, obviously. No more gardening this morning. 'Calm down,' said Ellie, sitting on the chair to ease off her gardening shoes. Where had she left her sandals? In the conservatory?

'But I . . . you don't realize . . . I think she's dead! Those poor children!'

Ellie felt faint. 'Who's dead? Not the baby?' Not little Mel, surely!

'No, not the baby, of course not. Oh, my precious!' The wailing noise increased. Had Felicity picked the baby up? Mel was only six weeks old but had a powerful set of lungs on her. 'Ellie, please! Come!'

Dear Lord, give me strength. Help Felicity, look after little Mel. Whatever's wrong, show me how to help them.

The phone went down and Ellie looked for her handbag, checking that keys, money and mobile phone were in it. Felicity lived the other side of the park, and Ellie didn't drive. Would it be quicker to phone for a cab and wait for it to come, or to walk over? She'd better walk. *Dear Lord, have mercy.*

Ellie opened the front door and took a step out before realizing she had no shoes on her feet. She went back for her sandals, then saw she'd left the back door and windows open, an invitation to burglars. She closed doors and locked up, put on her sandals, reached for a light jacket on her way through the hall, and hurried out into the sunshine.

Felicity had been left a wealthy widow after her first, and highly unpleasant, husband died. A second marriage to Ellie's older and charming architect cousin Roy was working well and had recently been blessed with the birth of baby Mel — short for Melissa. Felicity had proved a good if slightly anxious mother, though Roy was still ambivalent about becoming a father at his age.

If Mel wasn't in trouble — and her caterwauling down the phone seemed to indicate that her lungs were in full working order — then who was? What was all that about a woman dying?

After a hurried walk through the park, Ellie, panting slightly — she always intended to take more exercise — unlatched Felicity's front gate and saw her standing in the doorway, holding Mel. Felicity was crying and so was the baby.

'Gracious me,' said Ellie, holding out her arms for Mel. 'Give me the baby and find the tissues.'

'She's wet,' sobbed Felicity, clinging to the child still, 'and she's hungry. Tell me what to do.'

Reflecting that common sense didn't always go with beauty and wealth, Ellie urged her friend indoors and almost fell over the baby buggy, which had been parked askew in the hall. Felicity jiggled Mel. Mel howled; Ellie clutched at her temper and took charge.

'Felicity, lead the way to the kitchen, please.' The family more or less lived in the sunlit family room at the back of the house. There was more evidence of Felicity's disturbed state of mind on the way through the hall; a handbag sprawled open on the carpet, Mel's blanket lay half out of the buggy, the telephone had not been properly replaced on its stand. Ellie put the telephone back, sweeping Felicity and crying baby through into the kitchen.

'Give me Mel and I'll change her.' There was a changing pad and everything a baby that age could need on a table at the side. Felicity handed Mel over with a wail, sank into a chair and began to rock to and fro.

Mel was red in the face, her little fists screwed tight, her legs bent. Indigestion, croup? Hunger? Ellie changed the sopping pad, but Mel didn't stop crying.

'You'd better feed her,' said Ellie, carrying the baby over to Felicity.

Instead of taking her, Felicity doubled over. 'Ooooh!'

Had Felicity's milk dried up? But how? The girl had been so proud of her ability to feed the baby. Yet her blouse had been buttoned up awry, her hair was all over the place and she looked distraught.

'Has your milk dried up?'

Felicity only wailed the harder. Ellie jiggled Mel, whose cries had the penetration of a dentist's drill. 'Have you got any baby formula? A bottle?'

The girl shook her head. Of course not. Felicity had been boring everyone within earshot for weeks about the importance of breastfeeding, and naturally hadn't taken any of the usual precautions. Meanwhile, Mel was famished.

Ellie had only managed to carry one child to term and had been unable to breastfeed her so wasn't absolutely sure what to do. If she gave Mel some watered-down milk, would it agree with her, or would it be brought straight back up? Ellie hesitated. She knew you shouldn't put a strain on the digestive system of young babies. *Dear Lord, what do I do now?*

The answer came to the back of her mind. Boiled water. There was some water in the kettle and she switched it on. 'Have you a bottle, Felicity?'

Felicity shook her head, blonde mop flying.

Ellie investigated the cutlery drawer and found a teaspoon. Mel continued to scream. Ellie let the kettle boil, poured some into a cup to cool and made herself comfortable on a chair with Mel in her arms.

Ellie dribbled the first spoonful of cooled water into the baby's mouth. Mel gulped. Surprised. She smacked her lips, doubtful of the taste. Another spoonful. Accepted.

At least there was silence now.

Felicity raised her blotchy face from her arms. 'What are you giving her? You shouldn't be doing that.'

'It will fill her stomach till we can get some formula.'

'But I don't want her to . . . my milk will come back; I know it will.'

'Might. Might not.' Ellie continued to dribble water into the baby, and the baby's face lost its hectic tinge and began to regain its normal colouring. 'What caused this?'

Felicity took a deep breath, pushed her hair back out of her eyes. 'I don't know. It was so awful. Surely it can't be that serious, can it? I keep telling myself she'll be all right, she can't be dead; but there was a lot of blood, and . . . I can't stop thinking about it. I thought I might faint, but knew I mustn't because of Mel. It was getting near her feeding time, so I came straight back. Then I tried to feed her and I couldn't.'

'Shock,' said Ellie, spooning away. 'Have you given yourself some hot tea with sugar in it?'

'Roy's out of the office today,' said Felicity, taking no notice of Ellie's advice. 'I thought of ringing him, but he's finding it difficult, having a child when he didn't expect to be a father at his age. He won't help with her at all, saying it's my job, and of course it is my job, but he won't even pick her up or anything. Oh, I shouldn't have complained about him, and I'm not complaining really, but—' she got to her feet and gazed around, flapping her hands — 'which reminds me that I ought to be doing something about supper, because . . . but then I thought if I just drank a lot of water, I'd be all right. But Mel started to cry and . . .' She burst into tears all over again.

Ellie suppressed irritation. Felicity normally gave the impression of being a capable woman, but a legacy of her first marriage was that she could be thrown into a trembling state by criticism. Or shock.

Mel sucked the water down, pulling faces. It didn't taste nearly the same as her mother's milk, but she was so thirsty, it would do for now. She was a strong child. Such a prolonged screaming fit would have tired another child out, but not Mel. She took after Roy in being such a strong, healthy baby.

Ellie ignored Felicity's tears. 'From the beginning. You've been out with the buggy. You took Mel for a walk in the park? And then what happened?'

Felicity tried to speak, collapsed back on to her chair and began to hyperventilate. 'Hoo, hoo!'

Ellie needed three hands to cope with the situation; two for Mel and at least one for Felicity. Make that four hands. She put the teaspoon back into the cup and reached over to push Felicity's head down between her knees. Mel began to huff and puff. Ellie grabbed the teaspoon and dribbled another mouthful into the baby. Could she get hold of one of Felicity's neighbours to help her? But no, neither of them would be of the slightest assistance; one being too old and the other too toffee-nosed.

Ellie hooked her chair nearer the table, shoved another teaspoonful into Mel and made a grab for her handbag. Mobile phone. Who could she ring? She knew two other youngish mothers with babies, competent people both, who could take charge of Felicity and/or the baby, but both had older children in tow. She couldn't ask them to load their children into cars and come over to help.

However, her old friend Rose might be free. For years they'd worked together in the charity shop in the Avenue, while of late Rose had been acting as housekeeper and friend for Ellie's aged aunt Drusilla. Ellie dropped the teaspoon to press buttons, then held the phone in the crook of her neck while she resumed dribbling water into Mel's mouth. Felicity lifted her head and leaned back in her chair, eyes closed, her face greenish-white.

'Rose, dear. Ellie here. Are you terribly busy?'

'In the middle of making some soup, asparagus. Your aunt fancies a little home-made soup now and then, nothing too strong tasting. Is something wrong?'

'A storm in a teacup, I hope. Felicity's had a nasty shock. Her milk has dried up and she hasn't any baby formula. I can't leave her. I'm feeding Mel with boiled water but she's so hungry it won't hold her for long.'

Rose became anxious. 'Baby's not hurt, is she? Should I come round straight away? Miss Quicke won't mind if it's an emergency.'

'Bless you, dear. Can you take a cab — charge it to me — buy some formula and a bottle at the chemist's at the end of the Avenue and bring it over? Roy's out and Felicity's upset.'

'I'll be round in a jiffy.' Uncharacteristically terse, Rose put the phone down. Ellie hoped Rose would remember to turn the gas off under the soup she was making, because when a day started to go wrong, sometimes it kept on going wrong, and it would be just their bad luck if Rose forgot to turn out the gas and the house burned down. Ellie spooned the last mouthful into the baby and told herself not to be silly. Of course Rose would turn out the gas before leaving. She might look like a little brown mouse, but she was a very competent housekeeper and looked after Miss Quicke beautifully.

Ellie considered telling Felicity to pull herself together and discarded the idea. She had a horrid feeling that the girl had seen something that would unsettle the strongest of nerves. Mel smacked her lips thoughtfully, but when the next spoonful didn't materialize at once, gave a deep sigh and closed her bright blue eyes. Her head fell back, her limbs went limp and with a bit of luck she might sleep for a few minutes. Or should Ellie try to burp her first? Yes, it would be better to get her wind up first, after that bout of screaming. Ellie raised the child to her shoulder and was rewarded with a resounding burp, though Mel didn't even bother to open her eyes.

Well, let sleepy babies lie. Careful not to wake her, Ellie deposited Mel in her recliner and fastened her in.

Felicity opened her eyes, but her dull expression showed she was far from recovering her usual poise. 'Ellie, you should have waited till my milk came back. She's not supposed to take food from anyone but me.'

'Yes, dear,' said Ellie, understanding that Felicity was upset not only by whatever she'd seen that morning, but also because she'd not been able to feed her baby herself. Ellie switched the kettle on again. 'Now Mel will probably sleep for a bit, Rose will be here shortly, and I think you'd better have a nice hot drink and take a nap. Where is Roy, by the way?'

'I'm not sure. He's got this meeting, something to do with some flats he wants to convert and I ought to know where, but—' she lifted both hands to her forehead and beat on it — 'I can't think straight. He's bringing someone back for supper, which I haven't started yet. I did think of ringing him on his mobile, but he doesn't like being disturbed at work and that's how it should be. Anyway, I don't want Mel being put on a bottle.'

'No, of course you don't, dear,' said Ellie, making a mug of tea and stirring two spoonfuls of sugar into it. 'Drink this. Have you got any aspirin you can take?'

'I can't take aspirin while I'm feeding Mel.'

'Of course you can't, but a couple now won't do any harm. All gone by tomorrow, when we'll be able to see how we get on.' Ellie handed over the mug.

Felicity sipped. 'You shouldn't have asked Rose to come over. She's got enough to do, looking after that big house and catering for Aunt Drusilla.' Roy was Miss Quicke's illegitimate but acknowledged son. It had never seemed appropriate for Felicity to call the older woman 'Mother-in-Law'. So 'Aunt Drusilla' she had become, which suited all parties.

Ellie said, 'Can you tell me what happened now?'

Felicity shuddered from head to foot. Her colour — which had been returning — fled again, but she firmed her shoulders and her chin. 'I'm being silly, aren't I? It can't be that serious. I was going round the park with Caroline, who's another first-time mother, almost as old as me. I often see her when I go round the park. We were talking about the Music for Tots group, how soon I should take Mel. Then there was some shouting. I didn't take any notice. Kids are always larking about, shouting. I was adjusting the parasol on the buggy to keep the sun off Mel.

'Caroline went haring off, shouting something, I didn't hear what. I saw her bending over a woman on the ground. I thought someone had fainted. There were numerous kids running around, screeching. Caroline used to work at the hospital. I thought . . . an accident . . . the woman had twisted her leg or something. I thought Caroline could cope. Then I saw the blood . . .'

Felicity bent forward, dropping her head between her knees, setting the mug down clumsily so that some of the tea spilled.

Ellie pushed the mug further on to the table. 'Breathe deeply. Take your time.'

Felicity sat up again, hand to head. Her colour was still bad, but she was gradually regaining control. 'She must have been mugged. She was bleeding all over the path. Caroline yelled at me to get my mobile, ring for an ambulance. I . . . I . . . just stood there. I couldn't move. I thought, Caroline used to work at the hospital. She can cope better than I.'

'Yes,' said Ellie, gently. She understood that Felicity was now feeling guilt because she hadn't acted quickly. 'Then what did you do?'

Felicity shook her head, making her blonde hair swing. 'I wasn't thinking straight. I said I hadn't got my mobile with me, that I'd forgotten it. You know, I really thought I *had* forgotten it, although I found it in my bag when I got back. I expect she'd just fainted. I ought to ring Caroline, find out what happened. I feel so stupid! I shouldn't be going to pieces like this, it's ridiculous. I'm sure the woman is going to be all right. Mel was beginning to wake up and want her next feed. So I told Caroline I'd get someone to help, but I didn't see anyone on my way out of the park and so I . . . I came home. Only when I tried to feed Mel, I couldn't.' She tried to stand up but didn't make it. 'I ought to ring Caroline and apologize. I feel so awful that I didn't help.'

Ellie soothed her. 'You're in no fit state to go dashing around. I expect Caroline managed to report it all right. Do you know her second name, where she lives?'

Felicity gulped back tears. 'Can't remember. No, wait a minute. It's Tinker or Tiller or something like that. Something beginning with "T". Glenavon. That's the name of their house. On the next corner. Her husband works for the council. I've never met him but Caroline's nice. Oh, I'm all of a tremble. Do you think you could ring her for me?'

'I'll see what I can do,' said Ellie, helping Felicity to her feet. 'Now, up you go to bed and have a little rest while I look after Mel. Don't you worry about a thing.'

'I couldn't have done anything if I'd stayed, could I?'

'Of course not,' murmured Ellie, wondering what she'd have done in Felicity's place. Being in charge of a small baby alters your priorities. Felicity's instinct had been to look after Mel, and perhaps she was right. 'You go and have a good rest, and I'll see to everything.'

* * *

Mick slowed down as he reached his aunt's house, thinking he'd best stash the bike somewhere for the time being, if she were around. But no, her 4x4 wasn't in the driveway. Good. The uncle was away somewhere, business stuff, not due back for a couple of weeks, which was about as long as Mick could stand living here.

It was a big old house, stucco-fronted, detached. There was a semicircular driveway in front, and a converted coach house at the side with plenty of room for her absent son's old banger.

Mick took the bike through a covered passage to the back of the house, dragging Toby behind him. The aunt didn't like dogs and wouldn't let him in the house.

Once on the patio, Mick secured Toby's chain to a garden chair and put the bike in the garden shed. He wasn't sure if he should try to scrub the dog down or not. Some dogs liked a daily shower. Personally, Mick couldn't be bothered with all that washing, and he wasn't sure that he could handle Toby if the dog objected to being scrubbed down. On the other hand, there were patches of dried blood on the dog's coat which were a dead giveaway if the woman in the park decided to sue him for assault.

Maybe he should throw a bucket of water over the dog and be done with it. He drew a bucket of water from an outside tap and threw it over the dog, who went wild and shot off over a flower bed, taking the chair with him and cutting a furrow through the plants.

Mick screeched with laughter.

CHAPTER TWO

The boiled water had stayed the worst of Mel's hunger pangs for the time being but was not sufficient to keep her quiet for long. Even before Ellie had discovered from the phone book that there was neither a Tinker, a Tailor, nor indeed a candle-stick-maker living locally, Mel was grumbling. Fearful that the baby might wake Felicity, Ellie picked Mel up and jiggled her, carrying her into the study which overlooked the road.

A minicab drew up and Rose eased herself out, carrying aloft two large bags of shopping. Someone else painfully inched their way out of the minicab behind Rose, scolded the driver for not helping her out, and then scolded him for trying to do so. Drusilla Quicke, Ellie's wealthy and sometimes difficult aunt.

Ellie hastened to open the front door. Rose, encumbered by her packages, still tried to help Miss Quicke along. For once the old woman leaned heavily on her stick. A hip operation the previous year had worked well enough at the time, but it seemed to Ellie that every time she saw her aunt, Miss Quicke had shrunk yet again. It hurt Ellie to see her aunt ageing so fast.

Ellie had hoped Felicity had gone to bed, but on hearing the front door open, the girl appeared at the top of the stairs. She'd had a shower and was now in a white bath robe, barefoot. She was so pale she looked transparent. 'Ellie, did you speak to Caroline?'

Ellie called up the stairs. 'I will in a minute. Go and lie down again.' Felicity threw up her hands and disappeared into her bedroom.

Rose helped Miss Quicke over the doorstep. 'She would come,' said Rose, shaking her head as one does over a disobedient child.

'I need to know if something's upset my grandchild,' said Miss Quicke, stumping along the hall towards the kitchen, and seating herself in a chair with a sigh of relief. Ellie thought her aunt was probably in pain. Miss Quicke rarely left the house nowadays and it was a measure of her concern for her grandchild that she'd done so now. It would, of course, be as much as Ellie's life was worth to ask if her aunt would like a painkiller. Instead, Ellie put Mel back in her recliner and helped Rose to unpack her shopping. Mel was beginning to mew and fuss. In a moment or two, she'd be bawling her head off.

Rose was explaining what they'd bought. '. . . So we went to that good pharmacy in the Avenue, the independent one and not the chain store because they've got the best selection, and Miss Quicke said we should get everything, not just the formula for a baby, but the bottles and teats and this gadget for warming bottles to the right temperature, which is something I'd not thought of, and I think I'd better make up a bottle straight away, don't you think?' And to baby Mel, 'Coming, my cherub.'

Rose's own daughter showed no signs of producing a baby, and Rose had granny fever. Rose was looking forward to holding a baby in her arms again.

Miss Quicke used her stick to hook Ellie to her side. 'What happened?'

'Felicity had a bad scare in the park. Someone got mugged, there was a lot of blood and Felicity saw it. She got home, tried to feed Mel only to discover that her milk had dried up. She's in shock.'

'So she phoned you. Do I need to get my solicitor to look after her?'

'No, no. She didn't even see the actual assault. She was walking round the park with an acquaintance who went to help the victim. The friend asked Felicity to use her mobile to call an ambulance, but Felicity thought she'd left it at home, so couldn't. She wants me to ring her friend and find out what happened. I know where the woman lives but I can't find a telephone number for her. I wonder if I ought to pop round and find out what's happened. It's preying on Felicity's mind, rather.'

There was nothing wrong with Miss Quicke's brain. 'Feeling guilty about leaving her friend in the lurch, is she?'

Ellie winced. She wouldn't have put it quite so harshly, herself. Rose settled herself in a chair and picked up the baby. 'Who's a good girl, then?' said Rose, introducing Mel to the delights of the bottle. Rose was one happy bunny.

Mel's face indicated that she was unsure of this new procedure. Ellie held her breath while Mel considered rejecting the teat, but with the first squirt of milk inside her mouth, recognized proper nourishment and got on with the job.

Ellie let out her breath and picked up her conversation with her aunt, trying to defend Felicity. 'Small babies alter your perspective. Mel was her priority.'

The lines of Miss Quicke's face hardened. 'She phoned for an ambulance when she got back?'

Ellie was silent, frowning. She didn't think Felicity had done so.

Miss Quicke sighed. 'It all goes back to childhood, doesn't it? A selfish mother bullies Felicity, before passing her on to her first husband, who abused her in every possible way. Of course the girl takes the easiest way out when she's in trouble.'

'Not always,' said Ellie, 'and she was shocked rigid.'

'Yet I don't see you leaving a friend to look after a dying woman. Or Rose.'

They looked across at Rose, whose delight in Mel created an impression of sunshine at that end of the room.

'Itti-bitti-woo-woos,' cooed Rose. Mel's eyes widened. She'd never been addressed in such terms before, but the underlying love in Rose's voice was fully understood and accepted.

Ellie swivelled in her chair to look at the clock. 'I suppose I could pop round and ask this Caroline person what happened. It won't take a minute, and it will set Felicity's mind at rest.'

'Be off with you, then.'

Ellie rescued her handbag and left the house, closing the front door quietly behind her. A lovely summer afternoon. The park on the other side of the road shimmered in the heat, the trees almost but not yet ready to turn that blackish green which heralded the arrival of autumn.

The neighbouring houses were all detached, each one individually designed. Most were well kept. Some people had paved over the front garden to allow their cars to be taken off the road, and enclosed the parking area with electronically controlled gates, tipped with gold.

'Glenavon' sparkled with new paint. The owners had retained their front garden, which displayed a pleasing mixture of shrubs infilled with annuals. Ellie paused with her hand on the gate to appreciate the picture. The gate swung on its hinges without a sound and the bell push responded to pressure just as it should.

The woman who opened the door was even shorter than Ellie; a buxom lass in her late thirties, cradling a drowsy baby. Something brushed around Ellie's legs and she looked down to see a brindled cat contemplating the world outside.

'Don't let her out!' The woman tried to grab the cat while maintaining her hold on the baby.

'Got you,' said Ellie, grabbing the cat's collar. There was something odd about this cat. As Ellie picked her up, she squawked, but didn't try to fight free.

'That one has no sense and I'm worried she'll dash in front of a car.'

'I know, I know,' said Ellie, whose own cat was street-wise, but who knew of others which weren't. 'I'm so sorry to disturb you but I'm a friend of Felicity's, the girl you were in the park with. She got home safely but is in a bit of a state. She can't rest till she knows what happened to the woman who got mugged. I said I'd ring you and try to find out, but Felicity must have got your name wrong, and I couldn't find it in the telephone book.'

'I've seen you at church, haven't I? In the choir? I go sometimes with my mother who lives the other side of the shops. Didn't you used to work in the charity shop in the Avenue? Come in, come in.' The woman held the door open, while putting out a foot to stop a second cat — this one being fluffy and black — from investigating the great outdoors. 'I'm Caroline Topping, by the way.'

So Felicity hadn't got anywhere near the right name. 'Ellie Quicke. Yes, I worked in the charity shop for years.'

Caroline closed the front door, and bustled down a tiled corridor to a large, extended kitchen at the back of the house. This was a much older house than Felicity's but equally taken over by baby paraphernalia . . . and cats. Two more cats vanished through a cat flap into the garden as Ellie approached, while the fluffy black one followed the two women to where a line of feeding bowls had been placed on the floor. The cat in Ellie's arms struggled free and jumped down on to the floor. Only then did Ellie see that she was a hop-along, since one of her front legs was missing.

'Accident prone, that one,' said Caroline, depositing her baby in a bouncy recliner very like Felicity's, and pulling out a chair. 'Have a cuppa? I was going to. Feel I needed it. Just wait a sec while I feed the circus, then I'll be right with you.' She pushed her hair back from her forehead. 'Sorry, I'm a bit . . . you know . . . after . . . tired . . . not quite . . .' Her voice trailed away.

Ellie took charge. It was getting to be a habit. She pressed Caroline down on to a chair. 'You sit down while I feed the cats and make a cuppa.' The kettle had water in it, and the cupboard doors here were glass-fronted, which made it easy to see where everything was. The fridge was also easy to spot.

Two cats plopped back through the cat flap and watched from a safe distance as Ellie tipped food into their bowls and refilled the drinking water dish.

By the time the kettle had boiled and tea had been made, the cats were gulping down their food while Caroline had hoicked a tin of biscuits towards her and was tucking in. 'Carbohydrates,' she said, around a mouthful. 'Medicinal purposes. Two sugars, please; strong.'

Ellie walked around the black cat to deliver the tea, and seated herself, too.

'Stupid of me. Sorry,' said the girl, shaking her head at herself. 'Ought to be able to cope. Worked in reception at hospital for years. But that's different, isn't it?'

'You should see Felicity. Hyperventilating.'

'Nasty, very.' The girl crammed another biscuit into her mouth, closing her eyes, hands clutching her mug. 'I thought the police would never come. I was dying for a pee, too.'

Ellie said, 'Felicity feels really bad about leaving you.'

'It was OK. Like, I'm used to coping. Well, not used to . . . that. But on the whole, you know, I cope. Only, those kids . . . I wanted to bring them home with me and give them a cuddle. Common sense prevailed, just. Only think what my hubby would have said.' She tried to laugh, and almost made it.

'Kids?'

'Two boys and a girl. The eldest boy kept his head, sort of. Fetched her handbag for me so's I could ring for an ambulance. That's the last time I go out without my mobile fully charged, I can tell you. Jack's always saying, "You never know what will happen," and I'm always saying, "Well, what could happen?" And then it does happen, if you follow.'

Ellie nodded. The girl needed to talk. That was the way the shock was taking her.

'I still can't believe it.' The girl held out her hand, checking to see if it was still trembling. It was, slightly. 'I rang Jack's office. He was in a meeting. I said not to bother, I was perfectly all right, and I was all right at that point. Then I put the phone down and howled.'

Ellie glanced at the sleeping baby.

'Duncan's all right,' said Caroline. 'Trust him, the little beggar. I fed him straight off when I got home. Well, as soon as I'd got out of my clothes, and showered, that is. The fastest shower in the west, I can tell you. I thought feeding him would calm me down, and of course it did. A bit. Only as soon as he dropped off to sleep, it hit me.' She seized a piece of kitchen towel and mopped up. 'Dammit, I ought to have stopped crying by now.'

'Can you tell me what happened?'

Caroline did some deep breathing. 'We were in that quiet bit of the park where the river takes a bend, right? Almost the furthest you can get from the play centre and the swings. There were some kids larking about on a bike. I really didn't take any notice, you don't, do you? Just . . . everyday. Then there was some shouting. Not play shouting. Alarmed shouting. I thought uh-oh, trouble, and it crossed my mind then that my mobile might be flat, you know how it does?

'Felicity was talking about . . . I can't remember what, but she wasn't looking, and I said, "Did you see that?" And she said, "What?" And then . . . it all happened so fast, and we were too far away. I thought afterwards that if I'd left my buggy with Felicity and run, but I don't think I could have got there in time. I've never been much good at sports day and that, couldn't run a marathon to save my life.' She was trying to make a joke of it.

Ellie thought, Here's another one feeling guilty about not helping enough.

'I rushed over as fast as I could, cutting across the grass with the buggy, but by that time the kids' mother had . . .' She did some more deep breathing. 'The dog was big, really huge, and the boy was laughing! I couldn't believe it! It was so . . . like something in a cartoon, you know? Only you don't really see blood in cartoons, do you? I mean, a dog attacks in a cartoon and the hero shakes the dog off, or whacks him with a piece of wood, or . . . I'm rambling, aren't I?'

'That's OK. So it wasn't a mugging, then?'

Caroline stared at her. Then shook her head. 'Can you be mugged by a dog? Moot point. I'd say not, really, but . . .' She took a deep breath. 'I keep seeing it over and over. I wish I didn't.'

'Take your time.'

'That's what the police said. I don't know whether the lad, the thief, saw me coming or not, but he got on the bike and went off with the dog. By the time I got there, the woman was sort of . . . sighing. Dying in front of my eyes. I worked in the hospital for years. I ought to be used to it. But seeing it happen in the park with her kids around her, it got to me. Her kids were screaming for her to wake up. I thought, if I could only stem the blood . . . but I couldn't, though I tried. The artery was spurting blood, you see. It's very quick when you get an artery. The boy never touched her, by the way. Only the dog.'

Ellie shuddered. She was rather ashamed of it, but she really didn't like strange dogs. She'd been bitten by a dog once, when she was a child. Ever since she'd been more than slightly wary of dogs.

Caroline seemed to have come to a halt. Ellie prompted her. 'So you asked one of the kids to get his mother's mobile phone, and you sent for an ambulance?'

'And the police. The two boys were beside themselves, half understanding, half not believing. The little girl was mute, thumb in mouth. I took them to the bench where the mother had been sitting while we waited for someone to come. I asked them their names.' She hid her face in her hands. 'Oh, that's awful. They told me their names and I've forgotten them already. They had different surnames, I remember that. Different fathers. The little girl didn't belong to them but was being looked after by the woman who died. The boys were second generation Jamaican, or maybe from St Kitts. I wonder what will happen to the children now. They said their daddies came to visit but didn't live with them. Social services will take them, I suppose.'

'Who arrived first, police or ambulance?'

'Dead heat. A couple of joggers came by, and a woman walking her two golden retrievers. Nice woman, I've often seen her in the park, she's just had an operation on her knee. She asked what had happened, stayed with me till they came. I told them what I'd seen, which wasn't much, I couldn't even describe the boy with the dog properly. They said it might come back to me, and I suppose it might though I really don't want it to, if you know what I mean.'

Ellie nodded. She knew what Caroline meant.

Caroline looked around her, took a deep breath. 'So, life goes on, right? We're born, we live a while, and we die. I suppose we all hope to die in bed with grieving relatives around us, in the fullness of time, etcetera, but it doesn't always work out that way, does it? I'll be all right in the morning, I expect. Had better be. Duncan's just about sleeping through the night now, and he doesn't seem to have been upset by all this. Well, he didn't see any of it, did he? Lucky beggar, dozing in his buggy. You say Felicity was upset? Nice girl. A bit fragile. Hope she'll be all right.'

'Her milk dried up, but I got someone to take her round some formula.'

Caroline nodded. 'I'm a first-timer, too. Had lots of misses over the years, thought I'd have to be content with my cats from the rescue centre, which I love to bits, but then . . . whoops, surprise! This little packet came along just when I'd stopped thinking about it. I never managed to breastfeed Duncan, hungry little pudding that he is. I had to put him on the bottle before I left hospital, had a Caesar, you know, complications. But all right now. I'll call round to see Felicity tomorrow, shall I?' She got to her feet, indicating that the interview was over. 'Thanks for letting me talk. I do feel better now.'

Ellie rose, too. 'You're very kind, Caroline. I'm sure Felicity will appreciate it.'

'What are friends for, eh?'

* * *

Felicity opened the front door as Ellie turned into the drive. It didn't look as if the girl had allowed herself a rest for there were dark marks around her eyes, and her skin looked paper-thin. She'd managed to put on a clean T-shirt and fresh jeans, and had thrust her feet into flip-flops.

'Aunt Drusilla told me you'd gone round to see Caroline. The woman is all right, isn't she?'

'Afraid not,' said Ellie, wondering if she'd physically be able to pick Felicity up off the floor if she fainted.

'Oooh!' Felicity clutched at the newel post at the bottom of the stairs.

Ellie guided the girl into the kitchen and sat her down. Rose and Aunt Drusilla both looked up, questions in their eyes.

Ellie said, 'It was quick. A dog got out of control and savaged a woman, who died. Caroline borrowed a mobile and called the ambulance and the police. She'll try to pop round tomorrow, see if Felicity's all right.'

Felicity was trembling, pushing her fingers up through her hair, holding on to her head. How to calm the girl down?

Rose put Mel over her shoulder to burp her. Mel obliged. Someone used their key to open the front door and the man of the house called out, 'Yoo-hoo! Are you there, Felicity? We're a trifle early.'

Felicity shot to her feet, looking anguished. 'I forgot. Roy's bringing someone back for supper!'

Roy appeared in the doorway to the hall, six foot of silver-haired, blue-eyed charm. Roy was a successful architect, he loved his wife and mother dearly and would give the shirt off his back to someone in need, but he'd been brought up to expect calm and tranquillity when he got home in the evenings. He also expected supper on the table on the dot, especially when he'd brought a colleague home for a meal. Which is what he had done. A round-headed, dark-skinned man in a good suit.

Roy's experience of having a baby in the house had so far been without stress. Felicity was a domestic creature at heart, she'd had an easy enough birth and been able to provide for her husband and feed Mel at times which didn't inconvenience him. It had always been she who got up to feed Mel in the night, and she'd never asked Roy to change the baby's nappy or do anything other than smile at her now and again.

Now, instead of a quiet house, a wife prettily dressed and supper ready for the table, Roy was presented with a wife looking like a ghost, Ellie, Rose and his mother ensconced and no meal in sight.

'Oh, Roy, I'm so sorry!' Felicity dashed to the fridge, opened it, dithered, dashed to a cupboard. Didn't take anything out. Wept. At this rate, thought Ellie, Felicity would soon begin to apologize for her existence. As Miss Quicke had observed, Felicity had been trained to slavery by her mother and her first husband.

It would help, thought Ellie, if Roy would take his wife into his arms and comfort her, but Roy wasn't yet accustomed to being a father figure. He knew all about being a lover and a husband, but hadn't realized that a successful marriage requires either party to take on the role of parent every now and then.

He stood there, gaping, clearly not knowing how to cope with this unexpected situation.

'Yes, but . . .' said Roy, clearly not knowing what to do next. In his book the wife looked after the children, and the husband was the hunter-gatherer who left affairs of the household to her. He looked at the door through which they'd come, clearly longing to escape.

Ellie sighed. The older she got, the more chances she saw to interfere in other people's lives. Now was such a moment. If she didn't do something, Roy might well go off with his colleague, leaving Felicity in tears. Felicity would feel inadequate, Roy would feel hard done by, and he'd probably compound the problem by taking his guest off to a restaurant for supper, which wouldn't help Felicity, or train Roy to become a caring husband and father.

Ellie put her arm around Felicity and urged her towards Roy. 'Dear Roy, your poor wife has been so brave, but she's had a really nasty shock. I've told her she ought to rest, but she was worried about getting supper ready for you. Can you make her see sense, do you think?'

Roy took his cue from Ellie and gave Felicity a hug. 'What's the matter, then, Flick?'

Felicity began on a tangle of sentences about a mugging in the park and not knowing what to do and finding her milk dried up, and she was so sorry about supper.

Roy's colleague looked understandably embarrassed. 'What a dreadful thing. I can see it's not convenient, so . . .' He waved towards the hall.

Roy looked worried. Was this an important client? Did his business depend on keeping him sweet?

Ellie caught Miss Quicke's eye, and then Rose's. 'Supper will only be a few minutes. Felicity must go up and rest, but if you two men can just relax in the sitting room with the newspapers or the telly for a short while, we'll soon have some food on the table.'

Miss Quicke levered herself to her feet. She had vast business interests of her own, so if anyone understood the importance of a business contact, she did. 'Of course you must stay, Mr . . . whatever. The sitting room is the first door on the right down the hall. Make yourself at home there. Roy, your wife needs to be given a sedative and put to bed. Can you see to her? She'll be all right in the morning, but she needs to rest now. Rose, you'd better put Mel to bed and rustle up some supper for the men. Ellie, you and I are only in the way here, so you may ring for a cab and see me home.'

* * *

Mick was bored. The aunt had said he could use the guest room and smoke there if he must, but the telly in the guest room was one of the old-fashioned kind and he preferred the plasma screen in her sitting room. The aunt had weird ideas about him helping her at her parties and going to the youth club and dead boring stuff like that. As if.

He pulled out his last fag, lit up and rested his feet on the glass top of the coffee table. He'd fed Toby the last of the food he'd brought with him. Tich had made him promise to feed and exercise Toby properly, but where was he supposed to get the money for his food? Never mind he was out of cigarettes.

He perched a cut-glass bowl of salted cashew nuts on his stomach and practised throwing them up in the air and catching them in his mouth. Sometimes he missed. She hadn't got Sky TV, but he flicked through the channels on the remote. There was nothing he wanted to watch. If he'd been at home, he'd have been out with the gang, thinking up ways to get some cash. He wondered if they were missing him. He pulled out his mobile and tried raising his best mate. Only, he hadn't been able to pay his last bill, had he, and the phone was no longer any use to him. He threw it across the room where it nudged a vase of flowers over.

He didn't bother to clear up the mess he'd made. The aunt had a cleaner, didn't she? That's what women were for.

He was annoyed that Toby had caused a fuss in the park, because it was the easiest place for him to exercise the dog. As it was, he thought he'd better avoid the place for the time being. Especially if Toby had put that woman in hospital.

He grinned at the memory of her flopping around when Toby got hold of her. What a dog! He was getting quite fond of him.

CHAPTER THREE

'Home' for Miss Quicke was a large, late Victorian house on the far side of the Avenue. This was where she had been born and brought up, and this was where she intended to die. Everyone referred to it as her house though in fact it had been the property of her late nephew, and so now belonged to Ellie.

In recent years Roy had adapted and updated the unwieldy building, bringing out the best in the handsome reception rooms, renewing plumbing and electricity and redecorating throughout. It was a large house for a solitary woman, but he had carved out a well-appointed maisonette for Rose from what had once been the servants' quarters, and at the same time had converted the redundant coach house into offices for his growing architect's practice.

Ellie helped her aunt up the steps to the imposing front door and waited while she used her key to let herself in. Following her aunt into the large, tiled hall — which still retained its original carved mahogany features — Ellie looked at the magnificent sweep of stairs and worried about how long her aunt would be able to climb it unaided. It was one thing to appreciate high ceilings and lots of elbow room but quite another to expect an elderly lady to negotiate a slippery wooden flight of stairs twice a day. Several times Ellie had suggested that Miss Quicke install a stair lift, and had had her nose bitten off by way of thanks.

Miss Quicke made her slow, painful way across the hall and into the spacious sitting room at the back of the house, where she inserted herself into a high-backed armchair before the fireplace. Miss Quicke did not like anyone to watch her take her painkillers, so Ellie checked that there was a carafe of water beside her aunt's chair and busied herself letting up the blinds, which had earlier been pulled down to keep the sun out of the room. It worried her to see how small a space her aunt was now occupying in the big chair.

As soon as her aunt began to relax and closed her eyes, Ellie made her way into the large conservatory which led off the hall. This was Rose's pride and joy. Rose had lived most of her life in a tower block but loved flowers and since Miss Quicke had given her a free hand, she had filled the conservatory and the somewhat sterile garden with the brightest plants she could find. Miss Quicke didn't know one plant from another but was happy to indulge Rose in her passion.

Ellie sometimes wondered, in the odd idle moment, what she herself would have done with the garden and had to admit that her choice would have been for colours slightly less hectic. But there; Rose was happy, Miss Quicke was happy, and luckily Ellie didn't have to concern herself with the upkeep or maintenance of the big house and grounds. As to what would happen when Aunt Drusilla died — but there Ellie cut off her thoughts. She would not think about that till it happened, and she hoped it wouldn't happen for years.

Ellie saw that Rose had been in such a hurry to get to Felicity's that she'd been unable to finish dead-heading her geraniums that day. Ellie did it for her and was happily lost in this task when something scuttled across the floor. She let out a little scream and then scolded herself. So what if it were a mouse? She'd probably frightened the mouse more than it had frightened her. She would ask Rose what she was doing about it when she saw her.

Miss Quicke seemed to have slipped into a doze, so Ellie went into the kitchen to finish making the soup which Rose had intended for supper and made herself a cheese sandwich to go with it.

'Excellent,' pronounced Miss Quicke, managing only a couple of mouthfuls before setting the soup aside. 'You're a good cook, Ellie; almost as good as Rose. You must ask her to lend you the book on soups she's been using.'

Ellie was a reasonable cook herself but refused to take offence. She smiled and nodded.

Miss Quicke's head sank forward, and she raised it with an effort. 'You'll look after Roy for me, won't you?'

Ellie blinked. She didn't like the sound of this, not at all. She could feel her heart beat faster. She was going to reply that her aunt mustn't talk like that when Miss Quicke raised a claw-like hand. 'Don't play games. They exhaust me. Will you or won't you look after Roy for me? He's a good lad at heart but impulsive and every now and then he needs a touch on the reins to keep him on the right track. That wife of his hasn't the gumption to step in when he makes a fool of himself.'

Ellie knew what her aunt meant. Roy was just a trifle too trusting when it came to business, and had got into difficulties in that way in the past. She nodded.

'I'll hold you to that,' said Miss Quicke. 'Do you think there'll be any repercussions for Felicity from what happened today?'

'I don't see why there should be.'

'Neither do I, but I have a bad feeling about it. You'll see that they find the dog and destroy it, won't you?'

Ellie realized that she would very much rather not. She had the same uneasy feeling as her aunt about this affair. It was true that in the past she'd looked into various goings-on in the community, had managed to right some wrongs and put some wicked people behind bars, but surely this wasn't going to develop into such a case, was it?

It sounded as if a squabble between children over a bike had led to an accidental death. A dreadful thing to happen, but not criminal. The dog had obviously not been on a lead or muzzled as he ought to have been, but if it were the case — as it seemed to be — that a young boy had been exercising him and events had got out of hand, well, the police would find him, the dog would be destroyed and that would be that. Surely Ellie didn't need to do anything about it?

'Promise me?' said Miss Quicke.

Ellie held back a sigh. She nodded. 'I'll look into it, but I don't promise anything.'

'Good. I know I can trust you to sort it out. There's only one other thing I want to know; do you or do you not intend to marry Thomas?'

Ellie told herself that she ought to be annoyed at being asked such a personal question, but she felt only dismay. To anyone else, Ellie would have returned a laughing rejoinder, but if her aunt really were so poorly that she might . . . might die . . . ? There, Ellie had put her worry into words for the first time. She had to face facts; Aunt Drusilla was shrinking into herself, she was in constant pain, and she was way past her sell-by date. In such case, she deserved as much of the truth as Ellie could manage.

She fingered the heavy gold locket which Thomas had given her at Christmas. Thomas was their widower minister, bearded and with broad shoulders. A solid man in every way, a man of oak whom you could trust with your life. He and Ellie were comfortable in one another's company, and her first thought when in any difficulty was to call him on his mobile. They saw one another several times a week and the parish had grown accustomed to thinking of them as a couple though they were not formally engaged and there was no talk of wedding bells in the immediate future.

Ellie took a deep breath. 'Sometimes I think how very pleasant it would be to marry him, and I know he'd like it. Then I think how much I value my independence. I have my own dear little house and garden, plenty of good friends, more than enough to do and more than enough money to live on. I am so very, very fond of him. I haven't met anyone that I liked so well since my dear Frank died, but what sort of vicar's wife would I make?'

'A good one, I suppose, if you set your mind to it. I like Thomas. He comes in to see me every now and then, even when I don't specifically ask him to do so. I've taught him to play cribbage. I used to play with my brother, years ago, though he was a poor opponent. I wish I'd been kinder to him when he was alive but there, the past never goes away, does it, but keeps coming back at you . . .' Her voice tailed away. She began to inch herself forward in her chair, reaching for her stick.

Ellie stood, ready to help but not sure how to do so.

'Stand aside, girl. Let me get my breath first. Then you can help me up the back stairs. I can manage those pretty well because they've got grab rails on either side. You may bring up my pills.'

Of course. The back stairs in what had once been the servants' quarters would be more convenient for an elderly lady in pain. Miss Quicke leaned on her stick to cross the hall to the kitchen, and from there to Rose's part of the house. The old lady took her time mounting the stairs. Ellie followed, her mind whirling with thoughts of organizing twenty-four-hour care for her aunt, wondering if she should call the doctor, or get Rose back straight away. Rose was probably looking after Roy and his guest and Felicity and Mel at this very moment, and enjoying herself too much to remember that Miss Quicke might be in need of her. Which was all very right and proper — or was it?

A connecting door at the head of the stairs led into the broad landing which served the spacious bedrooms of the main part of the house. The master bedroom overlooked the garden, furnished with antiques even older than its current occupant. Ellie cast a housewifely eye around and was pleased to see that there was fresh linen on the bed, and that the furniture was dust free. Another large, high-backed armchair stood by one of the windows, with a small television set on a table nearby.

Ellie's eyes settled on a piece of furniture which looked totally out of place, and which she hadn't seen in this room before. A modern computer station had been installed near the bed. All the equipment on it appeared to be active, judging by the green standby lights on monitor, printer, fax machine and tower. Until now Miss Quicke had conducted her multitude of business affairs from the dining room below. Did this mean she now spent most of the day in her bedroom?

Miss Quicke saw where Ellie was looking. 'I find the dining room a little draughty at this time of year. It's convenient to be able to work up here when I feel like it.'

Ellie managed to show no surprise at this, even though it was now high summer and the dining room had never suffered from draughts.

'You may leave me,' said Miss Quicke. 'I'm a little tired tonight. All that fuss with Felicity and Mel has worn me out. Perhaps I'll have a bit of a lie-in tomorrow.'

'Shall I ring Felicity's, find out when Rose will be back to look after you?'

'Leave her. She's happy there, and I'm happy to be by myself for a few hours. Rose is a lovely girl and has made me very comfortable these last few years, but her shoes squeak and she will hover over me as if I were a baby.'

Ellie realized that she herself had just been about to hover. She smiled and departed. As she emerged from the driveway on to the road, she felt contradictory emotions. There was a sense of relief at leaving the house and the problems of her aunt behind her, but there was also dread as to what the future held.

She would check on Rose when she got back home. She looked at her watch. It was too late to phone Thomas tonight, but she would like to ask his opinion about her aunt's health.

She quickened her pace. She hadn't expected to be away so long from her little house, and her marauding cat, Midge, would be wondering why his provider hadn't refilled his bowl with tasty food. Midge had all the characteristics of a streetwise ginger tom. Although he could show affection for all of five seconds on rare occasions, he also knew how to make his disapproval felt if Ellie failed to fulfil what he considered was her part of the bargain. He kept her company when he wasn't engaged in his other pursuits and in return she fed him, providing a lap to sit on in the evenings and a comfortable bed at night.

Ellie reflected that it was a lot simpler dealing with a cat — however strong-minded — than a human being.

* * *

Anxiety gave Ellie a poor night's sleep. The birds' dawn chorus seemed to start as soon as she dropped off. Midge hadn't liked being disturbed by Ellie's restlessness in bed, and had made himself scarce early on.

Finally Ellie decided that enough was enough and she might as well get up and busy herself for an hour in the garden before she had to face the list of jobs she ought to be tackling. She'd always found that she could keep a big anxiety — like the one about Aunt Drusilla — at bay, by worrying about little things that she might be able to solve. She also refused to think about Felicity and the stupid mess the girl had got herself into. Or the fact that Ellie had promised to do something about it. What could she do, anyway?

Well, she supposed she could go into the park and have a word with one or two of the dog-walkers, who always knew everything about everybody, and who would be sure to know whose dog it was that had gone berserk yesterday. She shuddered. An attack by a dog sounded horrendous. It wasn't really surprising that Felicity had lost her nerve. Ellie was not at all sure — in spite of what Aunt Drusilla had kindly said about Ellie's bravery — that she'd have been any bolder, when faced with the equivalent of the Hound of the Baskervilles.

She took her breakfast into the conservatory at the back of the house, appreciating the tracery of green leaves across the roof and promising herself to dead-head the geraniums after she'd eaten. She thought she'd rather like to plant a vine in the corner by the fish tank. It would be fun to grow her own grapes.

She watched the rays of the sun travel down the tree in her garden till they illumined the sundial in the lawn. She hadn't really fancied anything much to eat, but having decided that she must keep her strength up, she'd made herself a boiled egg and 'soldiers'.

Her garden could really do with a proper dig over this autumn. When her late husband had brought her here, oh so many years ago, the garden had been a wasteland, a patchy stretch of lawn surrounded by straggly privet hedges. Now it bloomed with colour all the year round, but some of the herbaceous plants had got a trifle too big for their positions and needed to be divided and replanted. Some might even have to be thrown out. In particular there was one patch of Michaelmas daisies which had been bought as a dwarf variety and proved to be as tall as Ellie herself. Possibly she should replace Albertine with another variety that could be trusted to bloom even if it did suffer from a shower of rain?

Another problem popped, willy-nilly, into the forefront of her mind. Ellie's daughter Diana, who would have given Ivan the Terrible a run for his money. Diana the Demanding.

Diana had been very quiet for a while, which was a bad sign. Usually she was on the phone several times a week, wanting her mother to do this and that. All without a word of thanks. Ellie had always considered that politeness oiled the wheels of society and never failed to thank people herself. She'd tried to get Diana to say thank you for things when she was growing up, but there . . . Ellie sighed a little . . . Diana had always had a strong personality and it hadn't got softer with age, even though the girl seemed less abrasive now that her estate agency appeared to be taking off.

Think about something else. Think about her dear little house, for instance. The front gate was falling off its hinges, again. She'd had an odd-job man repair it a few years ago, but it needed a new gate post now. She must get on to the local handyman about it.

As for the interior of the house, did it look a little tired nowadays? She'd had the kitchen fitments replaced and they looked good, but she'd had no decorating done elsewhere since her husband died. Everything looked a little, well, shabby. While she was about it, perhaps she should replace the curtains at the back of the house, which had faded in the sun, and possibly — here was a daring thought — have a walk-in shower built into the bathroom? She'd heard the local builder even did wet rooms, whatever they might be.

The mess would be indescribable, of course. If she did decide to do it, then should she have the whole lot done at once, and take refuge in a hotel for a while? Or cadge a room with Aunt Drusilla, who might well have reached a point where Rose could do with extra help in the house?

She switched her mind resolutely away from the problem of Aunt Drusilla.

'I love my little house and garden. I've been very happy here,' said Ellie.

The front doorbell rang. One long, loud peal. Ellie closed her eyes and shuddered. Only one person ever rang like that. It would be Diana, checking in with Ellie before she went off to work. Diana never came round for a social visit, but always had an agenda. What would it be this time? Not a request for money; no, she'd learned from experience that Ellie was not into handouts.

Diana didn't have keys to this house anymore, because she'd tried to sell it over Ellie's head a couple of times. So Diana couldn't get in and Ellie could sit there in peace and quiet and have another cup of coffee. On the other hand, Diana was quite capable of leaning on the bell push till Ellie answered the door, however long it took.

Ellie dragged herself to her feet. Was this the day she collected her grandson from school and gave him tea? Was it Thursday? It might well be. Ellie usually had little Frank for tea at her place on Wednesdays, but for some reason the date had been changed this week. So she was definitely due to pick up little Frank from the school across the Green that afternoon and entertain him till it was time for him to return to his father, loving stepmother Maria and their new little family. Frank had settled pretty well into a routine of living with his father during the week and staying with his mother at weekends. Just occasionally, Ellie cringed at the thought of looking after a boisterous, demanding small boy but on the whole she looked forward to it.

Diana was another matter. Mentally, Ellie braced herself as she went to open the front door.

'Mother? Did you oversleep? I've been ringing for ages.' Diana brushed past Ellie and went straight into the sitting room, drawing back the curtains and opening windows. 'That's better. I can't stay long, we're terribly busy at the moment.'

'Coffee? Tea? Juice?'

Diana shuddered. 'I don't suppose you've got any proper coffee, have you? You really ought to get hold of one of those new coffee machines. They cost a bomb but at least you'd have something decent to offer.' Diana took a turn around the room, her sharp voice and sharper black suit suddenly making the room seem dated and even dingy. 'About time you did something about the décor, isn't it?'

'As a matter of fact, I was just thinking that . . .'

'Well, never mind that now.' Diana threw herself on to the settee and patted the arm of the big armchair beside her. She smiled, showing sharp white teeth. 'Sit down. I've got something to tell you.'

Ellie sat, uneasily aware that what Diana thought to be good news was not always so for other people.

Diana beamed at her. 'I'm going to revert to my maiden name. I am to be known as Ms Quicke in future. I can't be "Miss" because I've been married, and I can't be "Mrs" because I've got rid of Stewart. So, "Ms Quicke" it's going to be.'

Ellie was glad that for once she could endorse Diana's latest idea. 'I think that's very sensible, Diana. Good.'

Diana lifted her hand. 'And, wait for it, I'm going to have Frank's name changed to Quicke, too. That way Great-Aunt Drusilla can't possibly overlook him when she makes her will. He is, after all, the only male descendant in the family, and he'll bear her family name. The two brats that Stewart's got with his current wife Maria are both girls, and anyway, not of her blood, so there's no competition there. As for dear Uncle Roy, he's married money and doesn't need any more, and he's only got a girl, too.'

Ellie took a deep breath. She hated having to disagree with Diana, who could be really unpleasant when crossed, but experience had taught Ellie that sometimes it was necessary to do so. 'I don't think you can change Frank's name just like that, Diana. Stewart would have to agree, and I can't see him doing so.'

Diana brushed this aside. 'Don't be ridiculous, Mother. Of course he'll agree when he realizes how much it would mean to the old bat. I'm not having my boy miss out on all that money for the sake of a change of name.'

'I don't think Aunt Drusilla is likely to leave her money to a child of five.'

'Of course not. She'll leave it in trust for him, obviously, with me as trustee. I daresay she'll want to leave some token amount to Roy and maybe some jewellery or some memento of herself to you, since you've been at her beck and call for ever. I asked her the other day—'

'You've been to see her?' This was news indeed, for Diana hated the waste of time that was involved in visiting the elderly. Perhaps she no longer regarded visiting Aunt Drusilla as a waste of her time?

Diana flicked at a slightly threadbare cushion. 'You really ought to have these recovered or get rid of them altogether. This room is altogether too cluttered, too old-fashioned for words. Yes, of course I drop in to see her now and then, about once a week nowadays. Can't help seeing she's fading away. I don't suppose she'll be able to get up those stairs much longer. It's about time she accepted facts and went into a home. I left her some brochures on local places last time I was there. She can afford something reasonable with her own room, twenty-four-hour care, and all that.'

Ellie coloured up with annoyance. 'You shouldn't have, Diana. That's awful!'

Diana shrugged, took out her make-up bag, checked her lipstick. 'It's about time she had a reality check. Also, it's time Rose McNally was told to get lost. Fancy giving a mere housekeeper what amounts to a maisonette in that big house! She had a council flat before, didn't she? The sooner she applies for another, the better. Then when she's gone and Great-Aunt's in a home, the big house can be sold. The money will cover the fees for as long as she lasts, but there'll still be plenty over for us to inherit when she finally pops her clogs.'

Ellie clasped her hands together till the fingers turned white. 'Diana, I don't know where to start, but you've got it all wrong. Rose's future has been well provided for by Aunt Drusilla, and the house . . . well, the house is only Aunt Drusilla's on a sort of repairing lease. She doesn't own it.' Ellie knew she was being weak in not telling Diana that the big house actually belonged to her, but she'd always kept quiet about that, fearing that Diana would put pressure on her to sell it and give her the money. Diana could be as persistent as a mosquito when she got going.

'Oh, really?' Diana frowned, and two upright lines appeared between her eyes. Diana was not ageing well and looked older than her mid-thirties. 'Oh, that's a nuisance. Well, she owns some flats which she rents out, doesn't she? And a couple of houses? She can fund the fees for a nursing home easily enough.'

'She was born in that house and wants to die there. I don't see why she shouldn't.'

'Oh, mother. So short-sighted, always.' Diana put away her make-up, got to her feet, checked her image in the mirror over the fireplace, and twitched her collar into line. 'Must go, now. I want to arrange a studio photograph of four generations of the Quicke family: Great-Aunt Drusilla; you; me and little Frank. She'll like that, but I quite see that it's got to be done within the next few days or not at all. We don't want her leaving her money to the cats' home, do we? If I can fix it for later today, I'll give you a ring. Kiss, kiss,' said Diana, wriggling her fingers in a farewell gesture. 'Must dash.'

* * *

The aunt turfed him out of bed, screeching her head off. He couldn't believe it. It wasn't even ten o'clock, and he never got up till midday.

What was she screaming at him for? So he hadn't got up to feed the pooch that morning, and she'd had to give him some of her own fillet steak. So what? Toby deserved it.

So what if he'd stayed out till all hours and gone to sleep with the telly on? Didn't she realize how hard it was to get into pubs without ID, looking younger than his age? He'd had to try four places before they'd serve him, and then he'd only had enough money for a pint and a pack of ciggies. He'd been looking for a college student whose ID he could lift, but had been dead out of luck.

So what if he'd been smoking in the bedroom, which was going to make all her drapes stink? Might make the next person she had to stay in her place feel more at home.

She didn't let up, not for a second. Picked up his clothes and threw them at him, shouting that he might do as he liked in his own home, but this was her place, and he'd have to abide by her rules or crawl back to where he came from.

He was desperate to get back to bed, but she thrust him through into the bathroom and turned the shower on, giving him such a push that he landed up on the floor. He couldn't believe it. She was treating him like a child! Him, the terror of the town, the leader of the lost! No wonder his cousin had scarpered as soon as he could.

He stood in the shower, shivering, hating her.

He'd get even with her for this, if it killed him.

CHAPTER FOUR

No sooner had Diana slammed the door behind her than the phone rang. Felicity, who didn't seem to have calmed down much. 'Ellie, I need to talk. Can you come over?'

Ellie thought of the cooking she'd planned to do that morning. She'd be giving little Frank a high tea when he got in from school and she'd promised he could have his favourite, shepherd's pie. 'Is it desperate, Felicity? I've got one or two things to do this morning.'

Felicity sounded distant. 'I suppose not, really, although . . . I thought that as you'd seen Caroline . . . did she say anything about the dog? I mean, I didn't see anything, really I didn't, only the police seem to think . . .' Her voice had risen and risen during this.

The girl was panicking again. 'All right,' said Ellie. 'Give me half an hour and I'll be with you. How is Mel, and did you get a good night's sleep?'

'That's another thing.' The girl was holding back tears. 'You can tell her to stop, can't you? I mean, you're such old friends, and besides, she ought to be looking after Aunt Drusilla and not trying to turn Mel away from her mother.'

Now what? 'Calm down. Get some coffee on the go. Cook something. You know that always makes you feel better. What are you having for supper tonight, anyway?'

'How can I think about that when Rose has walked off with my baby without so much as a word?'

So Rose was trying to take over with the baby? With the purest of motives, of course. However, that's not how Felicity would see it. It would be best to give the girl something to do. 'I'll be over in half an hour and I'll expect freshly made scones, home-made jam and clotted cream. Right?'

'I don't have any clotted cream.'

'I'll make do with butter. Get on with it, Felicity, or I'll be there before you've taken the scones out of the oven.'

Ellie went round the house pulling blinds down against the sun. She scribbled a note for her next-door neighbour, Kate, who often dropped in with her offspring for a chat on Thursday mornings. As she sprinkled some fish food into the tank in the conservatory, she caught sight of someone waving at her from the path at the bottom of the garden. Ellie waved back. Her old friend Mrs Dawes — mainstay of the altos in the choir — was stumping along with her stick, making her way to the church hall, where she was due to give her Thursday morning class in flower arranging. At least, Mrs Dawes still considered herself in charge, though she couldn't stand for long nowadays, and had passed much of the actual teaching to a second-in-command. She'd recently giving up judging at flower shows, too.

Ellie held back another sigh. It was sad to see two elderly ladies gradually relinquishing their grasp on life, but as one passes on, babies come along to take their place. Kate's two were delightful, Mel was a treat and little Frank was growing up nicely, thanks to the loving but firm care he was given by his stepmother.

Just as Ellie was about to leave, the phone rang again. This time it was Miss Quicke. 'Ellie, dear, I've been deserted by Rose, who's been lured away by Felicity to look after little Mel. Don't get me wrong. Rose asked me if I'd mind when she brought up my breakfast tray, and of course I said to go ahead, because it gives me an opportunity to have a good rest this morning, but would you mind dropping in later on with some smoked salmon for me? I fancy some in a sandwich for lunch. And perhaps you could heat up some more of that asparagus soup Rose made for me yesterday?'

'Will do,' said Ellie, mentally rerouting her morning to include a visit to the shops after she'd been to Felicity's. 'How are you today?'

'There's nothing wrong with me. A little tired after all the excitement yesterday, that's all.' In the old days Miss Quicke would have described a boardroom battle and a company takeover as 'a little excitement', especially when the result led to an increase in her vast fortune. In the old days Miss Quicke had been the one to generate excitement. Now . . . ah well.

Ellie collected her handbag and a shopping bag on the way out. As she walked through the park, she noted the number of dog-walkers and joggers using it. Everything seemed normal. One or two women pushed buggies, one of whom had a terrier on a lead attached to her wrist. There were no really big dogs in sight, except for a slow-moving, ancient husky.

Ellie shivered, even in the bright sun. She really did not want to look into anything concerning large, fierce dogs, and she was relieved not to spot any. She kept a lookout for Rose and Mel, but didn't see them anywhere. Perhaps Rose had taken Mel to the shops? Or round the houses?

Felicity opened the door as Ellie lifted her hand to the bell push. Felicity was dressed in a white shirt and black jeans under a plastic pinafore with cats on it, but her hair looked as if it hadn't been washed for a couple of days, and there was a smear of flour on one cheek. She was flushed — possibly sitting on anger? She looked both ways down the road before ushering Ellie inside.

'Thank God you've come. I'm so . . . I don't know what to . . . how could she?' She made a visible effort to control herself and speak normally but her words came out in jerks. 'It's not your fault, forgive me if . . . the scones are almost ready and the coffee's on. You will deal with Rose for me, won't you? She really mustn't walk off with my baby just like that. Of course I understand that she's at a loose end, although really you'd think she has enough to do in that big house, but . . . oh, there's the pinger. The scones are ready.'

Still talking, Felicity led the way through to the kitchen. Breakfast things were piled on the centre unit, unwashed. Also a bottle of formula, empty. Ellie began to load the dishwasher, while Felicity rescued the scones and made some coffee for them both, still talking.

'I didn't ask Rose to come round this morning, really I didn't. Roy took her back home last night after she'd given Mel her ten o'clock feed, but of course I was out of it by then, didn't know what was happening. If he asked Rose to come in today, he had no right, because I'd have managed all right, of course I would. Rose had made up some bottles of formula and put them in the fridge — can you believe how cheeky? As if she were hoping that I wouldn't be able to feed her myself.'

'Could you?' asked Ellie, wiping down the centre unit.

'That isn't the point.' Felicity reached into the man-sized fridge for some jam. 'I just need a little more time, that's all. I've been drinking lots of water, and I'm sure . . . well, if the police would only leave me alone, I'm sure . . . It's true I did have to give Mel one of the bottles in the night, because I still couldn't, then . . . and I was so dazed with tiredness that I wasn't at all sure I was doing it right, but Mel didn't seem to mind. I should have been able to feed her myself this morning, but . . . then Rose arrived just as the police did, and it threw me right back, and if my milk never does come back, it'll be all their fault.'

Not her fault, she meant. Tears were running down her cheeks, but she went on transferring scones to a rack. 'Mel's not been out of my sight since she was born, and now . . . I don't even know where Rose has taken her, and supposing it rains and — oh, I can't bear it!'

Ellie passed a couple of mugs, plates and knives along to Felicity, and set the dishwasher going. 'The police. I suppose Caroline told them that you might have seen something?'

'I didn't. I wasn't looking.' Her voice rose to an almost hysterical pitch. 'I couldn't tell what kind of dog it was because my husband — my first husband — mostly had King Charles spaniels and he wouldn't let me take them in the park in case they got bitten or fleas or something, which was ridiculous, but . . . anyway, I really truly didn't see what kind of dog it was, and I didn't see the boys fighting over the bike. I didn't see them because I was looking at Mel. I told them, I'd completely forgotten I'd got my mobile phone with me because I'd been using it earlier and I thought I'd left it on the kitchen table.'

'Yes, of course,' said Ellie, urging Felicity to a chair and handing over the depleted box of tissues. 'Try not to get upset. Keep calm, for the sake of your baby.'

Felicity took no notice. 'They think, they as much as said, that if I'd used my phone, the ambulance might have got there in time, but it wouldn't have made any difference, would it? Oh, where do you think Rose is? I just can't bear it!'

'Have you tried her mobile phone?'

Felicity gaped. Obviously, she hadn't thought of it. She fell on her handbag, found a mobile phone and paused. 'I don't have her mobile number. Should I ring Aunt Drusilla?'

Ellie pulled her own mobile phone out, and pressed buttons. *Ring, ring. Ring, ring.* Rose answered.

'Ellie here. Where are you, Rose?'

Rose replied, 'Bother this thing. Have I pressed the right button? Is that you, Ellie? I'm in the little bandstand thingy at the end of the park. It's most entertaining. Did you know there's a group come here every morning to do exercises together? They've just opened the gates to the tennis courts, and people are starting to . . . what do they call it at Wimbledon? Knock up, knock about? With tennis balls, you know.'

Ellie hadn't spotted Rose on her way through the park, but the rather ramshackle open-sided shelter which looked as if it might once have been a bandstand was some distance from the path Ellie had taken. She held on to her patience. 'Can you bring Mel back straight away? Felicity is getting very anxious.'

'Tell her there's nothing to worry about. Our darling baby's fast asleep. She loved being walked through the park, looking at the trees waving about above her, and everyone who sees her says what a beautiful baby she is.'

'That may be so,' said Ellie, putting some iron into her voice, 'but Felicity didn't know where she was, and wants her back. Now.'

'Silly girl. She ought to be thankful I took Baby out for a walk. Tell her I'll be back directly.'

Ellie snapped off her phone. 'She's on her way back. Relax. Mel's asleep, as good as gold.'

Felicity was tense. 'Rose hasn't taken her into the park, has she? How could she, after what happened yesterday?'

Ellie took a scone, buttered and jammed it, and took a large bite. Delicious. Of course, if she were serious about losing some weight, she ought not to be eating scones and jam in the middle of the morning, but there, in times of stress, carbohydrates were good for you. She pushed the scones towards Felicity, who turned her head away as if the sight offended her, but then changed her mind and took one for herself. Ellie stirred sugar into their mugs of coffee. It was good coffee. Perhaps Diana had a point about instant versus ground coffee.

Would it distract Felicity to hear about Diana's plan to change little Frank's name to Quicke? Probably not. The girl was obsessed with her baby and that was understandable. Ellie remembered only too well how difficult it had been to leave Diana alone for as much as half an hour when she was first born. That's what babies did to you. They relied totally on their mothers for their well-being, so they made sure the mothers were totally hooked into the job of caring for them.

Besides which, Felicity was no money-grabber. She'd inherited a good whack from her first husband, which she was managing with the aid of kindly, competent Kate, the financial whiz-kid who lived next door to Ellie. Felicity was neither ambitious nor greedy.

Unlike Diana. Ellie was getting worried about the time, too. If she had to get to the shops, buy some food for Aunt Drusilla, take it to her, then return to cook for Frank's tea, she was going to have to depart very soon, but she didn't want to leave Felicity in such a state. The girl was gulping her coffee, eyes on the clock. Couldn't wait to be reunited with her baby. The dishwasher whirred into life, drained out and refilled.

There was a ring at the door. Felicity flew down the passage, expecting it to be Rose with Mel, but instead there was buxom Caroline with her baby in a buggy.

'I thought I'd just call round to see how you were. Are you all right?' Wasn't Caroline a nice woman, to think of Felicity at such a time?

'Come in, come in,' said Felicity, peering down the road again, and again failing to see the one buggy which might contain her treasure. 'It's just so awful, isn't it? Rose, she's a family friend, has just taken Mel for a little walk, and I was telling myself that she's perfectly safe in the park today, but . . . would you like a cuppa?'

'Of course, of course.' Caroline manoeuvred her buggy into the hall, checked that Duncan was fast asleep and followed Felicity through to the kitchen. Ellie rose to her feet, the two women exchanged smiles, and Felicity busied herself pouring out coffee for Caroline.

Caroline's good manners held. She smiled at Ellie. 'It was good of you to let me talk it all out yesterday. As I told Jack later, it was just like having my dear old mum back, God bless her.'

Ellie said, 'The police have been round to see you again?'

Caroline accepted a mug of coffee and eyed up the scones. With her figure, she oughtn't to be thinking about mid-morning snacks, thought Ellie. Felicity served Caroline the largest of the remaining scones, and Caroline's eyes rounded. 'You are a good cook, I must say.'

Felicity accepted the compliment with a smile. A tinge of colour came into her pale cheeks. Ellie could see that Felicity would be safe with Caroline, and made preparations to leave. She had just one question for Caroline before she went. 'Caroline, do the police have a lead on the killer dog?'

Caroline said, around a mouthful, 'I'm a cat person, don't know one end of a dog from the other. It was large and mostly brown, that's all I can say. It wasn't on a lead or anything, because then the boy could have controlled it if that were the case, couldn't he?'

Ellie persevered. 'You said someone came and sat with you, someone who was walking dogs. Maybe she recognized the dog? What was her name?'

'Mm? Oh yes, she had two — what do you call them? — golden retrievers. Beautiful creatures. The children were really upset, didn't want to go near them at first, but she showed them how loving and, well soppy, really, that they are. I suppose that little interlude might prevent them getting a phobia about dogs in future.'

'Yes,' said Ellie, being patient. 'What was her name?'

'Not sure.' She screwed up her face, trying to remember. 'She must have told me her name. Yes, I'm sure she did. Trudy something? She looks Scandinavian, come to think of it. Trudy . . . Wells? Yes, because I thought, Tunbridge Wells, but she said there was no connection.'

'What was the boy like?'

Caroline shrugged. 'Young teen? Shaven head or very fair — couldn't tell which at that distance — sweatshirt with some kind of logo or wording on it, sloppy jeans, you know? Not much taller than the boys whose bike he stole.'

Felicity attempted a smile. 'No baseball cap on backwards?'

'Now don't you start,' said Caroline, polishing off her first scone and reaching for another. 'That's what the police said, "Wasn't he wearing a cap?" And I said, "I didn't think so but if you go on like that, you'll get me all mixed up."'

'It all happened so fast,' said Felicity, sympathizing. She lifted her head, hearing something which the others had missed, and ran to the front door to let Rose push the buggy indoors. Swooping on little Mel, Felicity carried her back to the kitchen, crooning over her and then exclaiming that she was so wet, wasn't she, the little poppet.

Meanwhile, Rose disentangled her bag from the tray beneath, serenely unconscious that she had offended in any way, and was about to follow Felicity to the kitchen when Ellie held her back. 'Dear Rose, it was very kind of you to take the baby for a walk, but Felicity can cope now. I was just leaving and thinking of getting a cab back home. Can I give you a lift?'

'Doesn't Felicity want me to help her with Mel a bit longer? Just till she gets straight again?'

Felicity was cooing to her baby, who was beginning to wake and fuss. Ellie called back to Felicity that she was leaving now, and giving Rose a lift.

'Oh. Yes. Thanks, Ellie. It was good of you to come over.'

Yes, it was, wasn't it? thought Ellie, urging Rose out of the front door. Given half a chance, Rose would have stayed and got in the way, but Ellie wasn't letting her have that chance. Felicity might be foolish in some ways, but she needed to get on with her life as a new mother, and Caroline would probably be a better counsellor for her at the moment than Ellie could ever be.

'I can walk back,' said Rose, but then sat on the low wall at the bottom of the garden, very ready to be given a lift home. She wasn't young or even middle-aged anymore, though she was younger than Miss Quicke by some ten years or more. For the first time it occurred to Ellie with a pang that Rose was ageing as fast as her employer, and with that came another reminder that Miss Quicke was well past her three scores years and ten.

Ellie used her mobile to call the cab company with whom she kept a monthly account, and sat beside Rose on the wall to wait for their transport.

'It was lovely in the park, walking Baby,' said Rose, almost, though not quite, justifying the fact that she'd assumed it was all right to walk off with Mel, instead of properly asking permission. 'I'd forgotten how lovely it is there at this time of year.'

'Did you see anyone you knew? Dog-walkers, in particular?'

Rose thought. She might be a fluttery sort of person, she might ramble off the subject, but she could concentrate when necessary. 'All the women who were walking buggies stopped to look at Mel, I suppose because I look old enough to be her granny, and not her mummy, though there were some grannies walking toddlers, as well. I can't say that I'm really fond of dogs and of course we never had one when we were in the flat, because it wouldn't have been kind to have a dog there, though there was one woman, and I'll name no names, but she really ought to have known better, and she had two of those big, fierce guard dogs in a top-floor flat, would you believe? I think the RSPCA came and took them away, and did she make a fuss!'

'What you mean is, that those with babies in buggies talk to one another, and dog-walkers talk to other dog-walkers, but baby-minders don't talk to dog-minders?'

'Yes, dear, I suppose I do. There was one woman with three dear little doggies, and her hair was dyed blonde and at first I thought the little doggies had been dyed to match but it wasn't quite like that because I think they were natural, one brown, one grey and one white. Very pretty. And her coat was probably not real fur. No, I'm pretty sure it wasn't, not in summertime, anyway.'

'She stopped to talk to you?'

'Oh no, dear. Not stopped exactly. One of her little . . . I don't think they're miniature poodles . . . I did ask her and she said something like "bishops", which they can't be, can they? Anyway, they all wanted to get down into the river near the bandstand and have a splash but of course the woman didn't want them to do that — think of the mess, dear. She was calling and calling to them, the naughty little things, and they didn't take the slightest bit of notice till they'd played in the water long enough. Do you think she has to wash and dry them in the kitchen sink? I suppose you could use a hairdryer on them afterwards, but what a bother.'

'I expect they're like babies to her.'

Rose sighed. 'I'm not as young as I used to be, and that's the truth. I was thinking, when I woke up in the night and began to worry about whether Felicity would be able to feed Mel at four, that I don't know how these mothers do it. It was all right for me, walking over early this morning to see how they were, but it was good of you to offer me a lift home.'

'My aunt was enjoying her lie-in, but she wanted me to get something in for her lunch. Smoked salmon for a sandwich, she thought.'

'Really?' Rose revived a little. 'She hasn't fancied anything much to eat for some time. I'll get some on the way back, shall I?'

'We'll stop off in the Avenue and I'll get it for you, and then drop you back. I expect you could do with a little rest since you were up so early.'

'Thank you dear,' Rose said. 'Don't think I don't appreciate it, because I do. Was Felicity very upset?'

'I expect I'd have done exactly the same as you, if I'd been in your place.'

Rose managed to smile. She understood exactly what Ellie meant. The cab trundled along the road, the driver looking out for them. The women got in and were borne away.

* * *

Mick hated everybody and everything. The aunt had gone off to work, swearing that if he didn't turn over a new leaf she'd send him back where he came from. Then she'd stuffed a twenty into his top pocket, just as if he were ten years old. Twenty! Hardly enough to keep him going for a day. She'd told him to buy some food for the dog with it, and he supposed that was something he ought to do because he'd promised Tich he would, and you didn't let Tich down if you knew what was good for you.

He burned to revenge himself on her, but told himself he had to stay put for a while. Just till things calmed down back home. But to live properly he had to have money, and a new mobile phone.

If he got a good price for the bike, that would help. Only he didn't know where to take it. A small shopping parade would be the right place to start. The aunt had said there was one not far off, where she had some sort of part-time job — he didn't know what. Or care. He cycled along the pavement to the Avenue. Some old woman stumped by with a stick and yelled at him that he shouldn't be riding a bike on the pavement. He gave her the finger.

There were lots of poxy restaurants in the parade, not his style, a couple of coffee shops and . . . ah, that was more the sort of thing, a fast-food place doing the kebab trade, with a couple of lads idling around the door.

Mick looked the lads up and down. Both were bigger than him, but that didn't matter. Mick recognized the type and knew what they needed. They needed pointing in the right direction. They needed leadership. They needed him.

They'd sized him up, too. They strolled out to meet him on the pavement, fists deep in pockets, hoods flopping over their shoulders.

'Got a fag?' Mick said, striking the right note.

CHAPTER FIVE

Ellie's mobile phone rang just as the cab deposited the two women in front of Miss Quicke's house. The call flustered Ellie, who didn't normally keep her phone switched on. She realized she must have forgotten to switch it off after she'd phoned Rose in the park.

It was her friend Thomas, wondering if she were free for lunch. They often met at a local restaurant for lunch on a Thursday or Friday, dependent upon his workload.

Rose went ahead and unlocked the door, while Ellie unloaded the shopping from the cab, mobile clamped to her ear. 'I'm not sure . . . I had hoped, but what time is it? I must admit it would be good to . . .'

'Now what?' he sounded amused.

Ellie eased her shoulders. 'You're right, I'm making a big fuss about nothing. Can we make it early? I just want to check on my aunt, and then, oh dear, I promised to cook a shepherd's pie for Frank's tea. I'm running late, of course.'

'Raid the ready meals cabinet at the Co-op for the shepherd's pie and relax.'

She laughed. 'Twenty minutes, give or take?'

'The Italian restaurant for a change, right? I'll be there.' Come to think of it, she might be a bit late, but if she were, Thomas would understand.

She scurried into the kitchen after Rose and helped stow away the shopping, noting with alarm that Rose did indeed look thin and grey. Perhaps she'd overdone it this morning. Ellie had somehow thought that Rose would go on for ever, looking after Aunt Drusilla. Maybe Diana had the right idea, and Rose ought to retire before she wore herself out? But then who would look after the older lady?

Anxiety made Ellie ask, 'Are you all right, Rose? Oughtn't you to see the doctor?'

'Just a little tired, dear. Nothing to worry about. As Miss Quicke says, a little rest and we're ready to face the world again. I'll go through to my own little sitting room in a minute and have a nap. I have the internal phone there beside me and can be with Miss Quicke in no time at all if she wants me for anything.'

'You're avoiding the issue. Doctor, Rose. When did you last see her?'

'Last week, dear. Miss Quicke has her call round now and then. Private medicine is quite something, isn't it? Miss Quicke insists that I get checked out, too. Nothing to worry about, just the usual wear and tear. If it gets any worse, Miss Quicke says she'll fund me for a hip operation just like the one she had, but I tell her I don't really fancy it.'

Ellie hadn't known that Rose had a bad hip. She felt dreadful that she hadn't noticed. 'Oh, Rose! How are you managing the stairs?'

'We do well enough if we take our time about it,' said Rose. 'Miss Quicke had a man come to see about a stairlift, but she wants to talk to you about it first. Now I'll just make up a sandwich for your aunt, and heat up some soup in the microwave. Perhaps you can take it up for me, save me the stairs.'

Stairlift. Of course they must have one, and the sooner the better. But why hadn't Aunt Drusilla mentioned it to Ellie?

Ellie put a delicately pretty plateful of sandwiches — minus crusts — on a small tray with a mug of soup and, leaving Rose to settle down for a nap in her big chair, checked that Miss Quicke was nowhere to be seen downstairs, and ascended the wide staircase to the first floor. Halfway up she paused. There was something she'd meant to ask Rose about, but what was it? She couldn't for the life of her think what it was at the moment, and she was not going back down to disturb Rose, who probably needed a nap as much as Aunt Drusilla did at the moment.

The sun was falling across the polished oak floorboards on the landing, but the blinds had been drawn in Miss Quicke's bedroom. The old lady was half lying and half sitting in bed, her eyes closed. Ellie noticed that she'd been using her computer because there was a screen saver doing its bit, and she could hear the hum of the motor.

Miss Quicke opened her eyes and said, 'Oh, it's you, is it? What's going on? Is Felicity all right? What about little Mel? Is that fool of a son of mine doing his bit?' Ellie put the food down on the bedside table and helped her aunt to sit upright.

'Yes, yes and I'm not sure. Rose has been brilliant but she's a bit tired now and is having a nap. She said you were wondering about a stairlift. Of course you must have one. I'll pay, if necessary.' Now that was a foolish offer, because Aunt Drusilla probably had more funds at her disposal than the Chancellor of the Exchequer. Well, almost.

Miss Quicke's lipless mouth quivered into a smile. 'Dear Ellie, always a bit slow to catch on.'

Ellie felt herself redden. 'I'm sorry I didn't notice earlier. But now I have—'

'No need. I know what I'm doing, and so does Rose.'

'Perhaps we could fix you up with a bed downstairs?'

'Nonsense. I was born in this bed and I'll die in it. Understood?'

Nonplussed, Ellie gestured to the food she'd brought up. Miss Quicke shook her head. 'I thought I might fancy it but I don't, not now.'

Ellie took the old woman's hand in hers and stroked it. She realized that her aunt was drawing to the end of her life, and that she was fully aware of it. The last thing her aunt wanted was someone weeping and wailing over her, although that was exactly what Ellie felt like doing.

'No tears, by request,' said Miss Quicke, with one of her crocodile grins. 'Now, tell me what's going on. They say curiosity is one of the last things to leave you, and I must admit to hoping you can sort out this mess before I go. Whose dog was it, and have the police got him?'

Ellie's mind was going off at a tangent, wondering how long her aunt still had to live, and finding herself dismayed at the prospect. She tried to concentrate. 'Felicity will be all right, though I'm not sure her milk will come back in. She has a new friend called Caroline, who also has a young baby. Caroline will be very good for her. I don't think the police have a handle on the dog because Caroline isn't a dog person and Felicity never even saw it. Maybe the children will be able to give a description. There was also someone who went to help Caroline, and she was a dog person. Maybe she saw something.'

'You'll follow it up?' Miss Quicke's eyes were closing.

'Yes.' Ellie relinquished her aunt's hand. She wanted to ask her aunt if Roy knew that his mother was so near to her end, but she knew — or thought she knew — that Roy had no idea of it. Ought she to warn him? How would he take it? Badly, was the answer to that.

'I think I'll have a little nap now.' Miss Quicke slid further down the bed and turned her face away from the light. Ellie left the room to the green standby lights and the flicker of the screen saver.

* * *

Thomas was sitting by the window at the restaurant. He'd covered the table with sheets of paper on which he was working with a red biro. He was not on duty today and so was wearing a sage green T-shirt over jeans. The T-shirt was new; it had a white circle around what looked like a bullet hole over his breast, with the slogan, 'I was shot here!'

'Gracious me,' said Ellie easing herself into the seat opposite him. 'Where did you get that T-shirt?'

'Given it.' He grunted, underlining something in red. 'If only you'd agree to be secretary for the parish council, Ellie Quicke, I wouldn't have to spend hours correcting fairytales passing themselves off as minutes.'

Ellie felt herself relax. She'd declined the office several times in the past and had no intention of taking it on in the future, either. Thomas knew it. 'The T-shirt?' she reminded him.

He threw the red pen down and collated the sheets of paper. 'Someone on the Alpha Course who's just come back from America. Nice chap, colour blind.'

'Not just colour blind,' said Ellie. 'Let me guess; he's an aging hippie and he thinks you should join the club?'

He squinted down at the shirt. 'It's clean, I'm behind hand with the laundry and I'm having the afternoon off — theoretically, anyway. What's your excuse?'

Ellie looked down at herself. Was she wearing odd shoes? She hadn't given much thought to dressing suitably this morning. She'd pulled on a cornflower-blue cotton dress with some white daisies embroidered on the yoke. It looked all right, didn't it?

Thomas reached across and pushed the name tab under the material at the back of her neck. He grinned at her.

She grinned back. 'What a comfort you are. No one else saw it, or perhaps they didn't like to say anything.' She thought that normally Miss Quicke would have spotted it and said something.

'Penny for them?' said Thomas, handing her the menu. 'I'm hungry but I suppose you'll say I ought to have a salad.'

'So ought I,' said Ellie. 'But carbohydrates help when you're worried, don't they?'

He eyed her over the top of the menu. The short sleeves of his T-shirt revealed brawny forearms, on which Ellie always thought she might see seaman's tattoos. The fact that he was an academic rather than a mariner was beside the point. He said, 'You're playing hard to get today, aren't you, woman? I'll spring to five pence for your thoughts, but that's my final offer.'

'Aunt Drusilla. Rose. A black hole is opening up in my life and I don't like it.'

'Uh-uh. I'm popping in again this afternoon.'

She drew a deep breath. 'I hadn't noticed she was going so fast until today. I ought to have noticed, but somehow . . . I'm always so busy, which is no excuse, I know. I was shocked. She didn't tell me, and in a way I can understand why. She's tired and doesn't want people making a scene. I can see she's ready to go, but I'm not ready to let her go. Should I speak to her doctor? Yes, I'll do that when I get back. How long, do you think?'

He shrugged. 'Days, maybe.' He looked up as the waiter approached and gave his order. Ellie ordered a salad, too. They both watched as he wrote their order down, taking his time about it. He was a young lad, new and not above making mistakes.

When he'd gone, Thomas asked, 'Anything else worrying you?'

She tried to smile. 'You know all about the dog, don't you? That's why you said you were "theoretically" free. You've been called in to help in some way. Let me guess. Was the woman who was killed a parishioner? Would I have recognized her?'

He poured water for them both. 'Yes, she was, and yes, you probably would have recognized her. Her children were christened at church. Her name was Corinne.'

Ellie remembered Corinne. She was shocked. 'Oh, no.' Corinne was one of those people who always looked on the bright side, even though she had a hard enough life looking after two children unsupported by a husband. She did part-time child-minding and was a dinner lady at Frank's school. Her boys were occasionally noisy but there was no real harm in them. To think of lively Corinne lying dead in the mortuary!

'I can hardly believe it. Corinne, of all people. She always had a smile on her face. She'll be greatly missed.'

Thomas continued, 'One of the boys plays football on Sunday mornings, but the other is in Junior Church. The family have — had — a flat in that block of council housing at the end of the Avenue. It's a three-bedroomed ground-floor flat, and spacious with it.

'Corinne was an exemplary mother; the children were well looked after and attended the primary school on the Green. I was contacted last night by Corinne's sister, Leona, who lives on the Acton estate. She's got a couple of kids of her own but managed to find a babysitter and came over to look after her sister's children. They're all very distressed. I was there last night, and again this morning.'

Their salads came. Thomas poured dressing over his, which probably negated any advance he'd made towards having a fat-free meal. Ellie declined the dressing and tackled her salad without enthusiasm. She could tell in her bones that Thomas was leading up to asking her to do something about the children, though she couldn't imagine what.

'It's a cultural thing,' said Thomas. 'Not all men of West Indian origin think that way, of course, but many do. In their eyes, the women aren't much cop unless they can prove fertility, and even when they do produce children, it isn't considered necessary to marry them.'

Ellie nodded. Caroline Topping had said something about the children having different fathers. Ah, did that mean what she thought it meant?

Thomas poured another dollop of dressing on his salad. 'The eldest boy is ten, going on eleven. The father is a construction worker on the Underground, working nights, sees his son once a month by arrangement. He's moved in with another woman who's also given him a child. He came round this morning, says his new woman has agreed that they'll take the boy in. The boy likes his father's new woman, thinks it would be great to move over to Tower Hamlets "where the action is". Yes, that might work out.'

Ellie's mouth was dry. She took a sip of water. 'There was a girl, too?'

'Corinne was child-minding the girl after school. She's shocked but her family are cosseting her and she'll be all right, I think.'

Ellie speared a section of tomato and put it in her mouth. She wished chefs would skin tomatoes before putting them in salads but there, it was a fiddly business, and she didn't often do it herself. 'And the second boy?'

'You've got it,' said Thomas, gloomily chasing the last of his salad around his plate. 'Dad doesn't want to know.'

Ellie abandoned all pretence of eating.

Thomas eyed her plate. 'Shall I finish it?'

'Waste not, want not,' said Ellie, pushing her plate towards him. 'So, what is it you want me to do?'

He dolloped more dressing on to Ellie's salad. 'This salad's perfectly acceptable, if you put some dressing on it.' He took a mouthful and chewed it. 'Find the dog, obviously. This has all the hallmarks of blowing up into a gang thing and I'd like to stop it before it starts.'

'What! How do you make that out?'

'Leona's man came round to the flat this morning. He's not her husband, by the way. The husband seems to have disappeared some years ago. This is the current man in her life, name of Grant. He has "connections", as they say. Acton connections, luckily, not North Ealing. But still, he's threatening to summon some "friends" and go looking for anyone around here who walks the right sort of dog. Hot-headed is one word for him. Rash is another. He thinks the presence of a fighting dog in the locality means that a local gang must be preparing to stage some illegal dog fights. That's his assumption, not mine, and the police don't share it. But once Grant gets an idea into his head, it tends to stick. If you could find the dog, it might defuse the situation.'

'That's mad! Just because the dog was not muzzled or on a leash, you can't say he's been trained to fight. Surely it's more likely that the lad — whoever he was — was too inexperienced to know how to cope with a large dog? Surely it was a dreadful, tragic accident?'

'Try telling that to Grant. I've tried and got nowhere. I said I'd try to find out if there was any talk of dog fights being staged in the area, but I haven't heard a dicky bird. Have you?'

Ellie shook her head. 'Though I wouldn't, would I?'

'Which isn't stopping Grant from calling up the troops, and it isn't solving the problem of what to do with the younger boy, who's catatonic with shock, by the way. The older one is still on a high, bawling his eyes out one minute and the next looking forward to moving, but the younger one's not coping. His father's not responding to calls to visit him, either. In fact, he's insisting that the boy is taken into care.' He shook his head. 'I'm not happy about children being taken into care, however worthy the carers may be. So where do we start, Ellie?'

'I suppose the police will be doing everything possible, asking other dog-walkers if they know the lad and his dog?' She signed to the waitress and said she'd like some coffee. Thomas chose triple ice cream with extra cream on top. He was definitely off his diet, if he'd ever been serious about it, which she doubted.

Ellie propped her chin on her interlaced fingers. 'It reminds me of that old saying about the battle being lost for want of a nail. A boy thoughtlessly lets a dog off the leash in the park and in consequence many lives are changed. A woman is dead, leaving a gap in the community. Her sister grieves and no doubt her sister's children do, too. Her sister's man will probably end up in jail charged with grievous bodily harm to some poor innocent walking a dog who may or may not be the one who caused the bother in the first place.

'Then there's the men in Corinne's life; presumably they're going to be shocked rigid. Above all, two children lose their mother and their home, are separated from one another and one is taken into care. Also, though I'm sure Felicity will get over it, she's been unable to feed her baby and her milk may have dried up for good. The shock has sent her all doolally.'

'You've missed one. Grant knows where to get hold of a gun.'

Ellie said 'Oh!' soundlessly. 'Why can't things stay as they are? I feel like saying, "Stop the world, I want to get off."'

'I'm not sure about that. If you were given the opportunity, what time of your life would you like to live through again?'

Ellie remembered anxious teens, watching her father fade away. Then the struggle to earn a living as a secretary, with her mother's health declining . . . the early years of marriage to Frank, which would have been delightful if she hadn't had all those miscarriages . . . only baby Diana had survived from all those attempts . . . working in the charity shop beside Rose and all the other friends she'd made there. Those had been good years, but still, would she really want to live them over again? There'd been tension in the shop because of the inefficiency of the manageress, and at home she'd been oppressed by her failure to produce another child, had been bullied 'for her own good' by her husband and bullied not so nicely by Diana and even by Aunt Drusilla, who'd been a dragon in those days.

No, she wouldn't want to go back to those years. Since Frank had died and left her comfortably off, she'd discovered the delights of eating when she wished to do so, of visiting friends when she liked, of being in control of the television remote. She'd made new friends, played a part in sorting out one or two neighbourhood problems, joined the choir at church. She'd even learned how to say no to Diana every now and then. In short, she'd grown up and grown a new life.

'I suppose,' she said, dropping a sweetener into her coffee, 'that I'm happier at this moment than I ever have been, only I'm looking into the future and not liking it. Aunt Drusilla and Rose have been in my life for so long that I don't want to think what's going to happen when they . . . when they move on.'

Thomas chased the last of the ice cream around his plate and leaned back in his chair, replete. 'They're both very fond of you, you know.'

'And I of them.' Which was true. Ellie found a hanky in her purse and blew her nose. 'How about you? Would you want to relive a different age of your life?'

He shook his head. 'God is making use of me and I'm content. At least, I would be if the housekeeper you've foisted on me would do my washing twice a week instead of once, and you could find me a secretary for the parish council who can spell and retain some idea of what really went on in meetings.'

Ellie smiled, which was what he intended her to do. Then she looked at her watch. 'Well, this won't buy the baby any bootees. I've got to get back, sort out something for little Frank to eat before I collect him from school. Ugh. Nasty thought. Corinne's children were all at that school, and he'll know them. This is going to be a bad shock for him. Also the little girl that Corinne was looking after is probably in his class. But they won't be at school today, will they?'

'Leona's keeping the boys at home, getting them packed up for their new lives. We don't know when the funeral will be because the police can't release the body yet.'

Ellie grimaced. They split the bill in half as they always did and went their separate ways. Ellie collected some frozen meals from the Co-op in the Avenue and got home to hear the phone ringing. It was the secretary from the primary school on the line. 'Mrs Quicke, I'm sorry to trouble you. We've tried to raise Frank's mother and stepmother, but there's no reply from either and he says he's supposed to come to you today after school. Do you think you could pick him up a little early?'

Scenes of carnage involving Frank ran around Ellie's brain. 'What's happened? An accident? He's all right?'

'Yes, of course. He was in a bit of a scuffle in the playground at lunchtime, that's all, and his teacher thought it wisest if he calmed down before rejoining the others. So if you could manage to pick him up as soon as possible?'

'Yes, of course.' She glanced at the clock, thrust her shopping into the kitchen, fed Midge who had plopped through the cat flap as soon as he sensed someone was moving around in the kitchen — and made for the front door. She noticed that the answerphone light was flashing. Did she want to know what messages were on there? No, she decided she didn't.

Frank was in trouble. She didn't like to think what might be meant by 'a little scuffle in the playground'. He had his lunch early in the school day, didn't he? Could he have been involved in a fight while she and Thomas were taking their ease in the café?

As soon as she was out in the sun, she wished she'd stopped to collect a sun hat. It had been a warm morning and promised to be a scorching afternoon. Luckily it was not far to the school, which was just across the Green at the back of her house.

The playground was quiet as she approached. Afternoon lessons must have started. She pressed the buzzer on the gate and announced herself, to be let into the playground by remote control. Another locked door let her into the school building and as she pushed it open, the senior of the two secretaries came out to meet her.

'It's nothing to be alarmed about, Mrs Quicke. Just a bit of pushing and shoving, which the teacher on playground duty stopped straight away. Only Frank was a bit tearful, and we thought it best — come this way, will you? — to let him get over it quietly. I'm afraid everyone's a bit upset today and — here we are.'

She opened the door of a side room. Frank shot out and buried his head in Ellie's stomach. Her arms went round him. 'There, there.'

The school nurse appeared in the doorway. 'Mrs Quicke? He's been asking for you this last hour.'

Ellie let the implied criticism go by, asked if Frank had everything he needed, school bag, football boots, whatever, and being assured that he didn't need to take anything home with him, steered him out of the school buildings, across the playground and into the road. He kept his face turned to her side all this time, with one hand clutching her dress.

She didn't try to make him look at her but took him straight across the Green, into the alley and up through her garden to the house. Midge had never been too sure that Frank was a cat person so on seeing him being walked up the path, decided to make himself scarce by jumping on to the roof of the conservatory and doing an alpine trek to Kate's house next door.

The sun had made the conservatory too hot to sit in, because Ellie had forgotten to let down the blinds before she left that morning. She took Frank into the kitchen, sat him down and ran the cold tap. She wetted a kitchen towel and asked him to look up so she could wash the tears from his face. The nurse at school had looked after him, of course, but Ellie could see a bruise coming up on his jaw. Also, he'd torn his shirt and lost his tie. Diana would have something to say about that, but Ellie was more concerned with the fact that the little boy was still extremely distressed.

'I want some Coke,' said Frank, tears spilling over on to his cheeks.

'I'll get you something in a minute.' Ellie didn't have any Coca-Cola, but wasn't going to tell him that straight away, because it might precipitate a tantrum. 'Let's get you cleaned up first. That's a nasty bruise you've got there. Tripped and fell over, did you?'

'He pushed me. I hate him.' Frank wasn't one for a fight normally, and he hadn't talked about hating anyone at school before.

'Mm? Who started it?'

'He did. Yukky-picky-nose-snot. Horrible blue-bottle-crap. He's a pig, a pink-porky-pig and I'm not saying I'm sorry to him because he is!'

'You sit tight and I'll get you a drink. Could you manage a biscuit? Was this before or after lunch?'

'It was sausages and I felt sick. I sat in the nurse's room for a bit but then she said I'd be better off in the fresh air so I went out, and that's when he said . . . he said . . .' Tears welled up again. 'It's not true, is it? If Mummy died, my dad would want to keep me, wouldn't he?'

Ellie swooped on him and held him tight. 'Of course he would! Whatever have they been saying to you? But nothing's happened to your mummy, you know.'

'It happened to his. He's got to go and live with people he doesn't know, and never see his mummy again.'

'Oh, my dear. Your mummy's quite safe and your daddy would never, ever let you go. Believe me. Nor would I.' She sat and rocked him in her arms, the poor little mite. They must have been told about the death in school that morning. She knew that neither of the boys had been sent to school that day, but perhaps the girl had. Somehow or other the news had got round that one of the boys would have to go into care because his father didn't want him.

Frank sobbed and sobbed. 'That horrible pinky-pig, he said it, he said I'd be the one no one would want because my daddy had got two nice little girls now and wouldn't want to keep me if my mummy died. So I pushed him, and he pushed me over and kicked me, and I got up and kicked him back only I think I missed, then the teacher stopped us, and I wish I'd killed him and I will, too.'

'Frank, dear, nothing has happened to your mummy, and nothing will happen to her, and your daddy loves you so much, you know he does!'

'Daddy said—' A gulp. 'He said I ought to be more careful, that I'd hurt Yaz, even though I didn't mean to, but she was being silly and I had to stop her playing with my computer, didn't I?'

'Did you really hurt your little sister?'

'I just pushed her a bit, that's all, but she made such a fuss Daddy said . . . that. So he doesn't love me enough to keep me, does he?'

'You're getting all mixed up, Frank. Your daddy loves you to bits, so does Maria and so does little Yaz, you know she does.'

He hiccupped. 'Then she shouldn't play with my things when I tell her not to.'

Ellie rocked him closer. 'I expect she did it because she wants to be like you. She's only little and doesn't understand how grown-up you're getting. I know you're usually wonderful, looking after her and playing with her. Maria and your father are always singing your praises, saying what a good, loving brother you are to your little sisters.'

He sniffed. 'Then why did Daddy shout at me?'

'I expect you shouted at the porky-pig boy, didn't you? People do shout when they're upset.'

He relaxed a trifle. 'Porky-pig's father's never around. He went away and never came back, but he's not dead. He just isn't interested in Porky-Pig.'

'There you are, then. He's probably jealous because you've got so many people who love you. There's your mummy, and your daddy and Maria, and then there's little Yaz and—'

'Can I come and live with you if Daddy doesn't want me anymore?'

'Your daddy wouldn't like that one little bit. He loves you dearly, and so does your mummy and so does Maria.'

'If he didn't want me, could I?'

'I think I'd have to fight off your mother and your father and Maria and Yaz if you said that to them. And what about the new little baby? Didn't you say last week that she was even prettier than Yaz?'

He twisted in her arms to look up at her. 'But, could I?'

'Yes,' she said, and knew she'd made a rod for her own back, because he was going to play her off against Diana and everyone else from now on. She loved him dearly, of course she did, but he was just the teensiest bit tiring, and nowadays she was beginning to feel, when she saw him off back to his family at night, that she was glad to have a bit of peace and quiet. But, 'Yes,' she said.

* * *

Mick strolled down the Avenue with his two new friends, one on either side of him but a pace in the rear. They'd directed him to a house where a man they knew took the bike off him, no questions asked, in exchange for some useful ID and a fiver. So now Mick knew where he could get rid of anything he picked up. He could also get served in any pub thereabouts.

All he needed now was a new mobile phone and some cash. He'd look about for a well-maintained house without a burglar alarm, perhaps with just one old lady living in it. There were plenty of houses like where the aunt lived. There'd be electrical appliances he could lift from such a place, but he'd take it slowly, plan it out, not rush into anything.

What he'd really like to do was trash the aunt's place, because she really got on his wick. But no, he wouldn't do her over, not yet. Not till he could move on somewhere better.

The immediate problem was where to get some food for the dog. He explained to his new friends that he was looking after Toby for a mate who'd been called away sudden like. He didn't tell them Tich was in prison on remand. No reason to give them details. They said, 'No problem, get the stuff from the Co-op,' which he did.

He told them, 'Toby's a fighting dog.'

He watched them think about this. They were really stupid, no-brainers, but that suited him. He could do anything with them, tell them to keep lookout, help him smash his way into a house, help him carry away the stuff he lifted. They'd been in a gang before, but their chief had got an ASBO order on him, and his parents had sent him away somewhere. Mick had to laugh. He knew all about Anti Social Behaviour Orders, for he'd got one himself. As one goes, another fills his place.

One of them said, 'You don't half talk funny.'

That was a laugh, considering the way they slid the words out of their mouths. Mick said, 'Well, my dad's American. Not around, if you see what I mean.' Nearly the truth, if not quite.

They nodded. They knew all about dads not being around. The one with darker skin said, 'Did your dog kill that woman in the park yesterday? They said a dog did it.'

Mick took a deep breath. It hadn't occurred to him that she might have died. Did that make him a murderer? The thought gave him an uncomfortable feeling. He shrugged. 'Might of.'

Respect for him slid into their eyes.

CHAPTER SIX

It was mid-afternoon before little Frank released Ellie long enough for her to go to the bathroom by herself. Until then he clung to her side. She tried sitting him down with a video, she tried playing snap with him, she tried reading to him from a picture book. She tried everything. Finally he dozed off in front of the telly, and she escaped.

After a quick visit upstairs, she went into the study and closed the door to make a couple of phone calls. Diana wasn't answering her mobile and her partner, the steely, smiling Denis, answered the phone at the 2Ds estate agency. Diana was out with a client, he said. Ellie left a message for Diana to ring her. Ellie remembered that the answerphone light had been winking when she arrived back, and pressed play. It was Diana, her voice sharpening as she said she'd arranged for a professional photographer to be at Miss Quicke's at five o'clock sharp and would Ellie be sure to be there with Frank so that they could get the session over and done with. Ellie tried Diana's mobile, but it was still switched off. This time she left a message on it for Diana to ring her, urgently.

Diana might bother to ring back and she might not. Ellie told herself it would be best if Frank changed out of his school gear, no matter what. Luckily she always kept some clothes for him in the little bedroom upstairs, since he spent the night with her on a regular basis.

Then she tried Maria, who had returned home with her two youngsters by then. Maria was perturbed because her answerphone had registered the calls the school had been making to her and was just about to ring them when Ellie got through. Ellie explained what had happened and Maria responded exactly as she ought to.

'Oh, that's terrible. Please tell Frank we love him dearly, and of course we still love him even though he was a bit rough when playing with his little sister. But that doesn't make any difference to the way we feel about him. Should I speak to him on the phone?'

'He's just dozed off. I'll tell him when he wakes up, or get him to ring you so that he can hear it from you direct.'

'I was just about to take my two out to a birthday party with one of Yaz's friends. Shall I cancel it?'

'No, you go. I'll tell him when he wakes. The arrangement was that I'd keep Frank till Stewart collects him after work, and we'll stick to that.'

Ellie wanted to add how much she appreciated the way Maria had taken little Frank on, but didn't quite know what words to use. Diana tended alternately to spoil and neglect her son, but Maria provided him with a calm, loving environment while never letting him get away with bad behaviour. In consequence, a boy who might have grown up with a twist to his character, was coming along nicely.

Likewise Stewart, who'd been reduced to a pathetic shadow during his short marriage to Diana, was now a contented husband and father and was even putting on a bit of weight. To Diana's fury — because she'd considered herself the best and only candidate for the job — Miss Quicke had taken Stewart on to manage her empire of rented properties. Worse still, from Diana's point of view, he'd proved to be both conscientious and trustworthy.

'Maria,' said Ellie, 'you're a star.'

'So are you,' said Maria. 'What we'd all do without you, I don't know. But before you go, is there any news of Miss Quicke? Stewart's worried about her, says that if he asks her anything she tells him to use his own judgement, which of course he can do, knowing the business inside out as he does. But it's not like her.'

'She's tired, Maria. She knows she can trust Stewart to look after her interests, and she knows she can trust you to look after Stewart and Frank.'

Maria probed further. 'Tired? My father is getting tired and talks of retiring, but that's not quite what you mean, is it?'

'No, Maria. You're right. It's not.'

Maria sighed. 'Well, don't leave it too long before you come round to see us again, right?'

'One afternoon next week, perhaps? Oh, and Maria, Diana's arranging for a professional photographer to be at Aunt Drusilla's this afternoon to take a picture of the four different generations in the family. Would you like to see if Stewart can make it?'

'I'll get him to come back home first and put on a clean shirt. Should he bring some clean clothes for Frank?'

'I've got some upstairs for him. Thanks, Maria.' Ellie put the phone down to consider her next move. She was pleased with herself for putting a spoke in Diana's plans for the photo session. Now, should she check to see that her aunt knew about it? Definitely yes. After some thought, she rang Rose on her mobile. Rose was up and about with her radio — or perhaps the television — playing in the background.

'Rose dear, have you had a good nap? Splendid. Now I don't know if you've heard from Diana, but . . . you haven't? Right. Well, this is just to warn you that she intends to arrive with a professional photographer at five this afternoon to have the four generations of the family recorded for posterity. I'm supposed to bring little Frank over for it, and I'm checking that Stewart, Roy and Felicity will be there. Will you see if my aunt knows about it? I'm not at all sure that she'd want to be bothered . . . no, I agree, if she's resting she oughtn't to be disturbed, but I don't want Diana bursting in on her without warning. I'm taking Frank over to Felicity's in a while, but I'll leave my mobile on in case you want to contact me.'

Ellie put the phone down and went to see if Frank was awake and wanting to be fed, which he was. She usually gave him some home-made dish for tea, but he didn't grumble when confronted with something out of the microwave fact, he ate every scrap up, had bananas and custard for afters, and didn't even complain that she hadn't got any Coca-Cola in for him.

Ellie looked at the clock. 'I thought we could walk through the park to see how Flicky is coping with baby Mel. You are good with babies, aren't you? Perhaps Flicky will let you help give Mel her bottle.'

Frank screwed his face up. 'I'm not going through the park. That's where *it* happened.'

Distraction might work. 'That was yesterday. Why don't you run up and change into one of your new T-shirts?' She thought of Thomas's wild T-shirt and smiled to herself. All that guff about his washing not being up to date was just another way of saying he still wanted to marry her. Which was a comforting thought, even if she'd no intention of doing so. Or not yet, anyway.

'Oooh, must I?' The usual whine of childhood.

Her smile held, just. 'Yes, my dear. I want you to look your best when you go out with me. We might drop round to Aunt Drusilla's on the way back. Your mother wants to have a family photograph taken.'

Vanity was called into play, and he perked up. 'Can I wear the T-shirt with the Lion King on it?'

'Why not?' He scampered up the stairs and Ellie made sure she had her mobile phone, a comb and notepad in her handbag. Ought she to change for the group photo as well? No, her summer dress was good enough and it would take too long to change and do her hair and find some other sandals to wear. Diana would probably be in her fussiest black suit, portraying the successful businesswoman. Ellie would sit in the background and be grateful that her hips were not going to be on show. Her ankles were fine but there was no denying that she was finding some of her skirts a little tight around the waist and hips nowadays. But she did take the precaution of putting in an extra clean T-shirt for Frank. If he were going to have something to eat at Felicity's, he'd probably dirty whatever it was he was wearing now.

While waiting for Frank, Ellie rang Felicity to ask if it would be all right if they dropped by for a few minutes. Felicity sounded distracted, but said, 'Yes, all right.' She didn't sound very pleased about it, but she was at least warned that they were on their way.

'Don't want to go in the park,' said Frank, reporting for duty. 'Can't we take a cab to Flicky's? Mummy always goes in the car, and Daddy lets me sit up front beside him.'

'It's quicker to go across the park than to wait for a cab, and I know that Felicity's been baking scones today.'

'Flicky's a brilliant cook. Maria doesn't have time to cook like Flicky does. Do you think she'd let me have two scones?'

He talked about food as they took the road that led to the park, his eyes circling the vicinity on the lookout for dogs. They spotted a Pekinese, and Frank fell silent.

'Not that sort of dog,' said Ellie, who was also keeping an eye out for large dogs.

'Was it a big, big dog, with ginormous ears and . . . and *fangs*, like dragons' teeth?'

'I shouldn't think there were any fangs. Just teeth.'

He skipped along beside her, concentrating on putting his feet in the middle of the pavement slabs, and not treading on the cracks. Ellie was looking out for people walking dogs but didn't see any. When they turned into the park gates, Frank put his hand into Ellie's and kept close beside her. There were a few people with dogs in the park, but all the dogs were on a leash. Possibly there weren't as many there as usual? There were fewer people on the tennis courts and in the children's play area, too. Understandable.

'Would you like to go on the swings for a bit?'

He shook his head. Then looked to his right, where a black and white collie was being walked by a woman who also had a little terrier. Both were on leads. 'Is that the kind of dog it was?'

'No, I don't think so.' Ellie halted by the entrance to the fenced-off play area. No dogs were permitted in there, but a couple of spaniels had been tied up nearby in the shade while their owners took their children inside to play on the equipment. Frank was nervous, eyeing the dogs.

'Nor that kind?' he asked.

'Nor that kind,' said Ellie, who had spotted a woman walking a couple of glossy-looking golden retrievers, both on leads. This might be — if Ellie were lucky — the Trudy who Caroline had been talking about, and she was walking right towards them.

'Frank, why don't you go in and play while I talk to someone for a minute.'

'Don't feel like it.' He kicked the gatepost.

Ellie stepped forward to meet the woman. 'Excuse me, but are you Trudy Wells? If so, could you spare me a minute?'

The woman nodded, her eyes asking questions since she didn't know Ellie from Adam. Trudy was fiftyish, fair of hair and making no attempt to look younger than she was. She had the kind, strong features of a woman who lived a disciplined life, and Ellie could well understand how her very presence had helped Caroline the day before.

Ellie explained the connection with Felicity and Caroline, and how distressed everyone was, having known Corinne and her children from school and from church.

Trudy said, 'I didn't see it happen, you know. I only came along afterwards and tried to calm the children down while we waited for the ambulance.'

'I know that,' said Ellie. 'May I walk with you a little way? Frank, either you come along with us, or you go into the play area for a while. And no, these dogs are not the same as the one who did the damage yesterday, and there's no need to be afraid of them.'

'I'm not afraid of them!' But of course he was. He clung to Ellie's hand, walking on the far side of her from the dogs.

Trudy said, 'The police wanted to know if I'd seen a youngster walking a large brown dog, but I hadn't. I wish I could help, but I can't.'

'From what I've heard, the people who use the park fall into different groups. The dog-walkers talk to one another, the baby-walkers the same, and the joggers don't talk to anyone else but themselves.'

Trudy agreed. 'We all have our routines. Either my husband or I walk the dogs first thing in the morning, and again about this time of day. He's on shifts, so sometimes he does it, and sometimes I do.' One of the dogs was investigating a fast-food container on the grass beside the path. Trudy said, 'No, Skipper — come away. That's nasty!' She picked it up and dropped it in the nearby bin. 'Some people don't know what a rubbish bin is for.'

Ellie said, 'It was about this time of day when . . . ?'

Trudy nodded. A small boy on a bicycle fitted with stabilizers was wobbling along the path towards them, followed by an anxious looking mother on an adult bike. Trudy called her dogs. 'Skipper, Gemma. Sit!' They both sat at the side of the path to let the mother and son through.

'You've trained them well,' said Ellie.

Frank said, 'Will we be able to see the blood?'

'I hope not,' said Ellie, shuddering.

'I shouldn't think so,' said Trudy, but her eyes signalled a different message to Ellie, and she suggested they cut across the grass to sit on a bench under the trees. The dogs settled down in the shade, panting. It was a dustily hot afternoon.

Frank sat on the far side of Ellie from the dogs but since they took no notice of him, he began to move, little by little, towards them and finally managed to stroke the younger one's head. The dog permitted his advances without welcoming them.

'What's your interest?' enquired Trudy.

'One of Corinne's relatives is spoiling for revenge, and there's a danger it could spiral into a gangland episode. He thinks the dog was bred to fight.'

'You mean illegal dog fighting? There's none of that around here.'

'Would you know, if there were?'

'Oh yes, I should think so. We all talk to one another, we dog owners. Before I get to the park gates in the morning, I'll have met one or two of my friends who've walked their dogs already. They'd tell me if there was a problem, such as a bitch on heat in the park — which is not supposed to happen — or if there's a dog who's not properly under control. Then I'd know to keep my two on a leash. I do the same for them. Yes, we all know one another pretty well.'

'So yesterday afternoon you should have been warned about a dicey dog even before you got into the park?'

Trudy patted Skipper, who was nudging her knee. 'In a minute, Skipper. Normally I would, but as it happens I didn't see anyone I knew on the way in yesterday. Not all that many people want to bring their dogs out in the heat of the day. It suits my routine, but most of them will come later when it's cooler.'

'So you weren't warned and as far as you can tell, the boy and the dog were strangers that you'd never seen before?'

'I've been thinking about that. That poor woman must have brought the children and their bike into the park as soon as they were let out of school. You expect to meet primary school children in the park then, but you don't expect to see older lads, teenagers, maybe fourteen or fifteen. That's what Caroline told the police, that he was a youngish teen, smallish, definitely not of school leaving age.'

'Which means he was bunking off school?'

'Could be. Maybe it was the first time he'd brought the dog to the park, and didn't know how to control him. Only, one of the kids said—' she shot a glance down at Frank, who by now was crouching on the ground, patting Gemma's head — 'the oldest boy, he was in shock, of course, but he kept saying that the lad who stole his bike reminded him of someone in the local gang. One particular school near here has a very mixed intake, and there's a group of three or four lads who truant regularly and are often to be found hanging around in the park, especially in the evenings. They're into antisocial behaviour in a big way — graffiti, tossing stuff from the rubbish bins all over the paths, that sort of thing. The boy insisted that he hadn't seen this particular lad before, but he might be wrong. It sounds the sort of thing those lads might do, take a dog out without knowing how to control it, and then pinch a bike. Only that lot usually goes around in threes or fours. In my experience, it's unusual to see one lad all by himself.'

'I know what you mean.'

'The police will follow it up, of course, but if the boy's right, then they should be looking for a stranger, and how they find him, I don't know.' She got up to leave. 'Must go. Husband's supper to cook. He's on lates tonight.'

'Thank you.' Ellie scrabbled in her handbag for a piece of paper on which to write her phone number. 'If you think of anything else, or if someone else does, could you let me know? As well as the police, I mean. For instance, if you come across someone who was walking their dogs earlier than you yesterday and might have seen the lad, too?'

'I'll ask around. Gemma, Skipper, walk on.'

Ellie and Frank continued across the park. 'I was brave, wasn't I?' said Frank. 'I touched Gemma all over her head and she didn't dare to bite me. You'll tell Daddy how brave I was, won't you?'

Ellie smiled assent.

'And you won't tell him I was fighting in the playground, will you?'

'Maria knows all about it, already.'

'Oh.' They had to cross the path of a whippet, who was racing around its master like a frenzied yoyo in spite of the heat. Frank fell silent till they reached the far gate, when he said, 'I don't mind going in the park with you, Granny, but I still wouldn't want a puppy for my birthday. I think I'd prefer a snake.'

Ellie nearly had hysterics at the idea of Frank having a snake for a pet. She wondered how Maria would react to the idea and decided she could leave that sensible woman to deal with it.

Roy's car was not in the driveway when they reached his house, but Felicity answered the door with Mel in her arms, and a tea towel thrown over her shoulder.

'Won't she bring her wind up?' asked Ellie. 'Shall I have a go?'

Felicity looked hot and bothered. 'She wasn't like this when I was feeding her myself. Caroline says Rose may have got me the wrong formula.'

Of course Felicity would want to blame Rose. Ellie took Mel and put her over her shoulder, whereupon the baby obliged with a loud burp and dribbled a mouthful of creamy milk on to Ellie's shoulder. 'It brings it all back,' said Ellie, remembering just how it was when she used to feed Diana, who was now taller than her mother.

'Mel's very small,' said Frank, comparing her with his two half-sisters.

'You were that small once,' said Ellie, remembering.

'Want some tea?' Felicity was switching on the kettle in the kitchen. 'Roy's going to be late again, I think. Frank, do you want something to eat? There's some scones and jam.'

Frank took a stool and waited to be served.

Ellie rearranged Mel on her shoulder. 'Diana has arranged for a professional photographer to be at Aunt Drusilla's today at five, to take a four-generation photo. Has she checked it out with you? No? Well, do you think you could make it with Mel? And check that Roy knows about it, too?'

'A photograph of four generations? What a good idea, except . . . Roy did say his mother wasn't up to much nowadays. I was surprised she made it here yesterday.'

'She was worried about you.'

Felicity tried on a laugh for size. It fitted pretty well. 'I was completely out of it yesterday, wasn't I? Totally off this earth. I still don't like to think about it, but as Caroline says, we've got to think of the babies. They're important, and we're not. Or not in the same way, if you see what I mean.'

'I see what you mean. Frank, dear, come and look at Baby's eyes. Do you think they're changing colour already? Babies' eyes do change colour, you know. Do you think she's like your sisters?'

Frank leaned over to inspect the baby. 'She's all right, I suppose. Maria lets me hold the bottle at feeding times. Well, sometimes she does. Maria says I'm brilliant with babies, but they do take up a lot of time, don't they?'

Felicity and Ellie smiled. Yes, babies did take up a lot of time.

Felicity looked down at herself. She was wearing the same blouse and jeans that she'd had on that morning. 'I'd better ring Roy, remind him to be there, and I must change into something more suitable. I suppose Diana will be dressed up to the nines.'

Frank chomped his way through two scones while Felicity phoned Roy and then went to change. Ellie sat with Mel in her arms, thinking of this and that, thinking that she ought to sponge down the shoulder of her dress before they went to Miss Quicke's. She'd left her mobile on, but Diana hadn't bothered to contact her. Diana was not going to be pleased that her family photo was going to include Stewart, Roy, Felicity and Mel.

Ellie found herself smiling. Once she'd have quailed at the thought of rousing Diana's displeasure but nowadays she really couldn't allow herself to be disturbed by it. She sank lower in her chair. Mel was dozing, warm and cosy against Ellie's shoulder. The room was warm. A helicopter droned in the distance. Ellie's eyelids drooped.

She was a child again, visiting some friends of her parents in the country. One of the boys asked if Ellie would like to see the puppies which had just been born in the garden shed. Ellie knew very little about dogs, being a city child whose parents had never owned one. She followed the boy down the garden path, and he opened the door. Ellie peered in, curious, unafraid. The shed was dark. Something growled at her and she started back, turning to the boy for information, not sure what she was getting into, but the boy had disappeared behind the door. She could hear him laughing. A black and white bombshell burst out of the shed and Ellie ran, screaming. The dog fastened on to the back of her leg and hung on. Adults dragged the dog off and scolded the children for disturbing a nursing mother.

Later, she was lying face down on a wooden table, having a burning hot poultice applied to the back of her leg. The wound had gone septic. It hurt.

Half asleep, Ellie thought, I must find that dog . . .

Somebody was making a noise nearby. She jerked awake, thinking that if a dog had killed once, he was capable of killing again. It was desperately important to find him before he could do any more damage.

Felicity was combing out her fair hair and talking. '. . . So I think it's probably best if we take a dress with us and change her at the last minute.' Felicity had changed in to a low-cut, sleeveless cream silk dress which showed off her summer tan. She looked gorgeous.

Ellie tried to concentrate. 'That's a new dress, isn't it? You look lovely.'

Felicity laughed. 'I look like a cream cake, but I suppose it will do.'

Ellie's arm had gone to sleep, while she nursed Mel. 'Where's Frank? I brought a change of clothes for him. He's bound to have got jam on his T-shirt.'

'Garden. Talking to my next-door neighbour over the fence. The old one. She's picked up no end since her husband had to go into a home. I only have to go into the garden and she's there wanting to chat, poor old thing. I hope I don't get like that when I'm old.' She looked at her watch. 'We'd better get a move on, hadn't we?' She called out of the back door,

'Frank, it's time to go. What's that on your hands? Well, I expect it'll wash off. But what about your T-shirt?'

Ellie grimaced, her worst fears realized about Frank's ability to attract dirt. 'Suppose he waits to put on his clean T-shirt at the last possible moment. We must all look out best for the photo, mustn't we? Come on, now. We don't want to be late.'

* * *

The lads whined, 'What shall we do now?'

Mick understood that they'd been playing follow my leader ever since they began to truant from school, years ago. The one in the black hood lived in some high-rise council flats on the other side of the park. The one in the striped T-shirt lived in a dump provided by the social, at the other end of the Avenue. They'd followed their previous leader because he gave them some focus in life, thinking up things for them to do.

Mick tested them. 'What do you usually do?'

The one in the black hood shrugged. 'We keep lookout while he spreads his tag around. He used to get some of that paint that don't come off easy. Only, the shops in the Avenue won't sell us none of the good stuff, know what I mean?'

'Sometimes we go in the park, tip over the litter bins, watch the old ladies get upset.' This from the one in the pseudo army fatigues. 'That's a laugh, that is.'

Black Hood warmed to his story. 'He usedta do the play centre in the park, any old paint will do for that, and they don't half get cross when they see it in the morning! Only, after a while, they knew it was him, and they got really stroppy. It were only a bit of fun, weren't it? Something to do.'

'Is that all?' said Mick, thinking these lads were still in kindergarten as far as he was concerned.

Black Hood said, in defence, 'We let off some bangers in the park last year, when there was fireworks in the shops. That was all right, didn't half make people jump. But it's summer now and the shops ain't got no fireworks yet.'

'I can think of something better than that to do,' said Mick.

CHAPTER SEVEN

As they drove along in Felicity's car, Frank informed them that he liked the person who lived next door to Flicky. The old lady had agreed with him that little sisters were a pain and shouldn't be allowed to touch his things, ever. She'd promised that if he went to stay with her, he could play with his computer all night.

Felicity rolled her eyes at Ellie. 'What brought this on, Frank?'

'Nothing.' Frank was busy rewriting history. 'Yaz is a silly cry baby, that's all. Did you have a cry-baby sister, Flicky?'

'I was an only child so I didn't have that particular problem. Ellie, you're very quiet today.'

'I was wondering about dogs, you know.' Felicity swerved. 'Careful!' said Ellie. 'And that light's about to turn red.'

Felicity applied the brakes. 'Sorry. It's just, dogs, you know.'

'I know, but the problem won't go away. That dog has killed once and got away with it. Suppose he attacks a child in the street tomorrow, or a baby in a buggy?'

'Ouch!' said Felicity, throwing a glance over her shoulder to see that Mel was still in the car and unharmed.

'So,' said Ellie, 'do you know anyone in the dog world? Someone who breeds them, perhaps? Or, that might be a better line of enquiry, do you know anyone who likes to bet on the dogs?'

Felicity watched the lights and drove on when they turned green. 'I think Roy knows someone who goes to the races. Horse races. I don't know anyone who goes dog racing.'

Ellie nodded. Felicity was usually a careful driver, but today she was not giving her passengers as smooth a ride as usual. Felicity was coping pretty well with her trauma, but it was still there. They turned into Miss Quicke's drive and parked.

'Window cleaner,' Felicity said, undoing her seat belt. 'He's always on his mobile, placing bets. I'm not sure whether it's dogs or horses, but he might know something.'

'My window cleaner is the chatty type,' said Ellie, undoing her own seat belt, 'but I've never heard him talk about dogs or horses. How can I contact yours?'

'He comes when he feels like it, roughly once a month but on no set date. It depends on the weather. I don't have a phone number for him.'

By this time Frank had released his seat belt and was already out of the car and pressing the doorbell. The adults followed with Mel's car seat and the children's paraphernalia. They passed Diana's car, but neither commented on it.

It was Diana who opened the door, and predictably moved into scolding Frank. 'What's that on your T-shirt? How could you turn up looking like that! You're not fit to be seen!'

Ellie tried to lower the temperature. 'It's all right, Diana. I've got a change of clothing for him.'

'What? Felicity, what on earth are you doing here?'

Felicity blinked but carried Mel through the hall into the sitting room. 'I've come for the photograph of course. Roy should be here in a minute. Are we having it done in here?'

'Stewart's coming, too,' said Ellie, enjoying the look of baffled fury on Diana's face. 'Won't that be nice? All the family together.'

Diana's mouth stayed open. For once she had no words to express her displeasure. Instead, she took Frank by his upper arm and propelled him in the direction of the cloakroom. 'Get yourself cleaned up, this minute. Mother,' Diana tried to moderate her tone, 'I thought I could trust you to—'

'To do what, dear?' said Ellie, sorting out a change of clothes for Frank. 'A lovely idea of yours to have a family photo. I left a message for you on your mobile, but you failed to ring me back. I'm only concerned that Aunt Drusilla might not be up to it. Here you are, Frank. Best clothes for a best boy.'

The doorbell rang, shutting off Diana's retort. She switched to a smile, ushering in a photographer laden with paraphernalia. Diana explained that there would be a larger group than she'd expected but he wouldn't mind that, would he?

Close behind the photographer came Roy, Miss Quicke's son, whom Diana believed to be the chief threat to her inheriting the family fortune, and Stewart, her despised ex-husband. Both men were well turned out, and both were smiling. Neither gave Diana the attention she felt she deserved.

Ellie smothered a grin and dived into her handbag for a comb with which to tackle Frank's mop.

'Is that you, Roy? I'm in here,' called Felicity, from the sitting room. 'Won't be a mo. Just changing Mel.'

'Ah,' said Roy, exchanging knowing glances with Stewart. 'I don't do nappy duty, do you?'

'You get used to it,' said Stewart, proud father of three.

'Where . . . ?' asked the photographer, looking harassed.

'Sitting room,' said Diana, only to be contradicted by Rose, who appeared from the kitchen at that moment, pushing an old-fashioned trolley bearing everything a party of twenty might want for tea. 'Miss Quicke said she's not coming downstairs this afternoon, so if you want a photograph you'll have to go up to her bedroom. Don't take too long about it because she's wanting a nap before supper.

Afterwards, I'm serving tea down here for anyone who wants it.' Rose liked nothing better than to cater for people with large appetites.

'Up we go, then,' said Roy, indicating that the photographer follow him to the first floor. Stewart hung back to give Felicity a hand with Mel in her car seat, while Ellie took Frank's hand in case he slipped on the broad, polished stairs.

Diana brought up the rear, her mouth in a bitter line. 'Mother, you might have warned me you'd invited everyone and his pet dog.'

'I did try to, dear, but you'd got your mobile switched off.'

'I couldn't risk being interrupted when I was with a client.'

'Where . . . ?' asked the photographer, one of his metal boxes slipping from under his arm.

'In here,' said Roy, tapping on the closed door of his mother's bedroom. He raised his voice — 'Are we decent?' — and led the way in. The room was shadowy, the blinds down, but Miss Quicke had arranged herself in her high-backed chair in front of a carved Japanese screen which usually stood in a corner of the room. She was wearing a dark-red velour dressing gown and her hair had been freshly combed. Her eyelids looked heavy, but her eyes were as sharp as ever.

Ellie felt fear clutch at her heart. If the others didn't notice that the old lady was holding herself upright by leaning on her silver-handled stick, Ellie certainly did. A smaller chair and a bedroom stool had been placed on either side of Miss Quicke, showing that she'd prepared for the event.

'You,' said Miss Quicke, addressing the photographer, 'will kindly do your business as fast as you can. I do not intend to sit here for an hour while you fiddle with focus, understood? Ellie, you may sit here,' indicating the chair to her right. 'Felicity, you may sit on the stool with baby Mel. Diana, you may stand behind me. Roy is to stand at your right, Stewart to your left. Frank, come and stand in front of me and no wriggling. Cat got your tongue, Diana?'

Diana seethed but said, through her teeth, 'Of course not, Great-Aunt. You've arranged things admirably.'

Felicity kissed Miss Quicke, took Mel out of her car seat and fluffed out the broderie anglaise dress into which the baby had just been inserted. Mel stirred, rosy-cheeked, looking around her with interest.

Felicity was about to sit down when she gave a little shriek. 'Ellie, whatever is that on your dress? Is it from when you were holding Mel? Let me sponge it off for you.' She dithered, wanting to put Mel down but not wanting to give her to Diana, who happened to be standing nearest.

'Let me take her,' said Stewart. 'I'm used to babies.'

'No, no.' Felicity was distracted. 'Here, Roy; you take her.'

Roy looked alarmed but accepted the child without protest. Ellie wondered, as she was hustled off to Miss Quicke's bathroom, whether Roy had ever nursed his child before. Perhaps not. Felicity scrubbed away at Ellie's dress, muttering about the smell which always hung around people who had anything to do with babies. Ellie wanted to giggle; was Felicity turning into an authority on the subject? Well, perhaps she was.

By the time they got back, the photographer was checking his portable light, Frank was sitting cross-legged on the floor looking bored, Stewart and Diana were ignoring one another, and Roy . . . Roy was walking about the room smiling down at his daughter, his little finger stroking her cheek. The miracle had taken place, and Roy had fallen victim to his daughter's charms. Five minutes of looking into eyes which were the mirror image of his own, five minutes of admiring the tiny fingers that waved, trying to catch a sunbeam, and he was as besotted a father as any wife could wish for.

'Ah,' breathed Ellie. 'Will you look at Roy.'

Felicity smiled, cat-like. 'She's a little charmer, isn't she? I knew he'd come round to her in the end.'

Ellie noted that Miss Quicke was crouched lower than ever over her stick. 'Aunt is getting tired.'

'Can I go downstairs and get something to eat?' asked Frank.

'In a minute,' said Stewart, who also seemed concerned about Miss Quicke. He bent over his employer. 'Are you sure you're up for this?'

'Of course she is,' snapped Diana. 'It's an historic moment. Four generations of the Quicke family and their . . . their appendages.'

Roy laughed out loud at this. Felicity lifted her arms to take the baby from him. He let her go but followed her with his eyes. 'I think she's got your beautiful skin, Flicky.'

'Can we get on?' demanded Diana. 'If we have to have an extended family photo first, I want one with just the four of us *immediate* family next: Great-Aunt, Mother, me and Frank.'

'My patience is not inexhaustible,' observed Miss Quicke. 'You there,' she addressed the perspiring photographer, who was leaping from lighting to tripod and back again. 'Hurry up, or shut up shop. I want a rest before supper.'

'Ready, ready . . . all but . . . if you would all take your places?'

Ellie seated herself, conscious of the damp, scrubbed patch on her shoulder, but thinking it really didn't matter, though she'd have preferred to have gone home and changed, which would have taken far too long, and she really ought not to worry about such trivial things when she could see — as could Stewart — that Miss Quicke was holding herself erect with difficulty.

The group all looked at the photographer, except for Felicity and Roy, who looked down on baby Mel. One flash. A pause. 'All look this way?' Another flash. Another pause. 'Could Ms . . . ? The lady in black, could she manage to smile, please?' Another flash.

'That's enough,' said Miss Quicke.

'Oh, but—' said Diana. 'Just one with the four of us, something for Frank to remember.'

'I said, that's enough.' Miss Quicke tried to rise from her chair and failed. Stewart shot a look of alarm at Ellie, who took control.

'That's it, folks,' said Ellie. 'Time for Aunt Drusilla to have her nap, and time for us to have some tea. Frank, will you lead the way? Tell Rose we'd love a cuppa now. And go carefully. Felicity, suppose you let Roy carry Mel down. We don't want anyone slipping on those stairs, do we? Diana, will you settle with the photographer? And perhaps Stewart can help him with his bits and pieces, right?'

The room emptied out. At the third attempt, Miss Quicke managed to get to her feet, and on Ellie's arm made it back to her bed. Ellie saw the old lady comfortably settled, but when she would have withdrawn, a claw-like hand settled on her wrist. Ellie waited until her aunt had regained enough strength to speak. The bedroom windows were open, as were the windows of the room below, so she could hear the clash of teacups and murmur of voices from the tea party below.

At last Miss Quicke spoke, or rather, whispered. 'Promise me. No hospital.'

Ellie had been expecting this. 'Rose will need help, then.'

'You can see to that, details of nursing agency on my desk. I always thought, live alone, die alone. But maybe . . . maybe that's not best. Thomas said . . .' Her voice trailed away.

Ellie covered the old lady's hand with hers. Stroked it. 'Do you want to see him again tomorrow?'

'He makes me laugh. I've never known a man like him for putting one in a good temper. He seems to think laughter comes from God.'

'Where else would it come from?'

There was a long pause, while the old woman's eyelids drooped. When her eyes were almost completely shut, the weary voice continued. 'Roy will be all right now. Wife, child. He'll need a guiding hand now and then, so will she, but I trust you for that.'

Ellie thought with one part of her mind that she ought to say, 'Don't talk like that, you're going to live for ever,' and with the other part of her mind she knew that that was ridiculous. She made a 'Mmhm' sound in her throat.

'Diana . . . hah!' The old woman's voice deepened. 'She thinks I can't see through her.'

'The boy's all right. Stewart and Maria are doing a good job on him.'

'I do not believe in giving youngsters a lot of money. It prevents them from fulfilling their potential.'

'A trust fund . . . ?'

'I updated my will a month ago, and I'm satisfied with what I've done. I think I'd like someone to hold my hand when I go, but Rose will cry, I know she will, and I don't want that.'

'You want me or Thomas.' It was a statement, not a question.

The old woman relinquished her hold on Ellie's wrist. 'You may go now.'

On the landing outside Ellie blew her nose and wiped her eyes. She was going to miss her aunt. How she was going to miss her! She straightened her back. She had work to do. Now, how was she going to find that dog before it did any more damage?

Downstairs, the party was in full swing. Frank had wandered into the conservatory, dropping crumbs as he went, which would encourage mice to breed. Ellie made a mental note to speak to Rose about mice, soonest. Felicity was arranging for the photographer to take a picture of herself, Roy and Mel. Stewart was on his mobile, looking at his watch, saying he'd been held up but would be . . . wherever . . . in half an hour. Diana was restless, prowling around, touching the antiques with which the room was furnished.

Rose was pouring out second cups of tea and dishing out sandwiches. She was in her element. Ellie asked if Rose would like her to take something up to Miss Quicke, and Rose said she'd been ordered to take something up at six, not a minute before.

Ellie took her cup of tea and a sandwich over to where Stewart was fussing with some papers in his briefcase. 'Stewart, I'm sure you must be busy, but one word, quickly.

Do you use a firm of window cleaners, or different people for different buildings?'

'A firm, of course. Too much work for a one-man-and-his-dog setup. Frank!' He called out to his son. 'Time to go.'

'I haven't finished my tea,' said Frank, taking another slice of chocolate cake.

Stewart looked at his watch again. 'Look, son, I've got to drop some paperwork off on the way, but we don't want to be late for Yaz's bedtime, do we?'

'I hate Yaz,' said Frank, daring his father to make a scene in public.

'Of course you do, darling,' said Diana, seeing a chance to stir up trouble between father and son. 'You don't want to be bothered with little girls all the time, do you? Little girls are silly. You come home with me, and we'll watch a video together.'

Stewart began to look harassed. 'Frank had nightmares after he watched that war film at your place, Diana. Don't you think—?'

'What I think is that he loves his mummy best, don't you, Frank?' She stooped to caress his head. 'You tell Daddy where we're going in the summer holidays, then.'

'He's coming with us to stay with my family up north,' said Stewart.

'No, I'm not,' said Frank. 'I don't want to see your silly old people. I'm going to Disney World with Mummy.'

Stewart's mouth tightened. Of late he'd begun to stand up to Diana, but he didn't know how to deal with Diana and his son working together.

Diana was triumphant. 'Go and wash your hands, Frank. I don't want sticky fingers in my car.'

Stewart protested. 'He's not supposed to be staying with you tonight.'

Diana laughed, sure of herself. 'Do you want to go with your father, Frank? You'd have to wait around while he does whatever business he's got to do, and then you'd go home to find silly Yaz playing with your computer?'

'No way!' said Frank. 'I can sit up front in the car, can't I?' He ran off, leaving Stewart to protest again.

'Diana, you can't do this.'

'Watch me,' she said, and swirled out of the room after her son. There was an awkward silence. Roy and Felicity were packing up Mel's bits and pieces, ready to leave. Rose collected dirty china on to her trolley, her lips pinched in disapproval of Diana's tactics.

Stewart shouted, 'Frank, come back here!' and was answered by hearing a skitter of the boy's footsteps across the hall, and the thud as the front door closed behind him, opened to let Diana out, and shut again.

Ellie started to walk Stewart to the door. 'You know best, of course, but a solicitor's letter would remind Diana of the terms under which she has Frank to stay?'

'It's that pesky computer,' said Stewart. 'He spends hours on it, playing games, and he knows I don't approve. But Diana gave it to him and . . . he gets so irritable when he doesn't get enough sleep.'

She opened the front door and pushed him out. 'Let Maria deal with it. You go and meet your client.'

The tension left his face, and he smiled. His second marriage was a very happy one, and yes, Maria would sort it out for him.

Felicity and Roy left, too. This time Roy was carrying the car seat with Mel in it. Both looked happy, both kissed Ellie goodbye.

Ellie turned back into the house, which was now quiet and perhaps even a little sombre. Rose was clashing dishes in the kitchen and Ellie joined her. They were old friends, sharing the workload of putting crockery into the dishwasher as they'd once shared the workload at the charity shop.

Rose almost spat the word. 'Diana!'

'Yes, but Maria will deal with it.'

'I have a lot of time for Maria.'

'Stewart's OK, too. He's doing a good job for Aunt Drusilla.'

Rose was putting the rest of the cake in a tin, but her hands stilled. 'I'm not imagining it, am I? She is needing a lot more rest. She hardly eats anything, no matter what I cook for her, and only sips at the lemonade which I make fresh for her every day with real lemons and sugar and hot water, and then she hardly touches it and I'm so afraid . . .' She found a handkerchief in the waistband of her skirt, and sniffed into it.

There was no point pretending that Miss Quicke wasn't dying, because she was. Ellie emptied out the teapot and put it in the dish washer.

Rose put her handkerchief away. 'So. I've seen my mother die, and my husband, rest his soul, even though there were times when I wasn't sure he had one. A soul, I mean. Oh, what am I saying? Of course he had a soul, but he got short-changed in the kindness department, didn't he? Then there was my aunt that was so good to me and left me her china — not that I wanted it, but it was something she valued and heaven knows, we do value the strangest things, don't we?'

'We do,' said Ellie, cleaning surfaces. 'Aunt Drusilla doesn't want you wearing yourself out, caring for her, or you'll be ill. And that's the last thing she wants.'

'I'm all right,' Rose said angrily. 'It doesn't bother me, getting up in the night to attend to her, though I must admit we had a bit of a wobble on the way to the bathroom last night.'

'That's it,' said Ellie. 'You've done wonders, Rose. I couldn't have done what you've been doing, but now she needs someone young and strong to get her to the bathroom in the middle of the night. I'm to get some agency staff in. They'll take it in shifts to sit with her, and you'll get your strength back. Right?'

Rose sank on to a stool. 'She bought me an annuity; did you know?'

'I knew, and I think it's no more than you deserve.'

'She's also given me a ground-floor flat that's let out at the moment, but she says Stewart can get it back for me whenever I find this house is a bit too much for me and want to retire. I told her, I don't want to leave you yet, and she said, she said . . .'

'It's her that's leaving us. Yes.'

Rose tossed her head, gave another sniff and looked at the clock. 'I'll just take her up some fresh lemonade and see she has her pills, not that they do any good, and she says she's not in pain today, but it's something that we can still do for her, isn't it? The doctor's due at six, and then maybe Thomas will call round for a little while. She plays cribbage with him, did you know that?'

Ellie nodded. Yes, she knew that.

'Sometimes they sit and chat. Sometimes they just sit. When you go into the room, it feels . . . quiet. Oh, silly me. As if a room can feel quiet.'

Ellie gave Rose a hug. 'Dear Rose, you hit on exactly the right word to describe what happens in a room when Thomas has been there, praying. Now, I'll just pop upstairs and get that agency number, see when they can start.'

Ellie held on to the banister as she climbed the stairs. Really it would be better to have the stairs carpeted, much safer, but Aunt Drusilla has always liked the chilly splendour of polished wood. Ellie knocked softly on the door, but there was no reply. Her aunt was asleep, softly breathing. Ellie found the agency number on a flier where Miss Quicke had left it, already marked up in pen with the hourly rates, and a name to contact. Miss Quicke had thought of everything.

On the bedside table was a photograph in a silver frame, one that was usually kept in the sitting room below. The photograph was that of a young man, Roy's father. He'd wooed the plain young girl that Drusilla had been, thinking she was an heiress, only to abandon her when he discovered his mistake. The baby had been given up for adoption, and Drusilla had become a sour, miserly creature whose only God had been that of the wealth she'd accumulated through years of hard work.

She'd brought up her orphaned nephew Frank when his parents died, and perhaps she'd loved him in her own way, though she'd never shown any kindness to him or to his wife, Ellie, whom she'd treated like a skivvy until Frank, too, had died, leaving his widow to inherit the family house.

Only in her eighties had Aunt Drusilla come to appreciate Ellie's disinterested concern for her, and been further softened by the reappearance in her life of her son Roy. As a baby he'd been adopted into a loving family, had trained as an architect, and had only come looking for his birth mother after his first marriage had broken down, and he'd taken early retirement. Miss Quicke had never been so happy as in these last few years, not least because of Rose's gentle insistence on keeping the house bright and cheerful, and the delightful food she cooked.

Ellie gave the silver frame a rub with her skirt and returned it to the table, wondering if her aunt had ever managed to forgive the man who'd so drastically altered the course of her life. Still Miss Quicke slept, lightly, her breathing hardly disturbing the sheet over her tiny body.

The doorbell rang below, and voices murmured in the hall. Ellie took the agency details out on to the landing. Rose was climbing the stairs with a youngish woman carrying a medical case. The doctor.

Thomas had also arrived but was lingering in the hall, waiting for the doctor to be through with her patient. Thomas had changed into sober gear and was also carrying a case. Ellie's pulse went thump, thump. The case that Thomas was carrying was the one he took to the bedsides of dying men and women, to give them the last rites. Did he really think Aunt Drusilla was so close to death?

Rose introduced Ellie to the doctor, who nodded and went on into the bedroom. Rose went with her. Ellie went down the stairs, exchanged a greeting with Thomas and asked him to wait with her in the sitting room. Then, trying to be calm and organized, she rang the nursing agency. She was not altogether surprised to find that the agency already had all Miss Quicke's details on their computer, and had been on standby for some days, expecting to be called in. They could send someone over that evening about eight, would that be all right?

Ellie put down the phone, thinking that events were moving far too fast for her. The doctor came into the room, followed by Rose, who was weeping gently.

'She should be in hospital,' said the doctor.

'No hospital,' said Ellie, in chorus with Thomas.

Rose shook her head, gently sniffing and mopping. 'She made me promise. She made a living will, you know she did. You can't just whisk her off to hospital.'

Ellie indicated her sheaf of paperwork. 'An agency nurse is coming in tonight, at eight. Miss Quicke will have round-the-clock nursing from now on.'

Rose objected. 'I can manage during the day.'

'No, you can't,' said Ellie, giving her a hug. 'You have to keep your strength up, and chatter to her about the flowers and the garden and little Mel when she wants to listen, and look after yourself when she wants to rest. Ten to one she'll hate the nurses and prefer you to sit with her now and then, but there must be someone in the room with her all the time from now on.'

Thomas picked up his case. 'She asked me to call this evening.'

'She's waiting for you,' said Rose.

The doctor picked up her own case. 'I understand she's stopped eating, and barely takes anything to drink. She's dehydrated. If we had her in hospital—'

'No,' said Ellie and Thomas together.

'She's ready to go,' said Thomas, holding the door open for the doctor to leave.

The doctor gave in with a good grace. 'We doctors find it hard to admit we can't keep our patients alive indefinitely. I'll call in again tomorrow, or you can contact me any time.' Ellie heard the front door open and close, and the creak of the wood as Thomas mounted the staircase.

Rose put her handkerchief away with one final sniff. 'She asked me to give Thomas some supper when he's ready.

You too, Ellie; I know you only had a quarter of a sandwich at teatime, and there's plenty. I've got a nice lamb casserole in the oven with sweet potatoes and a savoy cabbage, which I know Thomas will enjoy, poor man, living in that poky vicarage all by himself, it's a thorough shame, that's what it is.' The newly rebuilt vicarage was far from 'poky', but of course the rooms didn't compare to these spacious surroundings.

'Oh, Rose!' sighed Ellie. 'Don't you start on me, too. I'll stay to see the agency nurse in, and then I'll be off home.' She thought of all the problems the day had brought . . . trying to find the dangerous dog and its owner; grieving for Corinne's family; wondering how to track down a window cleaner who might or might not know something about betting on dogs . . . Her mind leaped to the disturbing episode of Frank rejecting his father. Oh dear, people just went on making problems for themselves, didn't they?

'You sit down here,' said Rose, patting the back of Aunt Drusilla's chair. 'Take the weight off your feet. I'll bring you in a nice cuppa in a minute, and you can relax because if you go down poorly I don't know what we'll do, and that's a fact.'

Ellie laughed a little, but sat and found herself relaxing. Rose pushed a stool under her feet, and Ellie allowed herself to be cosseted for a change.

* * *

Mick strutted down the street with his two henchmen in tow, feeling like a kiddy in a sweet shop. No one knew him here, and all around were opportunities for a bright lad to get ahead of the game.

He said, 'You ever lifted stuff from shops?'

'Well,' said the one in the striped T-shirt, 'he used to, while we kept lookout, or we'd go in before him, tumble things over pretending it was an accident, and he'd make off with ciggies and stuff, sell them to that bloke we took you to for the bike. Only the shop put a camera in and caught him. That's when he got an ASBO and went away to his cousins up north.'

Mick could see he had a lot to teach them, but he wondered if they were ready for the hard stuff yet. Babes in the wood, they were. Graffiti and litter bins. Bangers and shoplifting. They hadn't even worked up to snatching laptops and handbags from cars, yet he'd seen plenty of good-looking cars around with stuff left on the back seats, ready for the taking. Well, it was up to him to educate them.

'You come walkies with me and Toby,' he said, 'and we'll see what we can find, right?'

CHAPTER EIGHT

Ellie made herself a proper cooked breakfast, which she practically never did nowadays. The fishmonger in the Avenue stocked soft roes in his freezer, and every now and then she fancied some, with bacon, tomatoes and a mushroom or two. She did draw the line at fried bread, though, and conscientiously had bread without butter on her side plate. Still, it was a very pleasant breakfast dish, topped off with a slice of toast laden with butter and her own home-made marmalade. Midge the cat enjoyed the soft roes, too, though he wasn't keen on tomatoes or mushrooms.

If she concentrated hard enough on cooking and enjoying the meal, she wouldn't have to think about dogs and little Frank, Diana and older people dying. She sank back in her chair in the conservatory and closed her eyes, resolutely not thinking about them. She wondered if her own window cleaner might know someone who bet on dogs. She didn't really think he was the type, if there was such a thing as a type who bet on dog races or dog fights. No, she really didn't want to think about dog fights, either.

It was a beautiful blue morning, the garden was overdue for some dead-heading to be done, and then there was the vexed question of the front gate coming off its hinges. Well, she could deal with that, couldn't she? She tipped her breakfast things into a bowl of water in the sink and went into the study to find the telephone number of her old friend Mrs Dawes' grandson, who was a fair to middling odd-job man and decorator.

Neil, his name was. She hadn't seen him around for a bit, but Mrs Dawes — who sang with Ellie in the church choir on Sundays — had told her that young Neil was doing all right for himself nowadays. Which was good news, since it was Ellie's small charity which had funded Neil when he set up in business.

She found his number and rang. Engaged. His mobile number was somewhere here . . . so many digits, how did people ever remember them? Ah, she'd got through. 'Neil, this is Mrs Quicke here.'

'Miss Quicke the elder, or Mrs Quicke the young one?' Well, he did do the odd job in the garden for Miss Quicke, too.

Ellie suppressed a giggle at being called 'Mrs Quicke the young one'.

'Erm, Mrs Ellie Quicke here. Opposite the church, you know? I know you're very busy, but my front gate is coming off its hinges again. I think I need a new gate post. Can you fit me in sometime?'

'Um, hum . . . Mebbe early next week? I'll call round early, eight do you? Mebbe Tuesday, have a look. Gran said your front gate needed fixing again, but I haven't been round your way in a while. Got a big job on the other side of the Avenue, fifteen doors and all the skirting to be done in magnolia, then papering hall, stairs, landings. Got an old guy working with me now, good at papering. I'd rather be outside in this weather, meself.'

'Good for you, Neil. Tell me, do you know anyone who bets on dogs?'

'Nah, can't call anyone to mind. Not my scene.'

'I didn't think it was. It's just that there's a rumour going round about a fighting dog come into the neighbourhood and, tell the truth, it's a bit scary.'

'Dogs is all right. Depends how you treats them.'

'Do you know anyone who keeps an unusually big dog?'

'I heard of someone keeps a python in her bath. She's a stripper in a club up in town. The lads in the pub were saying we ought to go see. Mebbe end of next week sometime.'

'Where . . . ? Oh, never mind. That's not what I was—'

'Or, there's this chap I heard about, got back to his place late and there was this great big bird in his front garden, and he thought he was seeing things, but every time he went to put his key in the lock, this bird hissed at him, and he couldn't get anywhere near, he thought he'd got the DTs—'

'Yes, but—'

'Turned out it was an ostrich that had escaped from the local zoo, gave him a fright, and when he called the police, they didn't believe him. Stands to reason, what?'

'Yes, it would,' said Ellie, trying to disentangle her imagination from Neil's story. 'But what I'm really after is news of a dangerous dog that—'

'Ah, the one in the park. Yes. Gran told me about it when I went up for me tea. No, I don't know nothing about that one.'

'Would you hear, if anyone was setting up a dog fight?'

'Might do. Down the pub. Want me to keep my ears open?'

'If you would.'

She put the phone down, and it rang again. Sometimes when it rang, she got prickles running down her spine because she sensed something nasty was coming her way. She got them this time.

It was Rose, panicky, her words falling over one another. 'Oh, Ellie, come quickly, I don't know what to do. She's locked herself in the bathroom so she's safe for the moment, but for how long? I did try ringing Thomas but he's out already and his mobile's not on, and I can't remember the name of her solicitor, silly me — what a day to forget, though I know it as well as I know my own name, I'm getting so hot and bothered I'll be going down with something in a minute—'

'Calm down, Rose. What's the matter? My aunt?'

'No, it's not her. At least, it is, but . . . can you come, quickly? It's Diana, and she's sacked the nurse, can you believe? I'll leave the front door so's you can get in — and oh, I've just thought, Roy might be in his office by now—' The phone crashed down. Ellie looked at the handset, and the clock. Half past nine. She replaced the handset. No point in trying to ring Rose back.

Had she got shoes on her feet? Yes. Handbag. Lock the back door, is her mobile phone in her handbag? Must check — no it isn't. Yes, it is. Lock the front door. Don't run. That won't help. It won't do you any good ringing for a cab, either. By the time they reached her, she could be almost there.

Across the Green by the church . . . no time for more than an arrow prayer. *Dear Lord, whatever it is, and you know better than I do, give me the strength to deal with it. Help Rose. Help me.* Something was very wrong for Rose to panic like that. *Please, dear Lord, look after Aunt Drusilla.* And why had Aunt Drusilla locked herself in the bathroom? Had she suddenly lost her senses? And had Ellie really heard something about Diana in the middle of all that? Diana? Why should Diana be there now, unless . . .

Ellie didn't like to complete that thought. She crossed the Avenue safely, despite two kids on bicycles whizzing along the pavement, shouting at passers-by to get out of the way. She was almost running and got a stitch, of course. She hoped little Frank had got to school safely and wasn't getting into any more trouble. She hoped Diana had managed to say the right things, to reassure him that he was much loved and that she'd always be there for him. You never knew how Diana would react.

She reached Aunt Drusilla's driveway and slowed down. Diana's car was there, together with a rather older, more weather-beaten vehicle. There was no sign of an agency nurse's car. The outer door to the converted coach house in which Roy had his office was open, and a draughtsman was adjusting blinds at the window. There was no sign of Roy's car. He must be late, for once.

Ellie didn't know what she might find and didn't want to announce her presence first, so decided to let herself into the house without first ringing the doorbell, which is what she usually did. There was no one in the hall.

As she pressed the front door to behind her, she thought of the name of Aunt Drusilla's solicitor. She'd met him once, years ago. Gunnar something. An enormously big man, probably not of British origin. She hadn't got his phone number on her, but she did have the name of someone in his practice. Mark Hadley. Partygoer. Young. Might be helpful if push came to shove.

The house was quiet. Too quiet. Where was Rose? Moving as quietly as she could, Ellie checked the downstairs rooms. There was no sign of life. She went into the kitchen. No Rose there, either. Some porridge had been set to cook in a double boiler on the stove, and it looked as if Rose had prepared a tray for Aunt Drusilla's breakfast, but not yet taken it upstairs. Rose wasn't in her own sitting room, either.

After a moment's thought, Ellie eschewed the main staircase, on which every footstep resounded, and took the back stairs up through Rose's part of the house. Rose wasn't in her bedroom. Ellie opened the communicating door on to the landing with care, to see that her aunt's bedroom door was ajar and voices were coming from within. Was that Diana's voice?

'If you don't unlock this door and come out, I'll have to assume you've lost the plot. Which means that I can send for a social worker and she'll have you sectioned.'

Ellie caught her breath. Was that Diana threatening Aunt Drusilla? Oh, no! That couldn't possibly . . . it would mean . . . no, not even Diana would go that far!

A man's voice was bleating. 'But Ms Quicke, this isn't really, I didn't expect, if your aunt really isn't of sound mind and—'

'She's as sound as you or I. She's just being awkward. Do you hear me, Great-Aunt? Come out at once, or I shan't be responsible for the consequences!'

Ellie took a deep breath, sent up another arrow prayer — *Lord, give me strength!* — and pushed the bedroom door wide open. Three angry, uneasy faces turned to her. Diana, incandescent with fury, was struggling with the door to the en suite bathroom. A middle-aged, dark little man in what had once been a good suit was holding a sheaf of papers, and a pallid girl in a poor-quality black suit had her fingers in her mouth.

'May I ask what's going on? Who are these people?'

Diana's expression passed through fury and calculation, to a welcoming smile. 'Ah, Mother. Just in time. Great-Aunt was just getting ready to sign her will when she decided she had to go to the bathroom. She's locked herself in and doesn't seem to know how to get out. Or perhaps she's fainted. Perhaps you can get her to come out of her own accord, because if not we'll have to get a ladder and send someone up it—'

'Not me!' exclaimed the dark little man. 'I don't do ladders.'

Diana cast him a look of contempt. 'I'll do it, if necessary. Mother, Great-Aunt always listens to you. See what you can do to persuade her to come out.'

'Perhaps she's fallen down and is lying there, helpless,' quavered the girl, taking her fingers out of her mouth for a moment.

'Nonsense!' Diana shot that one down. Then reconsidered. 'Well, if she is then the sooner we can get her out of there the better. We can do our business and get an ambulance to take her to hospital and we can all be out of here in two shakes. Now, Mother. See what you can do.'

Ellie found she'd placed her hand over her breast to still the rapid beat of her heart. 'Where's the agency nurse?'

'I sacked her. She was hopeless.'

'And Rose?'

A shrug. 'How should I know? She got the weeps and vanished. No help at all.'

Ellie took a deep breath. 'Who are these people?'

'A friend, who's a solicitor—' the little man ducked his head — 'and his receptionist. I needed two people to witness her signature. I thought Rose could be one, and this girl the other. Now Rose has disappeared, you can do it for me.'

'To witness a will? A will prepared by you? You say my aunt was prepared to sign a new will this morning? I think there's been some mistake. Diana, let's go somewhere we can talk privately.'

'I'm not leaving this room till she's signed.'

Roy, where are you? And Rose — come back, I need you!

Ellie tackled the weak link in the chain. 'Mr . . . I don't know your name, but I think you should know that my aunt updated her will only a short while ago, and told me yesterday that she's content with what she's done. I very much doubt that she's changed her mind. She is not the changeable sort. She has her own solicitor, of course, and if she wishes to make any changes to her will, she would undoubtedly use him and not someone who is a stranger to her. She certainly wasn't expecting a visit from somebody else's solicitor today, and forgive me, but for you to arrive like this, to shout at her . . . doesn't this sound like undue pressure?'

'Certainly not,' said Diana. 'She doesn't know her own mind, that's all. I'm merely helping her to see sense.'

'If she doesn't know her own mind, then she's not fit to make another will,' said Ellie.

'Mother, whose side are you on?'

'Hers,' said Ellie.

'Do you want to see your grandson cut off without a penny?'

'Do I want to see you in the dock for producing a fraudulent will?'

'That's outrageous!' bleated the solicitor. 'You mustn't say things like that, you know.'

'How dare you!' thundered Diana. 'I didn't ask you to be a witness first off, because I thought Great-Aunt might have left you a little something in her will, and beneficiaries can't be witnesses. Not that you need the money.'

'No, I don't need it,' said Ellie, trying to keep calm. 'I don't know what's in the will, but I trust Aunt Drusilla to be absolutely fair. I imagine that you came here with reasonably good intentions, if misguided. But as you can see, Great-Aunt is not receiving visitors at the moment, so perhaps you'd better leave.'

'Yes, yes. Another day, certainly. Come on, girl, get your skates on,' said the solicitor.

'You're going nowhere till we get this settled!' shouted Diana.

'Hello, hello. What's this mothers' meeting all about, then?' Roy strode into the room with a grim smile on his face. Rose hovered behind him, smiling anxiously.

'You!' said Diana, loathing him. 'What are you doing here?'

'Riding to my mother's rescue.' Roy, six foot plus of healthy manhood, towered over Diana's solicitor. 'I understand she's having trouble with the latch on her bathroom door. It's been playing up lately, hasn't it, Rose?'

Rose bobbed her head up and down.

Ellie found herself smiling. Clever Roy. Clever Rose. Defusing the nasty situation without effort. Ellie opened the door for the solicitor and his girl to go through. 'Shall I show you out? Oh, you know the way, do you? What a lovely day it's going to be, isn't it! Such a run of good weather, I just hope it won't be too hot later on.'

She stood at the top of the stairs till they'd traversed the hall and let themselves out of the house, then went back into the bedroom. Diana was now as red in the face as she'd been white before, and was taking her fury out on Roy. 'I might have known you'd try to do me out of what's mine by right! Creeping out from under a stone, smarming around your mother, conning her into thinking you're her blue-eyed boy—'

'But I *am* her blue-eyed boy,' said Roy, who was indeed the owner of a pair of startlingly blue eyes. 'And no, I don't want her money. I earn a fair screw, and Felicity has her own money, so no; I'm not aiming to cut you out of anything.' Maybe he even meant it.

The latch on the bathroom door clicked open and Aunt Drusilla stepped out, leaning on her cane and with her crocodile grin firmly in place.

'What a to-do about nothing. I'd completely forgotten that I needed to turn the little button on the handle to the right, or is it to the left? These modern appliances. Rose, I trusted you to look out for me, and you did exactly that. Now, dear, I was looking out of the bathroom window and I think the rose in the corner — I don't know what its name is, but I expect you do — has come into flower overnight. Would you cut some buds and put them in a vase for me? And bring up some of your home-made lemonade, too. Ellie, will you help me into bed?'

Rose disappeared and with Ellie's help, Miss Quicke settled herself on her bed. She was still grinning, but her voice was fainter than it had been. 'I enjoyed that. Better than seats at the theatre. Diana, rest assured that I have left you precisely what you deserve in my will.'

Diana didn't know what to make of that at first, but then relaxed into a smile, having a high opinion of her deserts; an opinion which was not shared by anyone else in the room. 'Oh well,' said Diana. 'Least said. I'm very happy to hear that you understand my position—'

'Oh, I do,' said Miss Quicke. 'Your little charade has been as good as a tonic, perked me up no end. I might even fancy some of Rose's scrambled egg for breakfast.'

'That's good,' said Diana, sourly.

Ellie held a glass of water to her aunt's lips, and she sipped a little. Roy stooped to kiss his mother's forehead. 'Sorry I was late arriving this morning. I got tied up, playing with Mel.' His expression was that of Fond Papa. 'So where's the agency nurse?'

'Gone,' said Diana. 'I told her I'd sit with Great-Aunt this morning.'

'You should be at work,' said Ellie. 'Did you get Frank to school on time, by the way?'

Diana shrugged. 'I dropped him off at his father's late last night, not that he wanted to go, but I had arrangements to make for today, and it wasn't convenient to have him around.'

Silence. Roy opened his mouth, presumably to make some observation about the wisdom of being consistent when dealing with a bewildered little boy, but closed it again. Diana had never taken advice from him before, so why should he ask for trouble now?

Miss Quicke closed her eyes, her grin fading.

Ellie said, 'Diana, you'd be the first person to admit you're not the nursing type and I'm sure they're expecting you at work. I'll get on to the agency and see that the nurse returns. Aunt needs to be quiet, now. No more visitors, unless she asks for them. Right?'

'I suppose.' Diana gave in ungraciously, but she did give in. She raised her voice. 'See you tomorrow, Great-Aunt. Give me a ring any time, and I'll be right over. Perhaps you'd like something a bit different from Rose's home cooking. I could drop into Harrods food department and pick up some delicacies.'

'Check with me first,' said Ellie, and saw the faint smile on Miss Quicke's face morph into a grin. 'So, Roy; you need to get to work, too. Will you see Diana out?'

Aunt Drusilla was not asleep, but she was not properly awake, either. Roy swept Diana out of the room and Ellie relaxed, muscle by muscle, feeling that she'd rather like to have a little weep as soon as she'd phoned the nursing agency. Ellie told herself that she was a big, strong girl now, and just fancy! She'd managed to defeat Diana in whatever nasty ploy the girl had had in mind. Ellie had a strong suspicion that Diana's solicitor had had a new will in his briefcase which left everything to his client. How far would Diana have gone to get such a will signed? Ellie shuddered. That didn't bear thinking about. One elderly woman, not all that sure on her feet, against strong-willed, able-bodied Diana?

If it hadn't been for Rose fetching help . . . and for Miss Quicke taking refuge in the bathroom . . .

No, it really did not bear thinking about.

So Ellie went over to the improvised business centre and rang the nursing agency to explain the situation. 'Not unheard of,' said the manageress. 'I'll send the nurse straight back and tell her that she's only to take orders from you in future.'

Ellie put the phone down and checked on her aunt, whose eyes were now open. 'Thank you, dear. Now you'd better go and comfort Rose and remind her about my lemonade. It's quite safe to leave me now. My bell's within reach and you'll be wanting to track down that killer dog, won't you?'

'I'd much prefer to sit with you. I'm not all that fond of dogs.'

'I daresay,' said Miss Quicke, 'but you'll be more use to the world finding that dog than babysitting one old woman who's too tired to talk for long. And yes, I'm sure that's what I want you to do.' She closed her eyes again.

Roy put his head around the door. Ellie shooed him back on to the landing and closed the door behind her. He wiped his fingers across his cheeks.

'She's very poorly, isn't she? I hadn't realized until just now. Such a shock. She's gone downhill so fast. Why haven't I noticed?'

'She didn't want you to worry. She's so pleased that everything's going well with you, that you have a loving wife and a beautiful little daughter.'

He wanted to blame himself for something. 'I ought to have been here earlier, have stopped Diana from intruding. I'm always here at half eight, only today . . . Flicky asked if I'd amuse Mel for a minute, and I took her around the garden and she turned her eyes from side to side and looked up at the trees, and then a bird flew across, and she jumped in my arms. I said, "It's all right, Baby," or something like that and she must like the sound of my voice because she looked up at me, such a look! So trusting! And she's so tiny that I felt . . . I've never felt anything like that before. And all the time . . .'

He blew his nose. 'I feel so guilty. I've not got anything desperate on this morning. I'd like to sit with my mother for a while, if I may. I promise not to talk or disturb her in any way, but I'd just like to, well, be there for her.'

Ellie understood that he needed to do that for his mother, and for himself. 'Thank you, Roy. If you could sit by the window, perhaps have some paperwork to do? Just till the agency nurse comes? That would be really helpful. Now, I must go to see how Rose is getting on.'

* * *

Rose had gone to pieces, as Aunt Drusilla had known she would. Rose was sitting in the kitchen, mopping herself up while trying to cut the thorns off the roses she'd culled from the garden. There were discarded strips of chopped-up fruit on the chopping board, and some freshly made lemonade was slowly filtering through into a cut-glass jug.

Ellie gave Rose a hug. 'You were such a heroine, dear. Goodness knows what might have happened if you hadn't kept your head and called up reinforcements.'

Rose's face tried to crack into a smile but didn't quite make it. 'It was Miss Quicke who knew what to do, because that Diana barged in before I'd a chance to stop her, practically knocked me over, and was up the stairs with those two cronies of hers in tow, and I think I screamed — yes, I'm almost sure I did — but by the time I got up the stairs after them, they were in Miss Quicke's bedroom, shouting at her. At least, Diana was shouting, and the other two looked as if they hadn't expected that but when I asked them to leave, they both looked at Diana who said they were there on business, and would I leave, instead, and of course I said I couldn't do that, and pointed out that they were upsetting Miss Quicke, who'd just been about to get out of bed to go to the bathroom, which is what she always does at that time of the morning and I hardly ever have to do more than give her my arm to get there . . .'

Rose took a deep breath. 'Diana said they wouldn't be a minute, just needed to get a paper signed and I could be a witness, as I wasn't due to get anything in the new will Miss Quicke was going to sign, and I knew that Miss Quicke had made her will a little while back with her own solicitor and him bringing two witnesses and me serving him the shortbread biscuits that he always likes and either proper coffee, black, no sugar, or a glass of Madeira.'

Rose gulped in a breath and continued. 'That's when Miss Quicke said she needed to go to the toilet and would I help her to the bathroom, and Diana said she'd help her to the bathroom and she did, although I thought she jostled Miss Quicke along far too fast, but then . . .' Rose began to laugh and cry all at once. 'Miss Quicke turned the button in the lock, I heard it, and knew what she'd done, because she's never ever turned that button since Roy installed them, not liking these silly, new-fangled devices, but that's what she did, sure enough. There she was inside and Diana couldn't get at her, only of course Miss Quicke couldn't come out, either, could she! So that's when I ran away and tried ringing you and Thomas and Roy . . . and then I thought Roy would be arriving any minute and went out to his office but he wasn't there and so I just waited for him, and prayed someone would rescue us. Oh, how I prayed. I thought of Thomas praying, and somehow that helped.'

'You did marvellously well,' said Ellie, hugging her again. 'You kept your head and you saved Aunt Drusilla from a nasty scene. It's no wonder you had a good cry afterwards, because I felt like it, myself. But it's all right now. My aunt's none the worse for her little adventure; in fact, I think it's cheered her up. Diana can't get at my aunt again. The agency has instructions not to leave my aunt unattended, and in future no one can dismiss the nurses except me. Roy is sitting with her now, until the nurse returns. So you see, all's well that ends well.

'I'm sure my aunt will love those roses; what are they called? I wouldn't mind a climbing rose like that in my own garden. Is it Compassion? Or Peace? They do look somewhat alike, don't they? And I know she fancies some more of your lemonade, and perhaps a little something to eat?'

'Oh yes, what must you think of me, I'm all of a dither.' Rose was gradually calming down. 'I'll take them up to her straight away. Oh, Ellie, I know she's your daughter, and I wouldn't say anything about her normally, but . . . how could she!'

'I wish I knew how to get through to her,' said Ellie. 'I wish I knew.'

* * *

Mick fed Toby a tin of dog food, and while he was eating, took the precaution of clipping on his lead. The others hung back, suitably impressed with the fierce demeanour of the dog.

'Some dog!' said Stripes.

'He's different from the dogs in the park,' said Black Hood.

Mick let Toby finish his food and lap his water bowl dry before trying to take him out of the shed. Toby was frisky, needed a long walk. Both lads kept well back as Mick yanked on Toby's lead to direct him out of the garden into the road. Good. Having Toby around was better than having a knife, or even a gun. Toby demanded — and got — respect.

'I'm taking him walkies,' said Mick. 'See what comes up. Mebbe another mobile phone. Mebbe a laptop. Portable assets, as they say. You both coming?'

They nodded, falling in behind him, their eyes round.

CHAPTER NINE

Ellie told herself that she ought to hurry home and sort out what should be done next, but her legs refused to obey. Her legs told her that she'd had a difficult morning and that what she needed was to sit down and have a good rest. Her stomach told her that what she needed was a large latte and a piece of carrot cake. She could stop off in the Avenue and get both at the Sunflower Café. Perhaps there might even be some gossip to be picked up, although the people who frequented the café were not, on the whole, the sort of people you associated with large fighting dogs.

It occurred to her that there was one place in the Avenue where they might know about dogs and fighting, and that was the betting shop. She'd never been in it, naturally. She'd never been in any betting shop, ever. It made her grimace to imagine what her dear, long dead husband would have said, if she'd proposed entering such a place while he was alive. He'd have been horrified. He'd never bought a lottery ticket in his life, or bet on the Grand National, or the Boat Race, or the possibility of there being a white Christmas in London. He wasn't the betting sort.

She wasn't, either. She took a deep breath. Would it kill her to enter a betting shop? Of course not. It might harm her reputation if she were seen going into such a place, but what was a dent in her reputation compared with discovering who might be harbouring a dangerous dog? Besides, who cared about such things as reputations nowadays?

Thomas had told a story some time ago which dealt with this very problem. A good man had been going into the vilest of places, seedy clubs and brothels, trying to help the poor people who worked there. He'd been asked how he could bear even to cross the threshold, never mind work in such conditions, and he'd said that he couldn't have borne it, if he hadn't known that Jesus was already in there.

So poop to people who might pull a face if she went into a betting shop. Besides, there must be much worse places in the world than betting shops. Of course there were.

She remembered that she'd felt faint at the thought of entering a pub locally some time ago and it had turned out to be a cheerful, accommodating sort of place, and not at all the haunt of vice she'd imagined it to be. She'd had lunch at the local pub at the end of the Avenue several times since with Rose, and with Thomas; also with a couple of old friends who'd dropped in for a visit unexpectedly. It hadn't killed her to go into a pub, and it wouldn't kill her to go into a betting shop.

Except that she really didn't know the right questions to ask.

'Oh! Oh, dear! Someone, please come! Help me!'

She'd just turned a corner to discover an elderly woman lying on the pavement in front of her, a basket on wheels tipped over on its side and the shopping spilling out. The wheels on the basket were still spinning, which meant the woman had only just fallen over. She was crying, holding on to an elbow, trying to sit upright and failing. The pavement was uneven. Presumably she'd tripped and fallen.

'Don't try to get up yet,' said Ellie, kneeling beside the woman. 'Can you move your arms and legs? Yes? You don't seem to have broken anything. You didn't bang your head, did you?'

The woman mouthed, 'Have they gone?'

Ellie looked around. This was a quiet road linking two larger streets, and there was no one — not even a car — in sight. 'I can't see anyone.' Had this been a mugging?

The woman was weeping. Ellie helped her to her feet and deposited her on the nearby low wall of someone's front garden. There were no cars in the driveway of that house or the next. The houses had the empty look of owners who went off to jobs in the early morning and came back after six. Ellie considered ringing doorbells just in case, but the woman was clutching her arm, breathing heavily. Very scared. Now she was upright, Ellie thought she looked familiar.

'It's all right,' said Ellie. 'I won't leave you and if you'll let go my arm, I'll find my mobile phone and ring the police.'

'They took mine,' said the woman, pushing back thinning blonded hair with a hand that shook. 'My purse, my travel card, my phone.'

'I know you, don't I?' said Ellie, sorting through the address book in her mind. Had they met at church? No. Some local organization?

The woman pawed with her free hand at her gaping handbag. 'Charity shop. We met last year. Anita said you used to work there.'

'I remember. Mae from the charity shop. You used to work in the post office till you retired, right?'

Mae nodded. Tears welled over her eyelids. Her elbow was oozing blood through dirt; her knee-high stockings were torn; and her skirt was above her knees. Ellie remembered a buxom dame with golden curls, as sprightly as they come, but that confident woman had been reduced to a trembling wreck.

'If you'll let go of me for a second?' said Ellie, trying to disengage her arm.

Mae ran her tongue around her mouth. Had the fall shifted the plate in her mouth? 'The dog jumped up at me. I tripped and fell over. The little one tried to snatch my bag, but I'd got it over my shoulder, so he pulled me along the pavement. Then he ripped it open. They were laughing! Oh, my brand-new mobile my son sent me — I haven't even worked out how to use it yet but he said I ought to have one for emergencies.'

'Yes, indeed,' said Ellie, feeling for her own mobile with her left hand as Mae wouldn't release the other. 'A boy with a dog did this to you?'

'Three boys. One was a hoodie. Oh, oh! My keys! Have they got the keys to the house?' She delved into the bag, upending it. The keys fell out. 'Oh, thank God, thank God! But I'll have to ring everyone, tell them, cancel . . . oh, oh!'

'Relax. We'll deal with it. A dog, you say? What sort?'

'Big.' Mae shivered, tears falling faster than ever. 'It happened so fast. It jumped up at me and I fell. It was horrible!' She began to rock to and fro.

Ellie punched numbers. Police and ambulance. Mae wept. She looked ten years older than the brightly efficient sixty-year-old Ellie had met at the charity shop some months earlier.

A car came along the road and turned into a drive nearby. A woman got out, read the situation correctly and hesitated, obviously wondering if she had time to get involved. To her credit, she came across the road. 'What's happened? Can I help? Oh, it's Mae, isn't it? Remember me from the bowling club?'

'Yes, yes. Oh dear. I've forgotten your name for the moment, but this kind lady stopped to help me and we're waiting for the police—'

'And an ambulance,' said Ellie. 'I'm Ellie Quicke. I knew Mae from the charity shop—'

'Oh, of course, I remember you from years back. I used to get all my children's toys there. Mae, wouldn't you be more comfortable in my house? A cup of tea, perhaps? Then I could have a look at that elbow.'

Mae struggled to her feet, looking with despair at the bits and pieces of her shopping spread all over the pavement.

'I'll bring those across for you,' said Ellie. 'You need a good sit down. The police will be here soon.'

Mae was still trembling, but knew what she wanted. 'I'm not going to hospital. I know what it's like there. Wait four hours and then be told to see your GP in the morning.'

'I know exactly what you mean,' said the neighbour. To Ellie, 'I'm a trained physio and I don't have another appointment till three. Mae'll be all right with me.'

Ellie nodded, recognizing the type of woman who thrived on emergencies. Ellie respected that. She only wished she were more like it herself. She righted Mae's shopping basket and rescued all her bits and pieces, trundling it across the road after the Good Samaritan and Mae.

On the doorstep Mae hesitated. 'Ellie, I'm due at the shop this afternoon. Will you tell them what's happened, say I won't be in today?'

Ellie nodded again, hoping that she wouldn't be asked to fill in for Mae. She'd enough on her plate without that. Perhaps she could drop a note through the door to avoid speaking to anyone inside, to avoid being asked to help?

No, she couldn't do that. Ellie scolded herself; it wasn't at all likely they'd ask her to help, anyway. She hadn't worked there for years, wouldn't even remember how to operate the till nowadays. Of course she must go in and tell them properly, to give them a chance to find someone else for the afternoon.

The people she'd worked with were lovely, and they'd be distressed to hear about Mae. They'd probably all sign a card for her, maybe take some flowers round. Well, everyone but Madam — as the manageress was called behind her back — would do so. Madam would probably say Mae had asked for trouble and didn't she realize how difficult it made Madam's job, if people inconsiderately went and got mugged on the day they were supposed to work in the shop?

Even as Ellie turned in to the Avenue, her mobile phone rang. She was surprised that she'd left it on. She didn't, usually, being afraid — like Caroline — that the battery would run down at some vital moment.

It was Thomas, but the sound quality was poor. 'Ellie, I'm on the Tube, on my way up to town for a meeting, but I should be back between four and five. Do you fancy supper at the Carvery, pick you up about seven?'

Friday was his one full day off, in theory. In practice, he often worked seven days a week. She said, 'That would be nice. It's been a tiresome day.'

His tone sharpened. 'You've had some news about the dog?'

'Not really. I've put feelers out in the community but no one I know has seen it. Although Mae from the charity shop has just been mugged by three lads with a dog in tow.'

'Are you all right?'

'Mm. Sort of. There was a nasty scene this morning at Aunt Drusilla's . . . but no, not to worry, she's all right. Tired, that's all. I'll tell you all about it later.'

'I've got to visit someone in hospital when I get back, and then I promised to see Leona and the kids. Any ideas about that situation?'

'Off the top of my head, it might not be possible, but would Leona take on the boy whose father doesn't want him? He is her nephew, and she's got a couple of kids herself, hasn't she? She'd get the Child Allowance for fostering, or adoption or whatever. If she did, perhaps she could move into Corinne's flat, which you said was spacious and is in a much quieter neighbourhood than where she is now. Then her kids could go to our local school, which everyone knows is one of the best in Ealing, so the whole family would benefit from the move. The boy could remain in his own home and continue in his own school with his own classmates.'

Silence from Thomas. Ellie said, 'I'll expect you'll say that there'd be so much red tape to unwind that it wouldn't be possible. I can't think of—'

The train went into the tunnel and she shut off her phone.

The contact with Thomas had re-energized Ellie, and she turned into the charity shop feeling that she could cope with anything. Well, almost anything. Madam was the sort of boss who flitted around touching things with her fingertips and pulling rank on her band of faithful helpers. If she had but known it, the staff only put up with her because she did the paperwork and wasn't in the shop that much.

Ellie's spirits took a dive when she saw that Madam was there, haranguing some unfortunate woman who was trying to take what Madam considered were too many dresses into the tiny changing cubicle at the back.

Fiftyish, well preserved, well dressed and well connected, it was rumoured locally that Madam only worked in the shop to get herself, some day, on to the New Year's Honours list.

In the old days Ellie had been the social glue that had held the little band of helpers together; she'd been popular with customers because she was always patient when they dithered, and she'd never minded the dirtiest jobs. Together with Rose she'd pretty well run the shop until she took a few days off after her husband died, when Madam had seized the opportunity to sack her.

Nowadays Ellie only considered entering the shop when Madam was absent. What bad luck that she should be there today.

Ellie spotted her old friend Anita on the till and went straight in, hoping to avoid contact with Madam, only to have the manageress touch her on the shoulder. 'You've not come to gossip, I hope. My girls don't have time for that.'

Anita rolled her eyes, but kept her mouth shut.

Ellie tried to keep her voice soft. 'I only came to warn you that Mae won't be making it this afternoon. She's been mugged. The police have been called. She's not badly hurt, but very shaken.'

'Oh, no. Poor Mae!' said Anita, hands to her mouth in shock.

'How very inconvenient,' said Madam, manicured fingernails tapping the counter. 'But if she's not badly hurt, perhaps she'll be able to make it, after all.'

'No, she won't,' said Ellie, being firm. 'Tomorrow, perhaps, but more probably she'll have to take the weekend to recover. She has to replace her cards and travel pass. They took her money and mobile phone, too.'

'She ought not to have carried them in her purse.'

Ellie tried not to be indignant. 'They ripped her bag open as she lay on the pavement. There were three of them, and a dog. She hadn't a chance.'

'Three of them!' gasped Anita. 'Oh, poor Mae! I'll take some flowers round to her this afternoon.'

Madam turned on Anita. 'I think it would be best if you stayed on this afternoon to help. Otherwise, we'll be short-handed.'

Anita took some money from a customer who was holding it out for her, and slammed the till shut. 'I'm so sorry. I'm on mornings only at the moment, remember?'

Madam's brow creased into the faintest of frowns. 'This is an emergency, and I know I can always rely on you in an emergency.'

'Mae's got an emergency, too, hasn't she?' said Anita, not quite smiling. 'Perhaps you, yourself . . . ?'

The frown deepened. 'Certainly not. I'm playing bridge this afternoon at the golf club and I wouldn't dream of letting my partner down. Well, you'll just have to find someone else. I understand that Ellie here is a lady of leisure nowadays. Perhaps she would give up an afternoon to help us. If we close we can't take any money, and that would affect our takings for the week.'

'Sorry, sorry,' said Ellie. 'No can do. Family problems. Aunt, etcetera. I only came in to tell you, must go, really must go . . .'

Anita winked at Ellie, turning her face away from Madam. 'Thanks for letting us know, Ellie. See you around, right?'

'Right,' said Ellie. 'I must go, got to visit the betting shop.'

Anita developed a hacking cough, as she fought not to laugh. Madam's face went rigid with shock horror.

Ellie thought, Now look what I've done.

Madam took in a deep breath. 'I always knew you were unsuitable for work in this place, but I didn't realize you were *that sort*!'

Ellie felt herself go red but managed to say, 'What sort do you mean?' before backing out of the shop. The last she saw of Anita was her bent double over the till, handkerchief to mouth.

Now you've done it, and it'll be all over the neighbourhood by nightfall! Ellie Quicke, gambler! They'll say, 'I always knew she couldn't be trusted.' Well, I might as well be hung for a sheep as for a lamb.

Ellie marched across the road and into the betting shop without allowing herself to think about what she was doing. The window displayed a horse-racing scene. Did they do dogs as well? She entered the shop, which appeared gloomy after the bright sunshine outside. She hoped they had some better lighting to use when they cleaned the place, or they'd never see how much dirt might have been traipsed in on people's feet.

There were banks of screens overhead and covering what would otherwise have been the shop window, all showing horse races taking place in different locations. There was a shelf for punters on the right; presumably they wrote out their betting slips there? On the left a grille protected a couple of men, who must be the ones who took in money from clients and paid out winnings where appropriate.

Ellie went up to the grille and asked to see the manager in a confident voice. Confident she was not, but now she'd got this far, she might as well carry on.

'Can you tell me, do you do dogs as well as horses?'

'Yes, of course. Dog racing, you mean? We do almost everything that people place bets on.'

'Snowfall, Doomsday, the date of settlement on the moon?'

'As I said, almost everything.' The badge on the manager's jacket announced that he was a Mr Patel. He was a pleasantly spoken, youngish man, competent and courteous. He didn't even allow himself a glimmer of a smile when faced with a silly middle-aged woman asking stupid questions.

'I'm not here to place a bet,' said Ellie, feeling more foolish by the minute.

He inclined his head. 'Then how may I help you?'

'You cover dog racing. I want to find out if you've heard of a dog fight being planned for this neighbourhood.'

Raised eyebrows. 'I'm afraid we wouldn't know anything about that. In all the years I've been here, no one's ever come in asking to place a bet on a dog fight. They're illegal, you see.' He was being kind to her.

'I understand that they're illegal, yes, but a friend was killed in the park by a vicious dog, and we thought that maybe he'd been trained to fight.'

He leaned his arms on the counter. He was interested. 'I heard about that. A bad business. But it's not likely anyone would try to place a bet on an illegal dog fight in here, because they'd know we wouldn't accept it. Perhaps you need to talk to a bookie — a turf accountant — or to someone who goes to the dog tracks.'

'There isn't any official dog racing around here, is there?'

He shook his head. She thanked the men and turned to leave, finding two large workmen behind her, looking as if they couldn't quite believe their eyes at seeing a middle-aged, respectable-looking little lady in there.

She flushed again, and told herself that she had as much right as them to be there, and anyway, didn't lots of people buy lottery tickets and scratch cards every day of the week, and what was the difference if they wanted to throw their money away on betting?

It gave the punters hope that their circumstances might change, allowing them to dream what might happen if this week they won the jackpot, or a hundred pounds . . . or even ten. It was no business of hers if they chose to spend their social security money on a ticket to heaven, rather than on food for their children.

She wondered, as she left the shop, if they were all going to burst out laughing behind her. She hoped not, but . . . was that a guffaw as the door closed behind her? Well, what if it was!

She swung over the road to her favourite coffee shop, and was about to enter when she spotted Felicity sitting on one of the black leather settees inside, giving Mel a bottle. She was chatting away to Caroline Topping, who had her baby Duncan sitting upright on her lap. Across from them sat Ellie's next-door neighbour, Kate, with her toddler who was trying to 'read' a lift-a-flap book, while her baby snoozed in his buggy at her side. It was a cheerful scene, but Ellie did not feel like joining it.

She continued down the road to the Italian restaurant. This had several steps up to it off the pavement, which deterred young mothers with children from entering. It was quieter there. She sat and ordered a latte and told herself she didn't need anything to eat. She really ought to watch her weight.

It was only yesterday that she'd sat here with Thomas, talking of this and that, and she was looking forward to seeing him again tonight.

It struck her that she'd given him some bad advice about Leona and the boys. She felt a wave of embarrassment. How could she have been so crass? Why should she think that Leona would want to shift from an area where she'd brought her children up and move to her sister's place, even if the council were to allow it? Then Leona's man was on the lookout for a gun. It was rumoured that guns were occasionally being handed around in Acton, but not in this safer, more law-abiding part of Ealing. If Leona moved to North Ealing then so would her man, and she, Ellie Quicke, would be responsible for bringing a gun into these quiet streets. It didn't bear thinking about.

She felt a hot flush rise to her forehead. How could she have been so stupid!

Well, Thomas hadn't had a chance to shoot down her suggestion this morning, and no doubt he'd be very kind and not make her feel stupid about it when they met this evening. He was like that. Always careful of people's feelings.

Still, she'd put up a whole list of blunders that morning, hadn't she? As for her foray into the betting shop . . . !

Least said. What a ridiculous thing to do. As if she'd ever have learned anything by poking her nose into things she knew absolutely nothing about. She drained her cup and set it aside.

Sniffing, she told herself that she was *not* wallowing in self-pity, but counting over her shortcomings, which were many and varied. *Please Lord, I know I'm such a fool, but you will look after other people and make sure they don't suffer from my mistakes, won't you?*

'Would you like to order?' The waiter was the same youth, speckled with acne, who she'd seen before. It would never do to snap at him, as he'd little enough confidence as it was. Thomas had observed only the other day that it didn't look as if the lad were going to last long. She looked at her watch and saw it was nearly twelve. Perhaps she ought to eat something.

'A salad?' he asked, removing her cup and starting to lay the table for lunch.

'A salad would be fine. You don't happen to have heard of anyone acquiring a fierce dog hereabouts?'

He started, knocked a knife on to the floor.

She tried to put him at his ease. 'I'm rather frightened of large dogs. First there was the incident in the park, and this morning an acquaintance of mine was mugged by three lads with a dog. An epidemic, you might say.'

He picked up the knife, took it out to the kitchens, and came back with a clean one. 'Cats, now. They fight all the time.'

'They do.' Ellie half smiled, thinking of her own marauding Midge, who'd seen off all the tomcats in the immediate neighbourhood.

'Dogs have to be muzzled, don't they? If they're the fighting type?'

'I don't know much about it. I imagine so.'

He placed a glass and jug of water on her table. A couple came in, and he distributed menus before returning to Ellie. 'My mum, now, she's thinking of calling the PDSA or the police or something, but she was only doing a favour, cleaning, twice a week last week and this, and she won't go back there after, not if she were offered all the tea in China, she says. Only, she doesn't want to get the wrong side of this woman, who's got a nasty temper by all accounts. It's a puzzle, isn't it?'

Ellie blinked. Presumably if she hung around long enough, he'd get to the point. Meanwhile two businessmen had come in, calling out they wanted the all-day breakfast. The place was getting busy.

The lad ran around, dropping a salt cellar, crashing plates. Ellie shook her head; he really was not going to make the grade, was he? Her salad came, she put lots of dressing on it, and ate. Thomas had been right. It was acceptable that way.

She ordered a coffee and when the lad brought it to her table, he went on as if there'd been no interruption in their conversation. 'It's a large dog, Mum says. She only looked through the window of the shed, mind. It's not chained up inside, so she couldn't go in to attend to it, but she could see his water bowl was empty and he howls something horrible. She did say something to the woman, who told her to mind her own business and so of course, she did. But it did get on her nerves, and she isn't going back there, no way José.'

'Where is this?'

He swung an arm in the direction of the Avenue. 'Over there. One of those big houses that stands by itself. Mum was filling in for a friend while she's away on holiday.'

'You don't know the address? No? What's your mother's name? The police are looking for someone who might be harbouring a large dog.'

'No, no.' He backed away. 'I wouldn't have said nothing if I'd thought you'd get nosy. Mum's all right, now. I don't want her having to go away again, do I?'

'May I ask why . . . ?'

'She gets bad with her nerves, like really really bad. She's been all right for a good while now, pleased as anything to bring in a bit of money to help, but questioning and police and people shouting at her; no, she can't do. That's why she won't ring the PDSA about the dog, although it's on her mind all the time, and she can't talk about nothing else.'

'Would she talk to me about the dog, do you think? Then I could go round to the house and if it's still howling, I could ring the PDSA, and your mother wouldn't have to come into it at all.'

He screwed up his face, thinking about it. 'Might, might not.'

'Will you ask her? Look, I'll write my phone number down and if she agrees to talk she can ring me, and we'll take it from there.'

'She don't use the phone.' But he put the paper in his pocket. 'Tell you what, I'll ask her and if she says yes, I'll phone you, right?'

* * *

Mick tied Toby's lead to a bench in the Avenue and sat down to share the loot with the others. Always reward your mates. Tich had taught him that.

He unfurled the roll of tenners he'd taken off the woman. She must have come straight from the post office, because she'd got near enough £150 in her purse. The mobile phone was brand new, too. What luck! He'd been wondering how he could get one. He'd sell her credit cards and travel pass later.

'For you,' he said, handing forty to Black Hood. 'And for you.' He held out another couple of twenties to Stripes.

Hood stowed the money away, grinning, but his companion was shifting, foot to foot, hands deep in pockets, looking at the sky, looking at the ground, not making eye contact with Mick.

'What's the matter? Got the runs?'

'Nah. It's just . . . using the dog. Seems . . . I dunno. She were dead scared.'

'A course she were. Who wouldn't be scared of Toby? Toby's an exterminator, in't he? If I hadn't been holding him back, he'd have finished her off.'

Stripes shifted his feet again. 'I'd best be off. Promised Mum I'd go down the dry-cleaner's for her.'

Mick didn't like the sound of this. Members of his gang didn't run errands for their mothers. 'That's baby talk. Come on, we're going to get rid of these cards, make some plans. The aunt wants me to go to some youth club or other tonight. You go there?'

Stripes took a couple of steps away. 'Mebbe. I'll have to ask me mum.'

Mick untied Toby's leash. 'You want I set the exterminator on you?'

Stripes backed away, hands raised to defend himself, knowing the dog could easily knock him over. Toby growled, understanding that he was going to be allowed to attack.

Mick laughed. 'Don't run, or he'll have you.' The lad stood still, sweat beading his spotty face. Mick knew he'd the upper hand. 'A course you didn't mean it. No need to be scared of Toby while I'm in charge. You sit down with us, and we'll work out what we're going to do next.'

For a moment the lad wavered, ashen faced. Then he gave in and sat down.

'That's my lad,' said Mick, patting him on the shoulder. He tied Toby up again.

CHAPTER TEN

Ellie left the café, mentally checking over the contents of her fridge, wondering what else she might need for the forthcoming weekend, and came face to face with a poster on a lamp post. 'Ferret Racing', it said. 'Back by popular demand', at a local pub.

Ferret racing? Ellie had never heard of such a thing. Ferrets were wild animals, weren't they? They weren't kept as pets, surely. How would you race wild animals? Her imagination wouldn't perform on this one.

'Gotcha!' said a voice she knew. Anita nudged Ellie, indicating the poster. 'We'll have to get you into Gamblers Anonymous.' Anita was laughing, waving a bouquet of pink carnations. 'You didn't half start something back at the ranch. Madam's thrilled! She's on the phone this minute telling her cronies that you've gone to the bad. I said to Donna that I bet you were on the trail of something nasty. Is that it? Go on, you can tell Anita. You know I won't say a dickie bird.'

Ellie found herself laughing, because Anita was enjoying the situation so much. 'Do you know anything about betting on dogs, or horses? Or, I suppose, on ferrets?'

''Course not. My old man would have a fit. I'd a cousin used to bet now and then, but it was like a hobby with him, and he only lost his pocket money. He's dead now, God rest his soul. So what's with you and betting?'

Ellie turned away from the poster. 'I was trying to find out about this dog that seems to have turned up from nowhere, attacking people. My friend Felicity was scared half to death because she saw what happened to that poor woman in the park who was savaged by a dog, and now there's this business with Mae.'

Anita hefted the flowers. 'I'm on my way to see her now. Want to come?'

'Why not? So you aren't working extra hours? Has Madam got to shut the shop?'

'No, she got Donna to stand in for her. And John — that nice man who used to do the books — he said he might be able to fit in a couple of hours later. Come on, we stay on this side of the road for Mae's.'

Ellie hesitated. 'Hang about, when I saw her she was over the other side of the Avenue.'

'She lives this side, though. When you saw her I expect she was taking shopping to her mum's, who lives in sheltered housing over that way.'

'Basket on wheels. Half a dozen eggs, loaf of sliced bread, butter, some processed cheese, bacon. Yes, and a package from the fishmonger.'

'Eggs. Ugh. Broken?'

'I don't think they were.' They turned off the Avenue into a tree-lined road crowded with small, terraced houses, each with its own pretty garden. Well, most of the gardens were pretty, although one seemed to be haunted by elderly and rather grimy gnomes. Anita rapped on the fourth door along. 'Hope she's up and about.'

They heard slow footsteps and the door opened on a chain. Mae was upright but developing some nice bruises on her face and arms. She let them in, trying to smile. 'Thought you might be the doctor. I'm all right, really. Just a bit tired.'

'I should think you would be.' Anita bounced into the tiny, many-angled hall. 'I thought you'd like some flowers. Take them through to the kitchen, shall I?'

Mae greeted Ellie with a wobbly smile. 'Thank you for picking me up. I was all to pieces, wasn't I?'

'It must have been terrifying,' said Ellie. 'I'm not all that keen on dogs, myself.'

Mae shuddered. 'If that lad hadn't been hauling the dog back, he'd have had me for sure. I could see in his eyes that he was dying to fasten his teeth on me.'

Ellie helped her back into the sitting room. In these houses — cottages, really — there was only one through room on the ground floor, with a small kitchen beyond and a cubby hole under the stairs for a vacuum cleaner. Mae collapsed into a chair, trembling.

'I got drops of his drool on me, and they stung. I had to wash and wash and wash to get them off, and I'll have the biggest bruise of my life on my back. But there, it's not the end of the world, is it?'

Ellie pulled a light rug over Mae's knees. 'What about your shopping? Do you need anything brought in?'

'I'd done mine. That was for Mother. The lady who took me into her house, she dropped it off for me when the police had gone. A nice young policewoman it was. But there, they all have iron nerves nowadays, don't they?'

Ellie pressed Mae's hand. 'You'll feel better after a good night's sleep.'

'I don't usually hold with taking anything to make me sleep, but perhaps I will tonight.'

Anita brought a cup of tea in from the kitchen, and set it by Mae's chair. 'Drink up, make you feel better. Your son going to pop in later? You did tell him about this, didn't you?'

'I'll ring him this evening. I don't want to disturb him at work.'

Anita dumped a vase containing the carnations on to the mantelpiece where they drooped to one side in a clump. Ellie ached to rearrange them but didn't. Anita was doing her best.

Anita plumped herself down on a nearby chair. 'We missed you at the shop, but Madam got Donna to cover for you. She was not sympathetic, as you can imagine.'

'She has her own problems,' said Mae, weakly.

'Humph! Like too much money and too much time on her hands,' said Anita. 'Enough of that. You take what time off you need, understand?'

Mae tried to smile and this time it looked more natural. 'I didn't think it was in me to be frightened of dogs, having been brought up with them, as it were. My last one was a terrier, such a pretty little boy and so intelligent. He lasted eighteen years. That's a good age for a dog. I still miss him, but I don't want to start with another at my age.'

'This wasn't a terrier,' prompted Ellie. 'What was it?'

'A pit bull mix, I think. Mind you, I only saw it for a second or two. They were walking up behind me and I moved to one side to let them pass when he says, the leader says, to give him my purse and my mobile. I suppose I froze for a minute, not knowing what to do, whether to scream or what, only there were three of them and two were big, and they were grinning. The smallest lad had the dog's lead wrapped round his fist and he just . . . set the dog on me! Not enough to let him reach me, just enough to make me stumble back and fall. That's when he tore at my bag and dragged me along and . . . oh, dear! I'm going all of a quiver again!'

'Yes, yes,' said Ellie, patting her hand. 'You were very brave. Three of them, you say. You remember what they looked like, of course?'

'The little one, he was cocky. Horrible. Funny accent. Not Welsh or Scots but . . . I don't know what it was. A shaved head and such a look in his eyes, as if he hated me but didn't really see me. Then one was Asian, I think. With a black sweatshirt. He had the hood up over his head. The third hung back, I didn't really see him. He was a big lad, bigger than my son, I should think. The dog was . . .' She shivered again, and Ellie helped her take a drink.

'I think I'll have a little nap now,' said Mae, sinking further into her chair.

'Yes, you should,' said Ellie. 'One last question, if you can manage it. What colour was the dog?'

'Liver coloured, with white patches, just like my own dear Jack. Only Jack never went for anyone like that.'

Ellie and Anita left Mae to her nap. Outside, a slight breeze was wafting through the streets, stirring the leaves on the trees. A mid-afternoon hush had descended on the neighbourhood, broken only by the thud and thump of a building team at work on a new loft extension down the road. Soon the streets would be alive again, when school was out for the day.

'Poor Mae,' said Anita. 'I doubt if she'll be back at the shop for a while.'

Ellie nodded agreement. 'I'll pop in to check on my aunt while I'm this way. She's having nurses round the clock, now.'

'They're all dropping off the twig at the moment.' Anita waved cheerfully and set off home to put on the tea for her teenage boys.

* * *

Ellie braced herself as she entered her aunt's house. Some people put their problems into boxes and could close the lid of them and move on to the next thing without carrying the first with them. Ellie wasn't like that. She was, she had to admit, something of a worrier, particularly about family affairs. Now she was trailing not clouds of glory behind her, but all the worries of the people she'd been talking to that morning and before.

She had a little struggle with herself on the door mat, telling herself to forget about the poor woman who had been killed, and the effect on her children. Forget about the attack on Mae and the conversations with Madam and Anita. Forget the embarrassing visit to the betting shop; forget, even, the intriguing matter of the ferret races, which couldn't possibly have anything to do with the affair of the pit bull.

She must, even, forget the weight of worry that she always carried with her about Diana and what the future held for her and for little Frank. One good thing; Felicity seemed to have found a new friend and to be coping better today.

Rose came into the hall, pushing back her hair, looking as if she'd just been roused from a nap. She held out both her hands to Ellie, and Ellie took them. They were not going to exchange kisses; they weren't that sort. But they clung to one another's hands for a long moment.

'No change?'

'She's been dozing on and off all morning. Roy's with her now, while the nurse has her lunch.'

The two women stood in the hall, looking up the stairs, listening for sounds from above. None were heard. The big house was quiet. You could even hear birds in the garden outside.

'I'll sit with her for a bit,' said Ellie. She went up the stairs, holding on to the banister.

Roy came out of Miss Quicke's bedroom on to the landing, leaving the door open behind him. There were silver tracks on his cheeks, but he was in control of himself. He gestured towards a couple of chairs in the window and sat down opposite Ellie. Keeping his voice low, he said, 'She's asleep. No pain. The doctor came again.' He shrugged. 'No idea how long, but my mother says she's ready to go.' His face contorted. 'I wish I'd come looking for her before my adopting parents died. I could have had many more years with her.'

Ellie took one of his hands in both of hers and stroked it. It seemed that people needed this sort of contact when faced with grief and injury and death. 'You've made her very happy these last few years, and she's so pleased that you have a kind and beautiful wife, and a stunning baby. She's leaving you in safe hands, isn't she?'

'Yes, but . . .' He took in a deep breath. 'I'm being selfish, aren't I? She's been in a lot of pain lately. I can't wish that to continue for her, can I?'

It was a rhetorical question. Ellie continued to stroke his hand. She thought, I can't ask him about ferret racing now, can I? Well, why not? It might divert him for a few minutes. 'Do you know anything about ferret racing?'

He blinked. Shook his head, frowned, and then half smiled. 'Oh, yes. It's on at one of the local pubs, isn't it? Some do to raise money for charity. They had it last year, too. They put the ferrets into one end of long plastic tubes and bet on which one will reach the end first. Someone from the office went, said it was a riot. Can't say it appeals to me, much.'

'Do you know anyone who bets on the races? Dogs in particular?'

He was not concentrating, his eyes on the bedroom door. 'What? Oh, probably. You meet all sorts. Not dogs, though. At least, I don't think so. Why do you want to know?'

His mobile phone rang. He'd muted the sound, but fished it out of his pocket anyway, listened to the message, nodded, cleared his throat, said he'd be right down. 'I have to go. An appointment made ages ago. I'm trying to rearrange my schedule but it's tricky, not knowing how long . . .'

Ellie nodded. Her own throat felt raw.

He looked around, fingering his tie into place, palming back his hair. 'There's one thing you might know about. She's on about a photo she wants, of Frank. I couldn't see any photographs of the boy downstairs. Do you know where it could be?'

'She must mean my Frank, my late husband. She brought him up after his parents died young, and our wedding photo is on the chiffonier in the sitting room. I'll get it for her.'

'I know the one. We look a bit alike, don't we?'

Ellie thought, No, they didn't look much alike, but there was no point arguing. Roy went on down the stairs, and Ellie went into her aunt's bedroom. The blinds were halfway down, leaving the room in shadow, but the air smelt fresh because of a half-open window. The sun lay brightly on the garden below, where Rose was dead-heading geraniums, wearing an ancient straw hat which looked as if it had been designed for a wedding guest, and which Rose had probably bought in the charity shop.

Miss Quicke opened her eyes. 'You took your time getting here. What have you been doing?'

'Been playing Brer Fox, have you? Poor Roy, he thought you were asleep.'

'Very tiring, people clinging on to you when you want to be off. I know I can rely on you not to make a fuss. It was a good day for me when young Frank brought you home.'

'You didn't show it.'

'That wasn't the way I was brought up. I know you realized that.'

Ellie thought, Did I? Well, it doesn't matter now. 'Do you want me to hold your hand?'

'Mawkish nonsense,' said the old lady. 'Prop me up a bit. That's better. Since it seems I'm still here, you might as well entertain me. What have you been doing this morning? Ah, I remember. The affair of the dog. Have you found it yet?'

'Not yet, but I'm wondering if there may be two dogs because there's been a second attack. The first time in the park, the thief was alone but accompanied by a large brown dog. He stole a boy's bike and got the dog to attack his victim's mother. Never laid a finger on her himself. This time there were three boys who set a liver and white dog on an elderly woman. They frightened but didn't hurt her and got away with her purse and her mobile phone.'

'Same difference. Brown is liver coloured. Robbery was the object of the exercise both times.'

'Possibly. I could check with the first witness to see if the dog had some white on him. I think she said it was mostly brown. But even if the dog is the same, how do you account for there being only one boy in the first instance, and three in the next?'

'Use your head, girl. The owner of the dog's the key. He's ambitious. He's building a gang. Next thing there'll be not three but five or six lads tailing along behind him.'

Ellie shivered. It was a grim prospect.

'I remember . . .' Aunt Drusilla's voice faded to a thread, and she slipped down the pillows. 'I had a cairn terrier, once.

It was given me by my godfather as a birthday present. I loved that dog. I went shopping for my mother one day, and when I got back, he'd gone. She said he'd run away but I always thought she'd got rid of him because his barking gave her a headache.'

A bee blundered into the room through the open window. Ellie persuaded it to return to the outside world, and when she returned to the bed, she saw her aunt had fallen asleep once more.

The agency nurse came softly into the room, checked her patient over, nodded to Ellie and went to sit by the window.

Ellie took a light chair to the bedside and sat, holding one of her aunt's hands in hers. Miss Quicke hadn't had an easy or a happy life. She'd been brought up in a loveless household which held women in low esteem and in which all the attention had been lavished on her feckless brother. Seduced and abandoned by the one love of her life, she'd been forced to give up her only child for adoption.

When she had come to undertake the upbringing of her nephew, she'd never known how to temper duty with love, and in consequence she'd received dutiful attention from young Frank, rather than love. To compensate for an arid personal life, she'd devoted her considerable brain and energies to the accumulation of a fortune. Her great-niece Diana seemed to have been born with much the same drive to acquire wealth, but so far had failed to exhibit the same talent for doing so.

Ellie was possibly the first person to penetrate Miss Quicke's defences. For years Drusilla had ordered Ellie about as if she'd been a slave, but after her husband had died and Ellie had begun to develop her potential, there had come a shift in their relationship. Ellie no longer feared her aunt, but respected and admired — even loved — the old lady for herself. It would have seemed impossible a couple of years before, but they had become good friends.

Then Roy had appeared on the scene, and his advent had softened the old lady further. Diana had always held the view that Roy was a fortune hunter and had looked his mother up because she was a wealthy woman. Diana was wrong. Roy wasn't like that. He loved his mother, he admired her, he didn't want to lose her. Oh yes, he wouldn't mind inheriting more money to help him develop bigger and better properties, but that wasn't his primary aim in life.

Miss Quicke didn't see her son through rose-coloured spectacles — she'd never had any time for such frivolity — but she had found it pleasant to have a son who was an affectionate, good-natured and presentable professional man. His marriage to Felicity and the production of a baby had enlarged the circle of people Miss Quicke could trust. Here Rose, too, had helped enormously. Miss Quicke had been better looked after in the last couple of years of her life than ever before. She had even, perhaps, come to believe that it was safe to accept the love of the people around her.

Someone tapped on the half-open door. Miss Quicke did not stir, but Ellie left the room to speak to the newcomer. To her surprise, it was Diana standing there. A Diana for once not too sure of herself.

'Diana? Has something happened to little Frank?'

Diana looked beyond her mother into the bedroom. 'He's all right, I suppose. I'd got an appointment this side of the Avenue, finished early. I thought I'd like to sit with Great-Aunt for a while.'

Ellie didn't know what to say. Could the girl be trusted? True, Diana hadn't got a solicitor in tow and she wasn't carrying a briefcase full of paperwork for Miss Quicke to sign but . . .

'Oh, I'll not bother her any more,' said Diana, with a shadowy smile. 'I trust her to see me right. It was silly of me to doubt her, quite unnecessary. I just want to sit with her for a while. I've been thinking about her non-stop. She's always been there, all my life, pulling the strings, ordering us all about. It's unnerving, to feel that she's on her way out. The end of an era. I can't spare more than half an hour, but I'd like to do it, if I may.'

Ellie looked back into the room. The nurse was checking on her patient, who did not stir.

'She's asleep, isn't she?' said Diana. 'I promise not to disturb her, or to throw my weight about with the nurse, or anything. If she wakes up, I'll call the nurse.'

'The nurse doesn't leave the room. If you're happy with that . . . ?'

Diana nodded and went through into the bedroom, her black suited figure blending into the gloom. Had the sun been obscured by cloud?

* * *

The lads took Mick to the back of the shops for a smoke. It was an alleyway that led nowhere, a dumping ground for all sorts of rubbish, clay and builders' rubble forming an uneven surface underfoot. There was even a mattress for them to sit on.

Mick tied Toby's lead to the knob of an old door that had been left there. Stripes was kicking things, not meeting his eye, still showing signs of wanting to split from the group. Mick couldn't allow that. He fondled Toby's ears, pointing him at Stripes, who cringed. Mick could feel tension running up and down the dog's back. Toby wanted to get at Stripes and worry the life out of him.

A car nosed into the alley and parked. A youngish woman got out and turned to look at them. Mick didn't like it when people studied his face, and this woman was peering at them, squinting. Ah, she was short-sighted, probably couldn't see their faces clearly. Oughtn't to be driving, he thought, virtuously.

He kept his hand on the chain around Toby's neck, wondering whether to let the dog at her, when she turned away to unload bags of shopping from the boot of the car. She must live close by. She had the keys to the car in one hand, hefting bags out with the other. One push and she'd be over and quite helpless. Should he go for her handbag?

He muttered to the gang to go on lookout duty at the end of the alley. They pulled up their hoods and obeyed, though Stripes took his time about it. The woman used her remote to lock the car up and disappeared around the corner into the street.

Aha! Mick spotted that the car had a satnav in it. He picked up a half-brick and smashed the car window, grabbing the prized item. Hood laughed, but Stripes froze.

'What you staring at?' Mick asked the weak link. 'You want a taste of what else I can do?' Mick reached for Toby's lead and Stripes took off, yelling fit to bring the filth down on them. Mick had forgotten he'd tied Toby's lead to a door. The dog was willing, tried to drag the door along with him, till Mick jumped on it and stopped him. By that time, both lads had disappeared.

The first time he showed them how it was done, and they ran out on him! Well, he'd catch up with them some time. They just needed a little more training, that was all. Meanwhile, he'd sell off the satnav. He was building up a nice little reserve fund.

CHAPTER ELEVEN

Ellie found the wedding photo of herself and her husband — how young they looked and how dated her wedding dress! — and took it back upstairs. Diana was sitting in the chair by the bedside, and for a wonder she was actually holding the old woman's hand. The nurse was flicking through a magazine, but keeping a wary eye on her charge.

Ellie placed the photo on the bedside table and went down to the kitchen. Rose was cleaning the cooker, which she had no need to do as Miss Quicke paid for someone to do all the cleaning in the house. Rose was keeping herself occupied, singing along with a cracked voice to the radio. The sky had clouded over and a breeze rattled some bamboo in a pot outside the kitchen window. Ellie took a seat at the table; Rose turned the radio down and made a pot of tea.

They sat on opposite sides of the breakfast table, two women who had been through much together, and who realized that their lives were going to change. Ellie reflected how pleasant it was to sit in silence with an old friend. Well, not in silence, actually, because Rose was burbling on about this and that, the nice plaice fillets she'd got from the fishmonger, a newly planted rose that had unaccountably died, and . . . and . . .

Ellie didn't have to listen or do more than nod occasionally. She wondered how Thomas had got on at his meeting, and what she should wear to go out with him that night. There was such a lot she had to tell him. Her thoughts wandered up to the bedroom in which her aunt lay, gradually withdrawing from life. Had it been wise to allow Diana to sit with her great-aunt? Visions of pillows being thrust over faces would keep intruding into Ellie's mind. But no. Diana wouldn't do that. Diana didn't lie. If she said she would do a thing, she did it. If she said she wasn't going to do a thing, then she wouldn't do it.

Rose was looking at her, expecting an answer to some question she'd asked, which Ellie had not heard. 'Sorry, Rose. What was that again?'

'It's best to think about something else,' said Rose. 'I can tell you're worried about Diana sitting with Miss Quicke, but the nurse promised me faithfully she'd not leave the room even for a second, or I wouldn't have let Diana go up there, and if there's a soft spot your daughter has for anyone, it's for her great-aunt, who's her role model in life, if that's the right word. They do have such odd ways of putting things nowadays, don't they?'

Ellie smiled. Yes, they did.

'What I was saying was—' Rose clattered the teacups into the dishwasher — 'do you think I could borrow Midge for a night or two? I don't hold with traps for mice, nasty sadistic things, traps, and poison I will not put down, not with so many birds coming into the garden, although it's not precisely in the garden, of course, but in the conservatory, which is almost worse because they could easily escape from there into the house, and though I can't say I'd jump on a chair if one ran across the kitchen floor, I might scream, just because you can't help screaming if a mouse runs over your foot, can you?'

Ellie blinked. 'Of course you can't. I knew there was something I meant to ask you, and that's it. I thought I saw a mouse myself when I was in the conservatory the other day, but I'm not sure about bringing Midge over. He looks after my own house and garden beautifully, but I wonder if he'd agree to come. I know it makes me sound weak at the knees, but if he decided he didn't like it here and tried to make his own way back to my place, he might get run over and I'd hate that.'

'He settled down in your place all right, when you took him in. If we locked him in the conservatory with some of his special treats, not too many so that he still had an appetite for hunting, and if he knew you were around, he'd clean the place up in next to no time.'

'Do you really think he cares about who provides for him? I've always thought he only tolerated me because I let him come and go exactly as he pleased, though of course he does sleep on my bed at night.'

'But you'll be sleeping here tonight, won't you?'

Ellie tried not to pull a face because she didn't fancy the idea much. However, if Rose were feeling so stressed about Miss Quicke dying that she asked for company, then Ellie must agree. Ellie held back a sigh and nodded.

'That's settled then. Remind me to give you the extra key for the dead lock.' Rose reached for some lemons to cut up. She sniffed and put the knife down. 'I am not going to cry; no, I am not. I keep thinking, Will she be able to drink any of this lemonade I'm making for her, because it's the only thing she asks for? I make it fresh every day, but she hardly touched it yesterday and today not at all, so what am I making it for again, I ask myself?'

Ellie was soothing. 'You're making it because it's one little job you can do for her.'

'One last little job,' said Rose, slicing the fruit. 'So, will you go and fetch Midge now? I've had the spare room bed made up with fresh sheets for nigh on a week now, so you've only to bring your nightie and toothbrush when you come.'

'I'm having supper with Thomas. I'll get him to bring us over after that, provided Midge hasn't seen fit to go walkies. Which reminds me that I need to ask that woman who saw the first attack about the colour of the dog. I'll use the phone in the sitting room.'

The sitting room was normally bright with sunlight at this time of day, but today cloud and a light drizzle had dulled the sun's rays. Ellie extracted Caroline Topping's telephone number from her bag and punched numbers, hoping that the girl would be at home at this time of day.

'Caroline? Is that you? Ellie Quicke here. You remember that I . . . yes, that's right. I'm sorry to say that something rather alarming has happened, another woman has been attacked by a lad with a dog . . . no, no! Not another fatality. She wasn't hurt, just scared this time. It may not be the same dog, but I wondered, would you describe the dog you saw as brown all over? Or black all over, perhaps?'

'Brown, mid-brown, with white patches on his chest and either one or two legs. In fact, quite a lot of white, I'd say. Brown on his back.'

It was the same dog, obviously. Aunt Drusilla had been right. Again. 'Thank you,' said Ellie. 'That's most helpful. Did you give that description to the police? Yes? Oh, good. I'm sure they can link the two cases, now. You haven't remembered any other little detail that might help, have you?'

'Don't think so.'

Ellie could hear a fretful wailing in the background. 'Must go,' said Caroline. 'He's teething, poor lamb. Oh, there is one thing, perhaps. I woke up in the night, sweating, worrying, you know the way one does, and it was flashing through my mind again, and I think I heard, though of course I can't be absolutely certain, but I think I heard the lad call the dog Toby. Like the dog in Punch and Judy, you know? Toby. It's not a fashionable name nowadays, so I think I've got it right. I don't suppose it helps at all, but for what it's worth . . .'

'Thank you,' said Ellie. 'Have you told the police about—?' But Caroline had rung off, needing to attend to her toddler. What was his name? Duncan? That wasn't a fashionable name, either. Caroline was a sensible, intelligent girl and Ellie would take odds on it that she'd remembered the name right. Not that it helped to find the dog.

Diana came down the stairs, treading lightly. 'I'll be off now. She hasn't stirred. I thought at one point she'd stopped breathing—' a light laugh which ended with a catch in her breath — 'but she hadn't. The nurse says she may be like this for days, or go overnight.'

Ellie scolded herself for having doubted Diana. Of course the girl could be trusted to watch over her great-aunt for a while. 'I'm sleeping here tonight. I'll let you know if there's any change.'

'Thanks.' Diana wasn't practised at saying thanks and it sounded awkward. She looked at her watch. 'Must go. Another client, another day, another sale. Wish me luck, Mother.'

'Yes, dear.' Ellie saw her daughter out, went up the stairs to tell the nurse that she'd be back later that evening, popped into the kitchen to say goodbye to Rose, and found her not there but in her own little sitting room beyond, listening to a soap. She waved goodbye, mouthed, 'See you later,' and left the quiet, so quiet, too quiet house.

A passing car in the peaceful road outside seemed louder than usual.

* * *

Ellie busied herself with getting her house straight for the weekend. No matter if the sky was due to fall in: shopping for meals had still to be done; appointments for the dentist to be confirmed; and a parcel collected from a neighbour. It had been another warm day, even if it had clouded over, so some watering had to be done to keep the busy lizzies flowering in the garden. There was no sign of Midge.

She held a short conversation over the fence with Kate, bringing her up to speed and letting her know that she would not be sleeping at home that night. Ellie was worried about Midge. Had Kate seen him? He did sometimes move into her house for an hour or two. But no, she hadn't seen him for some time. It was typical of Midge to go AWOL when needed. Ellie wandered around the garden calling for him, but he wasn't having it. Finally she had to give up. As she'd warned Rose, Midge was a law unto himself.

Ellie really wasn't happy about having to sleep at the big house that night, but she did understand that Rose would feel more comfortable if she were there. Ellie rang to make sure that all was well with Felicity, who hadn't known the old lady for long, but had always admired her. Felicity was gently sorrowing for her. On a more cheerful note, Felicity reported that little Mel had taken to the bottle wonderfully well, and they were going round to Caroline's tomorrow morning for a while. Ellie said she'd probably be sleeping at Aunt Drusilla's that night, if anyone wanted her.

Ellie rang Rose, who sounded as if she'd just woken from a nap. She said that Miss Quicke hadn't woken at all, but the nurses had changed over and was Midge looking forward to his mouse hunt that evening?

Well, no. Midge didn't know about it yet. Ellie called him again, but there was still no sign of him. She hoped he hadn't got himself shut in someone's garage or garden shed by accident. These things did happen. It was just one more thing to worry about.

She showered and changed for the evening. Thomas liked her in blue, and blue was her favourite colour, so a pale blue cotton dress with a pretty neckline would do fine. She didn't bother with jewellery, except for the locket he'd given her at Christmas to wear on a chain around her neck. He was hoping that one day soon she'd ask him for his photograph to go inside the locket. The thought amused her. Maybe she would, sometime. Not just yet, though.

It was going to be another warm evening, if overcast.

Thomas had a somewhat elastic sense of time when visiting bereaved families, so she didn't really expect him to be on time, although in fact he was only five minutes late.

She locked the front door and took her place in his car with a sense of relief. For a little while she could relax and enjoy being taken out by a good friend. He was wearing a black silk waistcoat over a fresh white shirt, no tie, well-cut black trousers. Very nice. Presumably that was what he'd worn to his meeting?

'How did your meeting go?'

'Interesting. Tell you when we get there.'

She relaxed, thinking the meeting would be some diocesan affair about rules and regulations, or budgets and statistics, or mission statements. About anything, in short, which she knew men took seriously, but which didn't affect her.

Neither of them wanted a starter, so both went up for the Carvery straight away, and ate their way through beef for him, and turkey for her. She told him her day's little adventures, keeping her tone light. He always wanted the daily trivia, said it put his job into perspective. He said he'd try to drop in on Miss Quicke later that evening if he could.

'What's the news about Leona? I'm sorry I made such a silly suggestion today. I hope you didn't take it seriously.'

'I always take your suggestions seriously. You see your way more clearly than I do when dealing with people. I've put it to Leona that she might like to move into Corinne's flat and keep the boy. She saw the advantages immediately, not least that her children would get into a better school than the one they're in now. She'd been feeling really bad for her nephew not being wanted by his father, and she thinks her kids would like her to adopt him as well. So she's going to talk it over with them, see what they think.'

'I'm surprised. Delighted, but surprised. I was afraid there'd be far too much red tape to disentangle, even if she did feel like taking the boy on.'

'I'm good at cutting through red tape. Now following on from that, have you found any traces of illegal dog fighting in the neighbourhood?'

'Nothing. No one seems to know anything about such things, and none of the dog-walkers have spotted the dog before. There's been another incident involving a dog today, luckily no great damage done. I did wonder if there might be two dogs menacing the neighbourhood, but no, it seems there's only one. It seems to be in the care of a teenaged boy who may or may not be part of a youthful gang. It's a bit scary, isn't it?'

He'd poured just one glass of wine for each of them. Everything seemed normal, though she thought afterwards that he might have been a little quieter than usual.

'So, your meeting?' She fingered the menu. Should she have an ice cream? He often had a treacle sponge. But not tonight, apparently.

'Something of a surprise.' He looked down at his interlocked fingers. 'I've been offered a new job. Even when I was shortlisted I didn't dare hope for much, thinking there'd be other people in the field far more suitable. After talking to the bishop today, I've accepted.'

Ellie couldn't think of a single thing to say. She watched her hand move towards her almost empty glass. She thought, I'm in shock! What do I say? I thought a gaping hole was going to open up in my life when Aunt Drusilla left, but this . . . this is far worse.

He looked around for the waitress and asked for a couple of coffees. 'Shall we have them here at the table?'

Ellie thought, I'd better not try to move. I'll fall down if I do. She managed to nod. She thought, I'm all of a tremble. I can't believe that this is happening. I thought he'd always be there, though that's absurd, but I've come to rely on him for everything.

He fumbled with his napkin. He was looking everywhere but at her. No, that was one sharp look he'd just given her. Assessing her reaction? He said, 'They want me to start in three months' time. Editor of an ecumenical magazine which at the moment is losing money. Justifiably. It's a right mess at the moment. They seem to think that with my background, teaching, bringing out a couple of books, writing papers, all that . . . and then my experience of running a parish for a couple of years . . . they think I could pull it round. I'm not sure that I can, but I can't refuse. It's quite a challenge.'

She managed to nod, even to smile. 'Congratulations.' She cleared her throat. 'I'm sure you'll be a great success.'

'The church wardens won't be pleased to hear I'm leaving, but they always knew I was here on a temporary basis.'

Ellie wondered how that fact had escaped her. She'd assumed he was going to be with them for ten years or so, just as his predecessor had been. But then, she'd never been on the parish council, or wanted to be, so didn't get all the insider news.

He said, 'There'll be an interregnum, of course, but the bishop has promised to keep it as short as he can. He's got a lively curate or two who could do with more experience. A youngish family man would be best. Luckily the vicarage has been rebuilt and is now an attractive option for an up-and-coming man.'

Ellie nodded again. She wondered what he'd do if she had hysterics on the spot, or burst into tears, or kicked the table over — no, not that. The tables at the Carvery were extremely solid. Her throat was dry. Where was the promised coffee?

'Where will you be based?'

He shrugged. 'I'll have to find somewhere to rent. Any ideas?'

She shook her head. The moment she stood up, her legs would give way and she'd fall to the ground, and what a stir that would make. She told herself she was hysterical. She told herself that this was not happening, that everything couldn't end like this. The waitress banged their coffee down before them and departed.

'I shall be very sorry to leave the parish in some ways,' said Thomas, ladling sugar and cream into his cup. 'I've made some good friends here, among whom I count your good self, Ellie. I don't know how I'd have managed, not being a terribly social, outgoing sort of person, if it hadn't been for you.'

Ellie thought, I'm going to scream!

He sighed, replete, patting his stomach. 'Which reminds me, I think I need my eyes testing. Can you recommend an optician?'

She shook her head. Telling herself that she could do it, of course she could, she put one small spoonful of sugar into her coffee and stirred it. There. She hadn't spilled her coffee, and her hand had stopped trembling. She drank her coffee, wondering if this would be the last time that she'd sit opposite Thomas, her very good friend, her more than good friend, enjoying his company. The prospect was bleak.

He looked at his watch. 'Would you mind if we called it a night? I've got a couple of calls to make still. Oh, by the way, the church wardens don't know about my leaving yet, so keep it under your hat till they announce it in church, will you?'

She nodded. She managed to get to her feet, steadied herself against the tabletop, and made her way to the door by concentrating on putting one foot in front of the other. He paid the bill but this time they didn't split it in half, as they usually did.

She managed to behave normally on the way home. At least, she thought he hadn't noticed that she was devastated by his news.

He dropped her off at her house before she remembered to ask if he could wait for her to collect Midge and take them both over to Aunt Drusilla's. Perhaps it was just as well, because he had other things to think about now. He had calls to make that evening, had drawn a line under their relationship and was moving on. She'd been a good friend to him, he said. She hoped she had. She hoped he didn't realize how much he'd just hurt her.

Of course he didn't realize. How could he? She'd always played cool whenever he'd warmed to her. She hadn't wanted him to get any closer, and now he was leaving her behind, for a starry future.

She unlocked the front door, unlocked the back door, looked around for Midge, who hadn't touched the supper she'd left out for him. Bother.

There were no messages on the answerphone for a wonder. Usually it was full of people wanting her to do this and that for them. Diana was due to take little Frank home this evening, so they'd probably be cuddled up on the settee together, watching a video and eating a takeaway meal. Stewart and his delightful Maria would be talking over the day, she telling him the latest that their children had got up to, and he saying how sorry he was that Miss Quicke seemed to be on her way out. Felicity and Roy would be relaxing over a meal, with the baby alarm on to hear if Mel stirred. Kate next door would be feeding her husband, with her two little chicks safely tucked up in bed.

Everyone was playing happy families except Ellie. She scolded herself. She was often alone nowadays and enjoyed her independence. She never had to share the remote control for the telly, or worry about what time she wanted to get up or go to bed. She could eat what she liked, when she liked, dress how she liked. She could work in the garden as much as she saw fit, she could plant whatever colour scheme suited her, and she had enough money to get other people to do things she didn't want to do herself.

On the other hand . . .

No, there was no other hand. She was very much better off as she was, rather than having to think about someone else all the time. There were lots of good fish in the sea, and anyway, she wasn't interested in getting married again. Certainly not!

Time was marching on. She retrieved Midge's basket from the cupboard under the stairs, gave it a brush down, shook out and replaced the old towel that lined the base and set it on the kitchen table. She put his toy mouse in it, thinking it might tempt him to enter, knowing it was a forlorn hope. Midge only went in that under protest nowadays, when he went to the vet for his shots. To get him into the basket, she usually had to sedate him first with an enormous meal.

There was still no sign of him. If Thomas had come in with her for a companionable cuppa as he often did, he could have helped her to look for the cat. Midge approved of

Thomas, who had a comfortable figure which allowed cats to take a nap on him in peace and quiet. No Thomas.

She glanced at the clock and went upstairs to find a small overnight bag and stuff various bits and pieces into it. She made sure all the upstairs windows were firmly shut and locked. It was no good sitting down on the bed and having a good weep. That wouldn't get her anywhere. Besides, Rose must be looking out for her already.

She went through to lock the back door and found Midge had emptied his food dish. So he must have come back while she was upstairs? He'd not only eaten, but jumped into the cat basket of his own accord. Did he really think he was going to the vet's at this time of evening? Ellie shook her head at herself as she fastened the lid of the basket. She didn't understand anything about Midge — or about men, for that matter.

She rang for a minicab, since there was no way she could carry Midge for any distance, shoved some cat tins into a plastic bag, and put out the rubbish for the dustman to collect in the morning.

She carried everything to the road as a large car drew up. It was one of those over-large 4x4s with tinted windows which, when parked badly, blocked the road for passing traffic, which is precisely what it did now. But there was no helpful Asian driver in the front seat. Instead, Madam from the charity shop wound down the electric window to summon Ellie to her side of the car.

'Just the person I wanted to see. I trust you're not leaving the neighbourhood yet awhile?'

Ellie cringed. She didn't mean to, but Madam's tone of effortless superiority had the desired effect. Ellie had been conditioned to fall in with other people's wishes all her life. Her own mother and father had expected obedience from her and got it. They'd sent her to schools which had been strong on discipline. A dominating husband had hardly helped her to develop an independent spirit, while Frank's aunt Drusilla and their daughter Diana had taken full advantage of her tendency to put others before herself. Needless to say, when she worked at the charity shop, Madam had homed in on this fault — if it were a fault — and treated Ellie the same way.

Of recent years Ellie had learned to stand up for herself; she'd managed to assert her own sphere of independence with Aunt Drusilla, and she'd come some way towards doing the same with Diana.

Being in a 4x4, Madam had another advantage; that of looking down on Ellie, who was not vertically challenged exactly, but who often bought her clothes in the petite section of department stores. One up to Madam.

Ellie glanced up and down the street. 'I can't stop to talk now. I'm in rather a hurry, expecting a cab.' She rather thought Madam had a passenger, but couldn't see him or her properly from the street.

'This won't take a minute. The thing is, that Mae's accident places the rest of the staff in a very difficult position this weekend, and I'm at my wits' end to find someone to help us out. Then I saw you standing there, and I remembered that I could always depend on you in an emergency.'

'I'm sorry,' said Ellie, consulting her watch, 'but I'm waiting for a minicab to take me over to my aunt's. Rose is looking after her, of course, but—'

'Rose! I blame you for persuading Rose to desert the shop, too. Of course it's understandable that she'd rather look after a wealthy old woman than help our wonderful charity, but—'

'It's not like that,' said Ellie, reddening. 'My aunt's dying and wants me to sit with her. Rose is worn out, looking after her in the daytime, and it's the least I can do, to sit with her overnight.'

'You're always using that excuse. First your husband, and now your aunt. Surely you can find time to help your old friends and colleagues out for an hour or two? I wouldn't demean myself to ask if it were not so important for the shop to be manned on Saturdays.'

Ellie wanted to say something about blood being thicker than water, but wasn't sure it was appropriate. She was trembling. Would this terrible day never end? Where was her minicab? Ellie pulled out her mobile phone and pressed buttons to check. She made one last attempt to even up matters with Madam. 'Surely you yourself could help out on a Saturday for once?'

'You have no idea what you are suggesting. This weekend is exceptionally difficult, and I simply cannot . . . but why should I have to explain to you? And you might at least pay attention to what I am saying, instead of trying to hold a conversation with—'

'I'm trying to find out why my cab hasn't . . . oh, is that . . . ? Yes, it's Mrs Quicke here and . . . Oh, I see. Yes, of course I understand. Another fifteen minutes, you say? Well, I am in rather a hurry so—'

'Get in, do!' Madam told her passenger to get in the back and shot the door open. 'I can take you over to your aunt's, I suppose, if it's not too far out of my way.'

* * *

Mick was ordered into the back seat. He went, fuming. There were days when nothing went right. He'd spent a lot of effort building up a team, and they'd gone and run out on him, just as he was beginning to get things started up. He'd thought it would be a doddle staying with the aunt, but she was such a cow, getting at him all the time. Now she was going to dump him at some poncy youth club while she went out with her friends, and worse still, she wanted him to play waiter at a big party she was giving this weekend. Fat chance.

So what if he hadn't got a gang at his heels? He'd got enough from the satnav and the woman with the shopping basket to fund him for a while; he'd got a new ID and a mobile phone. Why not give himself a break, get away for some action for a coupla days? Not home. No, not yet. But he could find out where the action was going to be this weekend, couldn't he? He could make some more dosh by entering Toby in a fight or two. Yes. Mebbe he could make use of the old banger one of his cousins had left in the garage back at the aunt's. He could borrow that, no problem. Yes, why not?

CHAPTER TWELVE

Ellie didn't particularly wish to accept Madam's offer but couldn't afford any further delay since it was long past the time she'd hoped to be with Rose. So she told the minicab firm to forget about her, slung her overnight things and the bag of cat tins up into the vehicle and climbed up with some difficulty, hauling Midge's basket on to her knee. Midge began to growl.

'What sort of animal have you got there?' asked Madam, driving off into the traffic without signalling her intentions in any way, and taking no notice of the indignant honks that followed her progress. 'And where precisely does this aunt of yours live? Not in council accommodation, I hope.'

Ellie held on to Midge's basket with one hand while trying to do up her seat belt with the other. 'Straight on, across the Avenue, third road on the right.'

'Oh. Not far from me, then?' Madam was reluctantly impressed.

Midge was heavy on Ellie's knee, and seriously disturbed. He began to keen. Ellie told him to stop. It was embarrassing enough that she had had to accept a lift from Madam; Midge's behaviour was making matters worse. 'Just past the next lamp post, the house with the semicircular drive.'

Madam braked sharply, turning in to the driveway without bothering to indicate. There was a muttered exclamation from the back. Ellie only caught a glimpse of someone on the back seat in her flurry to get herself and Midge out of the vehicle. Madam hadn't introduced her to her passenger, but that meant nothing; Madam considered herself above the usual social amenities.

Madam tried on a smile. 'I'm sure you'll find your aunt much improved, and I have your word that you'll see what you can do to help us out tomorrow, right?'

Ellie picked up the bag of cat tins and said she didn't think she could, but Madam had shut the door in her face. Ellie wanted to stamp her feet and have hysterics. She felt like putting up two fingers as Madam's car disappeared . . . and then she noticed that in her haste she'd failed to retrieve her overnight bag from the car.

She wanted to cry with frustration. First Thomas was moving away, and now Madam wanted her to . . . well, sucks to Madam, so there! But what was she going to do about her overnight bag? She couldn't think.

She heard the front door open behind her. Rose said, 'So there you are!' And at that moment Madam's car reappeared, backing up to where she stood. The door shot open and her overnight bag landed at her feet. Presumably the passenger had discovered it when he or she switched back to the front seat.

Was there anything broken inside? Possibly, but she couldn't care less. She was beyond caring about anything much. Except Midge, perhaps. Whatever had possessed him to behave like that? He was still growling and seemed to weigh more than usual, though Ellie didn't understand how that could be.

She swiped the back of her hand across her cheeks, and with an effort turned to the next job in hand, switching anxieties.

'My aunt?' she asked.

'Dozing,' said Rose. 'Was that Gloria Goss?'

Ellie began to laugh. 'Do you know, I'd forgotten her proper name. Gloria Goose, you used to call her, didn't you? She used to frighten the life out of me. Still does, in a way.' She picked up Midge in his basket, Rose collected everything else, and they went inside.

* * *

Mick now knew of a couple of houses worth a visit. He'd taken special note of the one where they'd picked up the Quicke person, which was going to be empty that night. The usual sort of semi-D, you could easily smash a window at the back to get in. No alarm box in sight.

Better still would be the pickings at the big house they'd just left. A huge house, well-maintained, also without an alarm box on the front. Just two old women sitting beside a deathbed. Easy-peasy. In and out. This really was going to be a doddle. So which should he do that night?

* * *

Ellie tried to pay attention to what Rose was saying as she led the way into the conservatory, but most of it passed over her head. She gathered that Roy was sitting with his mother now, that the latest nurse was an uppity little thing, and that Diana had rung a couple of times to ask if Miss Quicke would like to see little Frank that evening, to which Rose had replied it wouldn't be a good idea to bring him over as the old lady was asleep most of the time now.

Rose clucked over Ellie's overnight bag, but really there was very little damage and Rose said that it didn't matter at all that Ellie hadn't thought to bring more than one change of undies, and she could easily pop the ones Ellie was wearing now into the wash that evening, fresh for the day after tomorrow if she were to stay for more than one night, and if she had forgotten her hand cream, she could borrow some from Rose, couldn't she?

'Thanks,' said Ellie, trying and failing to concentrate on what Rose was saying. She put Midge in his basket in a cool, shadowy place under the staging, and set out his food in his own dishes. At least he'd stopped growling and keening.

Rose pointed out where she thought the mouse nest was, and talked about buttering Midge's paws to keep him put, though Ellie doubted that would stop Midge if he decided to go walkabout. She opened the lid of the cat basket, and Midge's head rose into view as he elongated himself to twice his usual size. Grumbling, he decided to stay put in his basket. He was nothing if not contrary.

'Let's leave him to it,' said Rose in a stage whisper.

Ellie rubbed Midge's head at the back of his ears, by way of reassurance. He met her eyes with a look which she could interpret only too easily; Midge felt she'd betrayed him. He'd been prepared to be taken for a ride in a minicab as usual, well and good. Instead she'd transported him, willy-nilly, in a strange vehicle which had really upset him and now he was being asked to leave his sheltering basket, and for what? To chase a mouse? Yes, he could smell mice. Of course he could. Any cat could. So what? Was he a mechanical cat who could be switched into the 'kill' mode with the offer of a saucer full of his favourite biscuits?

'I'm sorry,' said Ellie, to her cat.

'What was that?' Rose was holding the door open, ready to depart. 'Shall we leave him to it?'

Midge sank down in the basket and turned his back on Ellie, which made her feel even more miserable than before. With a sigh, she followed Rose into the main body of the house.

Roy was coming down the stairs. He looked pale, but maybe that was because the hall was in shadow. 'No change,' he said, looking at his watch. 'I must go. I promised Felicity I wouldn't be late.'

He kissed Ellie's cheek, gave Rose a hug and left, letting the front door bang to behind him.

'Men,' said Rose, indulgent. 'I don't know why they can never shut a door quietly, which reminds me that I must give you another key — don't let me forget, will you? Now I've put clean towels out for you in the spare bedroom, and I'll bring you up a cuppa in a while. That new nurse wants a cuppa on the dot every two hours, camomile and ginger, if you please, but at least she brought the teabags with her. Will you be all right, Ellie? You look a little peaky, if I may say so, though I suppose it's no wonder, things being what they are, and if I hadn't been able to have a little nap this afternoon, I daresay I'd be feeling it, too, and I've promised myself that I'm not going to cry again, and I've almost managed it, haven't I?'

'You go and watch the telly for a bit. I'll be all right.'

'That nurse wanted the telly on up there in the room, but I said to her, "Are you being paid to watch telly or to watch your patient?" And she didn't have an answer to that, did she?'

Ellie picked up her overnight bag and climbed the stairs, holding on to the banister. She was so tired she wasn't sure she could make the first-floor landing. But she did.

Her aunt's bedroom was quiet and shadowy, the sash windows open at the top, the blinds half drawn. A Philippine nurse was sitting by the window, hooked up to an iPod. Swarthy, compact, no nonsense.

'Any change?' whispered Ellie, feeling limp.

The nurse shook her head.

Ellie left her bag out on the landing and seated herself by the bed. She would have taken her aunt's hand in hers, until she noticed that the aged, wrinkled fingers were fluttering over the top sheet. Ellie had heard that that sometimes happened when someone was near death. Was the end so near? She wished she could feel something; pity, sorrow, anything. But she couldn't. She was empty. She wondered what she'd do if Thomas came to call this evening. Nothing, of course. She'd smile and back away and hope that no one would notice that she was dying inside.

The nurse sat immobile. Ellie could hear the scratchy sound coming from the iPod.

Rose opened the door and brought in a cuppa for Ellie — which she didn't want — and something in a china mug for the nurse, who rose, announcing in a repressive whisper that she'd take her break outside on the landing.

Ellie sat on. Miss Quicke's hands stilled, and Ellie took one in both of hers. A slight scratching sound at one of the windows alerted Ellie to a visitor. Midge had escaped from the conservatory and climbed up to the first-floor window. How on earth had he managed that? She supposed he'd got on to the conservatory roof, and from there leaped to the window. Well, it was no good worrying about him falling because if he'd got that far, he wasn't going to fall now.

As Ellie watched, he gathered himself together on the windowsill, leaped to the top of the window and plopped down inside the bedroom.

'Hi, Midge,' said Ellie softly, thinking how much the cat's antics would have amused her aunt, if she'd been conscious.

Midge ignored Ellie, not being prepared to forgive her as yet. He strolled around the room, sniffing at the legs of the chairs on which the nurse had sat, and made his way to the foot of the bed, leaping on to it with skill and precision. He fixed his eyes on Miss Quicke. Ellie wasn't sure she should allow Midge to stay on the bed. She was absolutely sure the nurse wouldn't like it.

Midge liked beds. He always slept on hers. In cold weather he'd sleep at her back, and in warm weather he'd curl up at the foot of her bed where the tiniest of breezes from the window cooled the air. Was this what he was doing now?

No, he wasn't curled up. He was sitting upright, tail fastened around his forepaws, ears pricked but not uneasy. Waiting . . . for what?

Miss Quicke's hand jumped in Ellie's clasp.

Her eyes opened. Did she see Midge? She moved dry lips. Ellie hastened to moisten them.

Miss Quicke muttered, 'Are there animals in heaven? Ask Thomas.'

So she'd seen Midge? The frail eyelids sank. The sheet hardly stirred as Miss Quicke breathed in . . . breathed out. A long pause. Ellie held her breath, too. The old lady breathed in again, the faintest of rustles, the slightest of movements.

The nurse returned but went to sit in the window again. Hadn't she seen Midge? Ellie exchanged a conspiratorial glance with the cat, who blinked but didn't move. Anyone trying to take Midge off the bed would meet with resistance, claws hooked into the sheet, yowls of annoyance. Ellie wasn't going to risk his making a scene. He was worse than a fractious toddler when in a mood.

She sank lower into the chair. She couldn't hear her aunt breathe. How long was it since . . . ? Ellie counted to ten. Still there was no breath.

Miss Quicke's hand was still warm.

Another breath.

Quietly, Drusilla Quicke was slipping away from life.

Ellie closed her eyes, praying. *Let her go quietly. Dear Lord, take her quietly into your hands. She's had a difficult life and it made her hard, but she seems to have found some comfort, some consolation in recent years. She's been coming to church, she's been talking to Thomas, she believes in heaven. Dear Lord, I don't know how you judge people, but one thing's for sure, you know how my aunt's mind works, you know how much she's changed these last few years, and only you know what she believes in. I can surely trust you to be . . . not kind, that sounds silly, but . . . merciful.*

Ellie sank lower in her chair. Time passed. She prayed now and again. Perhaps she slept for a while.

A touch on her shoulder. She was half lying on the bed, her head cradled on one arm, while her right hand still clasped that of her aunt.

'She's gone,' said the nurse, iPod not crackling for once.

Ellie started. Had she dozed off? There was no sign of Midge. Had she dreamed the cat had been there?

The room was bright. The nurse had put on the overhead light. Evening had darkened to night as Ellie had dozed and watched, and dozed again. She was stiff from sitting in one position for too long. The hand she'd been holding for so long was cold to the touch. Yes, it was over.

Her aunt's face was peaceful. She was almost smiling

Ellie stretched, this way and that.

The nurse was clattering around the bed. 'If you'd like to leave me to do the necessary?'

Ellie nodded. She stroked her aunt's hand one last time, and went out of the room, unable to think straight. Unable to feel. Knowing there was much to be done, and not knowing how to do it.

She went down the stairs, taking her time about it. There was a dim light in the hall from a lamp on the hall table. The door into the conservatory was still firmly closed and there was no light on within. Had she imagined Midge's presence upstairs a while back? Possibly.

If he had been there, would Midge have returned to the conservatory, or started on the journey back home? Ellie couldn't bear to think of his making that journey across so many busy roads, across the Avenue with its buses, braving the dogs that might be taken for a walk in the dark. She couldn't bear to lose Midge as well as Aunt Drusilla. As well as Thomas. And there, grief struck, almost physically.

She held on to the newel post at the bottom of the stairs, telling herself that this would pass, that everything passed in due course. Tomorrow she would feel better, she would have absorbed the hurt, the loss. Tomorrow, or perhaps the day after, she would be able to smile again, to talk to people normally.

She switched on the lights in the conservatory and went in, forgetting to close the door behind her. Midge was lying on a cushioned cane chair, tail gently twitching. The slightest of breezes was coming down through a half-open window in the roof. Was that how he'd got out earlier? It would have been quite a jump even for Midge, but she wouldn't put it past him. He hadn't touched the food she'd left out for him.

She picked him up and huffed into his fur. He was warm and comforting to hold. He rumbled a purr, loose-limbed in her arms. 'Oh, Midge,' she said, her voice catching in her throat.

He lifted his head to rasp her cheek with his tongue. Only then did he stiffen, to remind her that he was no lapdog and didn't tolerate being cuddled for long. She set him on the floor and looked around to see if he'd started on the mouse problem. There were no dead mice to be seen, nor any sign that he'd caught and eaten any.

Instead, she saw his upright tail disappearing into the hall. 'Midge, come back!'

Fat chance. Well, she had to trust that he was merely in search of Rose and scraps of human food. The front door was shut, so he couldn't get out that way. She looked at her watch, shook it, couldn't interpret what it said. Was it really past midnight?

She went into the hall, to see Midge pawing at the door which led to the kitchen. Of course. She opened it for him, wondering how long it would take for him to learn how to open it for himself. He could open any door that had a handle and not a knob. Knobs did defeat him still. There were low lights still on in the kitchen to illuminate the work surfaces. Rose had left out a tray laid for supper, with sandwiches wrapped in cling film. A pot of soup sat nearby on the Aga. There was no sign of Rose herself, but soft music came from her sitting room next door.

Rose was dozing in her chair, in dressing gown and slippers. Ellie wouldn't have woken her, but Rose gave a start, and opened her eyes. 'It's over?'

Ellie nodded.

Rose gave a great sigh. 'You'll want some food inside you.' She struggled up out of her chair even though Ellie said she could manage by herself, honestly she could.

'I can never take anything solid at this time of night,' said Rose, taking no notice of Ellie's disclaimer. 'But you'll need something. Is the nurse . . . ?'

'Coping,' said Ellie, seating herself at the kitchen table. Midge had taken up his station on top of the fridge. If everyone else thought it time to eat, he wanted his share, too.

Rose ladled out soup and set it before Ellie. 'They'll be coming and going all night now. First there'll be the doctor to tell us what we already know, and then they'll be taking her away to rest, poor dear lady. I hope she went easily.'

Ellie nodded. She wasn't hungry and would have declined the soup, but that somehow or other Rose was making sure that she got it down her. It was delicious. Rose fed Midge, rubbing behind his ears and praising him for being a good boy. Ellie wasn't at all sure that Midge had been a good boy, but she didn't say anything. Perhaps she'd imagined his presence at the deathbed.

'Sandwiches, cream cheese and smoked salmon,' said Rose, removing the cling film and placing them before Ellie. 'With something a little extra. Just try one. See if you can tell what it is I've put in it.'

Ellie tasted, tried to smile appreciation. 'Chives?'

'I was going to get a herb bed going in that sunny patch where we've had the men in to pollard that prunus, drat it, nasty thing — never flowered properly and the flowers always look artificial, don't they?'

'I'm sure Aunt Drusilla won't mind,' said Ellie, without thinking. And then, 'Oh dear. Sorry. How stupid of me.'

'Up to bed with you,' said Rose. 'A quick shower in the en suite, a good night's kip and you'll feel better in the morning. Don't you bother none about letting the doctor in, or the nurse out, or anything. I've had nigh on four hours' sleep, which is as much as I usually get these days, so I can deal with all that. Look, Midge is waiting for you to go up now, isn't he just the little darling?'

Sure enough, Midge was waiting at the door to the back stairs. Ellie allowed herself to be wafted up the stairs, Midge at her heels. The landing above was ablaze with light, the nurse speaking on the phone to someone. Ellie didn't bother to listen. She took the corridor down to the spare room. It was a delightful room with a canopied bed. The walls were pale greeny-blue, and the blinds, curtains and bed linen were cream with bluish exotic birds and sprays of Chinese-type flowers on them. In some hands the effect could have been over-pretty, even childish, but Miss Quicke's taste had always been good; the colour of the walls was more cerulean than cornflower, the flowers were Audubon rather than cabbage rose, and the effect was adult rather than childish.

The bed had been turned down already. Her overnight bag lay on the table nearby. There were clean fluffy towels in the bathroom beyond. Every movement was an effort, but Ellie got herself out of her clothes, in and out of the bathroom, and into the bed. Midge was already curled up there, lightly snoring.

Ellie reached out a hand to turn off the light, thinking she was far too tired to sleep. And lay there, with one arm outstretched to the lamp, forming prayers of thanks and pleas for endurance even as she slipped sideways into the darkness . . .

. . . And was woken by someone shaking her arm and calling her name.

She struggled to open her heavy eyelids.

'Ellie! Wake up, do!'

Ellie got her eyes half open. The light was still on by her bedside. Hadn't she turned it off? She couldn't remember. The bedside clock was a digital one and it said 3.45 a.m. She blinked.

Rose was shaking her arm. 'Ellie, I'm sorry dear, but you've got to wake up. I wouldn't wake you if it wasn't necessary, you know I wouldn't, but it's bad news I'm afraid, and it won't wait till morning.'

Ellie's fantasy mind put up the thought that perhaps Aunt Drusilla wasn't dead after all, and was now stalking through the rooms of her old house, wondering aloud why there was a nurse at her bedside.

Ellie shook her head with both hands. 'Bad . . . ?'

'Kate, your next-door neighbour, dear. She's here, downstairs, waiting for you. There's been a bit of a fire at your house. The fire engines have been called, but Kate thinks you ought to . . .'

Ellie clutched at Rose's hand. It couldn't be! No, no! Not possible.

Rose nodded, holding on to Ellie as fast as Ellie was holding on to her. 'I'm afraid so, dear. Could you scramble into your clothes? She's in the hall, waiting to take you over there now.'

'I'm dreaming.'

Rose shook her head. 'She rang and rang. I couldn't think who would ring us at this time of night. Luckily I was just dozing in my chair, not in bed properly. So many people coming and going. The doctor. The nurse. And then to take her away, you know. Up and down, in and out, thinking I'd have a good lie-in tomorrow. I don't think it's too bad, Kate heard the alarm straight away.'

'How . . . ? Who . . . ?' She couldn't believe this was happening. It was unreal. She struggled out of bed and made her way into the bathroom. As she came out, Rose pushed a mug of tea at her.

'The cup that cheers. Drink up. Three sugars for shock. Whatever would poor Miss Quicke have said to all these carryings-on? One thing, it was lucky you have such good neighbours, or the whole house might have gone up in flames.'

The tea burned her mouth. Ellie stumbled into her clothes, was handed her handbag by Rose . . . where was Midge? . . . nowhere to be seen. Presumably he could look after himself, he usually did.

Kate was waiting in the hall, a long brown cardigan over her pyjamas. She looked drawn and pale. She gave Ellie a quick hug. 'Armand's looking after the children. Both were teething, or we might not have heard the alarm, sleeping so lightly, you know. I suppose it was an electrical fault.'

Rose unlocked the big front door, Ellie was swept out to Kate's car, and they drove through the quiet, dark night to where the sky was lit up with no less than two fire engines in front of Ellie's little house. And a police car.

They'd brought lights to help them. The sitting room windows had been smashed in, the front garden trampled over. Two high-pressure hoses snaked across the garden, but were now being curled up by large men with loud voices. Most of the houses round about had lights on in their upper windows, and there were even some onlookers in the street, probably thanking God that it wasn't them being burned out of house and home.

A fireman came out of the house through her front door, and left it open. The hall looked dark and unwelcoming.

Foxy-faced Armand loomed up beside Kate's car, their wide-eyed baby cradled in one arm, a sleeping toddler over his shoulder. 'The fire's out, Ellie, but I'm afraid your sitting room's gutted.'

Ellie got out of the car, and walked down the slope, looking into an unrecognizable front room. Black, black, black. It stank. She couldn't think. Or feel. She wanted to cry. Was too worn out to do so. Knew her mouth was agape.

Shock.

Kate brought up a fireman, introduced her. Ellie nodded. 'How . . . ?'

He was cheerful. 'I'm just going in to have a look-see. You were away?'

Ellie nodded.

'At a quick look, seems like the settee might have caught fire. You a smoker?'

She shook her head. He disappeared into the house. Flakes of soot drifted out of her living room and settled on her arm. She was cold, wearing nothing but a summer dress.

'Don't cry, Ellie.' Ellie hadn't realized she was crying. Kate put one arm around Ellie's shoulders, and hugged her. The toddler was now safely in Kate's strong right arm, still sound asleep. Ellie tried to speak, to say something about taking the children back to their beds, but couldn't get the words out.

Another fireman came up, and Armand accosted him. 'Look, we've got to get the children back to bed. It's all right to take them back into our house next door, isn't it?'

'Hang about a bit. The boss is just making sure there's no cylinders of gas around, no paint, no chemicals. The fire's out now, but we need to be sure. Why don't you all go and sit in your car for a bit, or go into a neighbour's?'

Kate and Armand conferred. Neighbours had offered to take them in, but their house seemed untouched by the fire, so they decided to wait in the car to see if they'd be allowed back soon.

The fire chief emerged from the house, conferring with a colleague. They plodded up the slope to where Ellie still stood, clutching her arms. Armand went to meet them. The fireman's words floated back up to Ellie.

'Sure you can go back into your house. I've turned off the gas, water and electricity at the mains, and there's nothing else there that could cause a problem. The fire was confined to the sitting room and didn't touch the rest of the downstairs. The two halls being next to one another, you should be quite safe next door. There was no burning upstairs, though the smoke probably would have done for anyone sleeping there tonight.'

Armand bustled up the slope. 'Kate, it's safe to go back in. Best gets the babes into their own beds. Will you stay with us, Ellie?'

Kate looked anxious. 'Do they know what caused it yet? Yes, Armand, you take the babes. Ellie, he's right, you'd best doss down with us tonight.'

The thought of the cool green bedroom back at the big house shimmered into Ellie's mind. Rose would be waiting up for her, anxious to hear what had happened. And dear Aunt Drusilla might still be there — or rather, her body might.

'No, I must get back. Rose is all alone and . . .' To her own ears, her words came out distorted, but the others seemed to understand, and nodded.

The fireman held up his hand. 'Just a minute, if you please.' He came up to Ellie. 'How come you were away tonight, Mrs . . . what's the name again? Mrs . . . ?'

Ellie went on staring at the wreck that had been her home. 'My aunt was dying. She died. I was to stay overnight so that Rose — her housekeeper — wouldn't be alone. Can I go in?'

'I wouldn't advise it. Now, if you could just answer a couple of questions? Mrs . . . ?'

‘Thirty-two years,’ said Ellie. ‘Or is it thirty-three? We had a flat at first, and then we moved here when we had Diana. My whole married life is there. Everything. I don’t understand.’

‘Looks like the fire started in the sitting room, in the settee. Might have smouldered for hours and then . . . whoosh! You’re a smoker, I take it?’

Ellie shook her head. ‘No, never.’

‘Are you insured?’

‘Mm? Oh yes. Kate sees to all that for me. I think it’s a new-for-old policy. Funny, I was thinking I needed to do some decorating, but not like this.’

‘Did you take care to shut all the doors inside when you went out?’

‘I don’t think I did, no. I don’t usually, and I was in a hurry to catch Midge and put him in his carrying basket . . . that’s my cat . . . and, oh, if I’d left him here, he’d have died, wouldn’t he?’

‘Probably, yes. Now, what time did you leave?’

She tried to think. ‘I’m not sure. After supper. I’d gone to the Carvery for supper. After that, then. Does it matter? Do I get the windows boarded up, or do you?’

‘Do you remember locking up front and back when you left?’

‘Yes, I suppose so. I mean, yes, of course I did.’ The meaning of what they were implying trickled through to her. She couldn’t believe her ears. Did they really think [illegible]? ‘You think I was responsible for the fire?’

‘There are suspicious circumstances, shall we say. The fire investigation team agrees with me. So we’d better bring the police in on this, right?’

* * *

Mick trudged home, weighed down by a couple of carrier bags, but pleased enough with his night’s work. With what he’d got already, he could afford to move on to his next scheme, which was to back Toby in a proper fight.

What a bit of luck, his aunt giving a lift to the Quicke woman. Stupid old cow, she'd left her tool shed unlocked, and he'd forced the back door with her own spade. He'd hoped to pick up a laptop or a mobile phone at the very least, but the place was a dump. The computer was so old it wasn't worth anything, ditto the television, out of the Ark both of them. He couldn't find any mobile phone or her credit cards, but he'd got her passport and chequebook. They'd fetch a few quid, plus the clock from the mantelpiece, and some jewellery from upstairs. Old-fashioned stuff, but they might fetch a few quid.

After he'd found the jewellery, he'd sat down for a smoke and a flick through the television channels. Before he knew where he was, he'd dozed off. A clock in the hall — too big for him to lift — had woken him by chiming three. His lighted cigarette had fallen on to the settee, but he didn't bother to stub it out. If it did burn the cushion, it served her right for not leaving her credit cards for him to find. He decided to get going, because he'd planned an early start next day.

He'd contacted his old mates up north on his new mobile phone and found out where the action was going to be that weekend. Not far from home, though he wouldn't bother to go back there, not with the ASBO still in force, not with his mum shacking up with a different bloke every night. Would he be glad to see his mates again! And would they be glad to see him, with a fighting dog in tow, a dog he could put in the ring, knowing it would win, win, win! He could hardly wait!

He hadn't dared take the old banger out tonight in case the aunt heard him, but he'd found the keys for it in the kitchen, and checked there was enough petrol in the tank for his needs. She'd never dare report it stolen and he'd bring it back in due course. And when he came back, he'd have a go at the big house where they'd left the Quicke woman.

CHAPTER THIRTEEN

Two large uniformed men stood on either side of Ellie, so close that she felt intimidated. She realized that they really did suspect her of having set a fire in her own house. She felt a moment of dislocation when she wondered if she were going to faint. So much had happened, so quickly. One moment she'd been chasing after mad dogs while worrying about her aunt, and then . . . and then Thomas had said . . . *that!* And her whole world had slid sideways from being a comfortable sort of place into the bleakness of despair. *Oh, Thomas, I wish you could be here now!*

She must be strong. She mustn't let herself weep any more, but that loss had knocked away the underpinnings of her life. Then dear Aunt Drusilla had made the journey into the future so quickly, without any fuss, just as she would have wanted to go. Painlessly. Going to sleep. Leaving them all behind. And now her own dear little house, her shell, her refuge from the world, was gone.

One of the men was talking, but she couldn't make sense of his words.

She said, 'I think, if you don't mind, that I need to sit down.'

Someone bustled up with a woollen throw in a bright tartan pattern, putting it around Ellie's shoulders. A neighbour whom Ellie knew only slightly. How kind of her. Ellie said, 'Thank you. So kind.' The kindness of neighbours restored some of her faith in the future. *Dear Lord, help.*

The warmth of the woollen throw gave Ellie a moment of comfort. Kate darted out of her house and called up the slope. 'Come on in. I've got the kettle on.'

Kettle equalled tea equalled more comfort. Was this God showing her that all was not lost? Yes, she'd lost Thomas. Yes, she'd lost her aunt. But there was still kindness in the world, and comfort of a sort.

Ellie took a deep breath. She was tired beyond reason, but there was a core of strength inside herself which she hadn't known she possessed. *Not in my own strength*, she prayed. *Lord, give me strength to deal with this. Give me the right words to say. Help me to stay sane.*

One of the men was insistent, repeating questions, but she couldn't make out what he was saying. She walked down the slope to Kate and Armand's house next door, and the two large men followed her.

In the hall there was a mirror. She looked into it. She was hollow-eyed, her hair all over the place. She thought she looked seventy. Poor old dear, she thought. And then she had a thought which twitched the corners of her mouth upwards; Aunt Drusilla was in her eighties and she had never ever let anyone get her down. If she were here now, she'd pulverize these two idiots of firemen or fire investigation team or whatever they were.

She said, 'May we use your sitting room for a few minutes, Kate? And could you bear to sit in with us?'

'When I've brewed the tea. Hot and sweet for everybody?'

A wail from a waking toddler drew Armand up the stairs. Ellie turned into the sitting room and selected an upright but cushioned chair for herself. All the furniture here was modern and brightly coloured, unlike that in Ellie's house. She corrected herself: Unlike that which *had been* in my house.

'Now,' said the largest of the firemen, 'let's go through it again, shall we?'

'Let's have some tea first. Also,' said Ellie, diving into her handbag, 'I must ring Rose and tell her what's happened. She'll be going frantic.' Rose wasn't answering her phone. Ellie hoped this meant that her old friend had managed to snatch a few hours' sleep, and left a message for her that she'd be back as soon as she could.

'You have somewhere else to stay tonight?' said the smaller fireman, who reminded Ellie somewhat of a pork butcher, though she couldn't exactly say why. Perhaps because he had a strong resemblance to some picture cards dating back to her childhood? Anyway, were there any pork butchers nowadays? There was no 'proper' butcher in the Avenue anymore, unless you counted the organic butcher who charged such high prices that Ellie never went there.

'I'm staying at my aunt's. At least, the house was where my aunt lived, but it's mine really and . . . oh, that doesn't matter now, does it? My aunt was dying and I was staying there to be company for my aunt's housekeeper, who is an old friend.'

'So you've inherited it now your aunt's dead?'

'Not exactly. Oh, don't bother about that. Tell me what you think happened to my house next door. I'm confused.'

'You are fully insured for your house next door?'

Ellie nodded, taking a large mug of tea from Kate, and trying to give her a smile in gratitude. 'Yes, Kate deals with all that sort of thing for me, and I'm sure it's all in order.'

'Certainly is,' said Kate, tucking the woollen throw further around Ellie. 'I've turned the heating on again, so you should warm up soon.'

Ellie turned to the pork butcher. 'Did you say you've turned off the gas and electricity next door? Oh dear. How can I clean the place if there's no gas or electricity?'

Kate was soothing. 'You'll get Maria, Stewart's wife, to organize it through her cleaning services.'

'Of course. Silly me. I'm not thinking straight. What time is it? Soon be dawn and then I suppose I can get in, see how bad it all is. I've only got these clothes that I stand up in and . . . oh, if they've turned off the electricity, I suppose everything in the fridge will go bad, and the freezer . . . oh dear.'

'Mrs . . . ?'

'Quicke. Mrs Quicke.'

'Right. Well, I don't think you'll be allowed back in for a while. You'll need a structural engineer in first, to make sure the first floor's safe.'

Her eyes rounded. 'There's that much damage?'

'We did pump a lot of water in, and then there's the smoke. If you'd closed all the doors when you left, the fire wouldn't have done so much damage, but there it is. That three-piece suite of yours was pretty ancient, had the old type of upholstery which sends off lots of toxic fumes. I suppose that's why you decided to spend the night elsewhere, so it wouldn't get to you.'

Ellie passed her hand across her eyes. 'Sorry, not with you. I had no idea till about teatime that I'd be called away. Are you trying to make out that I set the fire myself? Well, I didn't.'

'Of course you didn't,' said Kate. 'That's ridiculous.'

'Look at it from our point of view,' said the butcher. 'Here's a lady living in a pretty run-down sort of house, with a load of tatty furniture, insured to the hilt. She suddenly decides to spend the night away and takes her cat with her, as well—'

'Midge was needed to deal with some mice—'

'—and most conveniently, there's a nasty fire while her back's turned. And remember, she's fully insured.'

Ellie started to laugh and stopped herself with difficulty. Kate had gone red in the face. Ellie put her hand over Kate's and pressed it to prevent an outburst. 'It's all right, Kate. He's only doing his job.' And to the butcher, 'Now tell me, how could I possibly have set a fire when I wasn't there?'

'A match tossed on to a settee—'

'Wouldn't that have gone up in flames within minutes? I left after supper and sat with my aunt till she died. When was the alarm given? Hours and hours later.'

'It's obvious what you did. You sat with your aunt for a while, then came back here, broke in through the back door to set the fire—'

'What! What was that?'

'We found a spade just outside the kitchen door, which had been used to force open the door into the house. Once in, you—'

'What spade? I don't—'

'Presumably from the tool shed at the bottom of the garden, which is open to the elements, the padlock hanging on a hinge.'

'Oh!' said Ellie, clapping her hands to her forehead. 'I was in the garden on . . . when was it? It was Wednesday afternoon, I think. I was using the secateurs which I'd taken from the tool shed, and that was when Felicity rang . . .' She turned to Kate. 'You remember, she rang about the dog, and I had to rush over there and . . . I'm not sure, but I suppose I might well have left the padlock off the tool shed door, because I had to leave in such a rush.'

The butcher was not appeased. 'So you admit you were the last one in the tool shed?'

'I don't know about "the last one" but I think it's possible that I didn't put the padlock back on, yes. I heard the phone and rushed up into the house, and I must have dropped the secateurs on to the kitchen windowsill instead of putting them back in the shed. Or did I leave them in the hall when Felicity phoned? I really can't remember. I'm sorry. That was careless of me.'

Kate said, 'It was an emergency. Anyone would have done the same.'

'I'm a bit inclined to forget things I know, but . . . that was Wednesday and this is Friday, isn't it? No, Saturday morning. Surely I'd have noticed between now and then. Although, come to think of it, so much has been happening, and I've been in the house so little that maybe I didn't. The dog, you know.'

'What dog?' asked the butcher's colleague. He had tufts of black hair springing from a large nose.

Ellie reminded herself it was rude to stare. 'A woman was killed by a savage dog in the park, and my friend witnessed the attack. It upset her considerably, and she phoned me to go over there in a hurry. It seems so long ago now, and I'm very tired. Perhaps we could call it a night?'

Kate drew back the curtains to let in a greyish light. 'The blackbird's on the rooftop again. Dawn chorus, here we come.'

They all turned to the window, and fell silent. The blackbird was singing his heart out. Ellie observed that their faces looked grey in that light. A few streets away, Rose would be dozing, and waking to grief. A few streets away, the undertakers might even now be taking Miss Quicke's body from the house in which she had been born, had lived for eighty-odd years, and finally died. Ellie knew she was going to miss her enormously. What sort of funeral ought there to be? Should there be a memorial service? Would she have to see Thomas to discuss it? Ellie cringed at the thought of meeting Thomas again when he'd be so full of plans for his future, a future in which she had no part.

Perhaps Aunt Drusilla had left detailed instructions. That would be like her.

Ellie stood up. 'I must go. Kate, my aunt died last night. There'll be so much to do, so many people to tell.' She had an impulse to offer her hand to the firemen to shake, and had to sit on a giggle. This was not the moment for that sort of polite nonsense. She was pleased with herself that she was able to see the funny side of things, even for a second or two. 'Gentlemen, if you have any further questions for me, you know where to find me.'

'Now where would that be?' The two men rose, towering over her.

Ellie gave them the address. 'I suppose I'll have to stay on there for a bit, borrow some clothes, get what I can in the Avenue.'

'The police will want a word.'

Ellie shrugged. 'Send me someone with brains and I'll give him a cuppa. Now, Kate, you ought to be in bed. I'll ring for a cab to take me back to my aunt's and pray Midge hasn't gone walkabout. It would be the last straw if he decided to try to come back home through the streets in my absence.'

* * *

She made it back to the big house — she must stop thinking of it as her aunt's — as the sun came up, bringing colour back to the world. Then found she couldn't open the front door.

She stared stupidly at her keys. There were the keys to her own house — but they weren't much use to her at the moment. Then there was this much shinier, more solid key, which opened the door to the big house. Only, it didn't.

She turned it round and round, thinking that perhaps she hadn't used it properly. Still it didn't open the door. She put her arm to her forehead, telling herself that this moment would pass, that the door would open by itself, that at some point in time she would get herself to bed, that life would get better.

She was seeing double. There were two locks on the front door, where there ought only to be one. It was her eyes. They were giving up on her, like everything else.

The door opened. Rose was there, still wearing her dressing gown and slippers.

'Dear Rose.' Ellie went into Rose's arms and they clasped one another, patting one another's backs, murmuring words of comfort. 'There, there.'

'So silly,' said Ellie, trying not to cry again. 'I couldn't make my key work.'

Rose went off into some tirade about keys which Ellie was too tired to understand. She tuned in again when she heard her aunt's name mentioned. '. . . And oh dear, one of the last things she asked me to do was to make sure you knew about it and then I forgot, and oh dear, oh dear, are you all right? Silly me, I can smell the fire on you, the smell gets into your skin, doesn't it? Was it very bad? Don't answer, I can see that it was. You must be exhausted, poor dear, come into the kitchen and I'll find something for us to eat, and then you must go to bed and sleep it off.'

Ellie allowed herself to be swept into the kitchen, her mind a tangle of questions which she started in her head and never completed. She could make sense of some of what Rose was saying, but the rest passed gently over her head. She was persuaded into a chair at the table, while Rose, still burbling away, made a giant pot of tea.

'Dear, dear Rose,' said Ellie, beyond constructive thought. 'Oh. Midge?'

'Enjoying himself mightily, the little dear. Two little mousies he's caught already and laid at my feet, luckily they were quite dead because I don't think I could cope with catching a live mouse today, and he's asleep on my bed at the moment, at least, he was the last time I looked. But I'm forgetting myself; do you fancy a sandwich or some scrambled eggs?'

'Nothing, really.'

'Now you're not to worry about anything because everything's in order, and the doctor's been and pronounced her dead and the nurse has tidied up and, and her own dear self has been taken away and I'm going to have the cleaners give the room a thorough turnout when they come next week.'

'There's people we have to tell, people who ought to know.'

'We must tell that big fat man as well, the executor, Gunnar something, though he doesn't look Swedish, does he? A great friend of hers. He'll help sort things out. Now you get that tea down you. Everything else can wait till they get up in the usual way and then we'll tell Mr Roy and he'll come over and help us out.'

Ellie nodded. Of course Rose was right. Roy would be a great help. Gunnar something. She ought to know who that was, but for the life of her she couldn't think straight at the moment.

Rose poured out another mug of tea for herself. 'I tell myself that we'll get round to everything else in due course. There's no hurry now, is there?'

No, there wasn't. 'Dear, dear Rose,' said Ellie again.

'Now don't you worry about anything,' said Rose, taking a plate of sandwiches from the fridge, and setting them in front of Ellie. 'You eat up, then have a wash and a good sleep, and we'll take it gently. It's bound to be hard going, but we'll manage between us. There's only one thing I have to say, here and now, which Miss Quicke told me as a secret and to keep it to myself, right at the start of my moving in, that this house really belongs to you, and that when she died, I would have my own little place to move into, which she has had me go to visit a couple of times and it's really nice, I must say. So I'm quite prepared to move out any time and you've no need to worry about me in any way, but we won't even think about when that will be till the worst of this is over, because it's clear that your moving in last night with Midge was meant and I'm going to be here for just as long as you'd like me to help and not a minute longer.'

For the third time Ellie said, 'Dear, dear Rose.'

Rose pushed a box of tissues across the table. 'Mop up, Ellie. We've been good friends for years, haven't we, and I can't count on the fingers of my hand the number of times you've picked me up and put me right after I'd had a bad time and the least said soonest mended, and I'm sure I don't know whether Mr Roy knows that you own this house, nor yet that Diana does, but we'll meet that bridge when we come to cross it, right?'

'I haven't a stitch to wear, apart from what I've got on.'

'You'll let me have everything to wash in a minute, and I'll have it clean for you by the time you get up.'

Ellie's thoughts tangled up. 'This blue dress isn't suitable for . . . I've got a nice white top and a black skirt at home, but I don't suppose they'll let me have them yet.'

'They'll need cleaning, if the smoke's got at them. I'll ring Felicity in a while and she'll sort you out something. Even though her skirts are too short, they'll be long enough for you. Now if you don't fancy those sandwiches, would you fancy a spot of toast, cut into fingers?'

Ellie shook her head. She drank her tea and stopped thinking altogether until Rose somehow got her to her feet and led her back to the main hall and up the stairs to her own green, peaceful room. She was not particularly surprised to find Midge already there, curled up in a ball with his tail over his nose, at the foot of her bed.

She looked around her, taking it all in. What a pretty room, and how lucky she was to have it, and to have Rose fussing around her. She got into bed as Rose drew the curtains at the windows. Thank you, Rose.

Dear Lord, thank you for looking after me. Thank you for arranging that I wasn't at home last night when I might easily have been killed. Thank you. Please look after dear Thomas for me. I'm sure he's working too hard, as usual. How I'm going to miss him. I didn't realize how much he meant to me till he said he was leaving and now it's too late. Someone said that 'if only' were the saddest words in the English language. I see what they mean.

Help me to be strong. Rose says I used to help her when she was in trouble and I suppose I did help a bit, though not as much as she seems to think. That's my future, Lord. Helping other people. Let me not think too much about my own loss . . .

* * *

She woke to find the sun had found a way through a gap in the curtains and was throwing a bright ray across her bedding. That was all wrong. The sun didn't come into her bedroom till evening, did it?

Then she remembered. She lay still, drawing in her breath, recalling the watch by her aunt's bedside, the nightmare journey with Kate to her own home, the gutted, stinking house, the investigator's suspicion that she might herself have set the fire. She heard herself groan.

Then she shook herself more or less awake, got herself into the shower and investigated what clothes Rose had left out for her. She'd brought a change of underclothes with her, so that was all right. The ones she'd worn yesterday had disappeared and were probably washed and hanging out to dry by this time.

Rose had laid out an outfit for her: a cream linen V-necked blouse which fitted well enough, with a black skirt which was rather on the long side and rather tight at the waist. Undoubtedly they'd come from Rose's own wardrobe. Ellie's own sandals, which were not black but blue, had been cleaned. Her watch announced the hour of nine thirty.

She didn't feel particularly lively, but she'd manage. She did hope that Rose had snatched a few hours' sleep for herself. Midge had disappeared. She wasn't worried, because the sash window was open at the bottom and Midge had proved he could come and go as he pleased from his new home.

She went down the wide stairs, appreciating the beauty of the high ceiling and the spill of greenery in the conservatory. Midge was sitting in a patch of sunlight in the middle of the hall floor, giving himself a good wash. She bent to rub his ears but he wasn't interested in being caressed at this time of day, and removed himself to continue with his toilet elsewhere.

'Four mice so far!' exclaimed Rose, as Ellie entered the kitchen. 'What a good boy he is. I told him, he'd better show me where he wants a cat flap put in the conservatory, for we don't want one in the front door, do we, allowing him to get out and run into the street?' Rose was fully dressed and hardly showed that she'd been up most of the night.

Ellie didn't bother to point out that Midge was more streetwise than most adults, and that included Rose, who'd been known to step out from the kerb without looking before now.

'Breakfast here or on a tray in the sitting room?' asked Rose. 'Or what about the morning room, so called? I could set up a small table in there for you, no trouble. We've never used it because it doesn't get the sun in the mornings, which seems to me a very silly thing, to have a morning room without any sun. But there it is. Here or there?'

At that point the phone rang. 'Leave it till you've eaten,' said Rose.

Ellie shook her head. 'It's probably Roy, wanting to know the latest. I'll take it in the sitting room, if you could bring me a cuppa there?'

It was Roy. She told him the news and he took it quietly, having half expected it but still grieving. He said he'd be over as soon as he could. Ellie had a quick word with Felicity at the same time. Felicity had been fond of Miss Quicke and would also grieve for her. Ellie tried to keep a report of her own problems to a minimum, but they had to know about the fire. Felicity immediately said Ellie should come to them, an offer which Ellie declined, saying Rose had taken care of her.

Tea came, with toast cut into strips and buttered. Ellie nibbled and sipped and hoped she'd said all the right things. Rose drew back the curtains, pulled down the blinds, took a vase of drooping flowers out. Ellie made a list of people to ring and started on it. Rose returned with a vase full of heavy-headed roses.

Ellie rang Diana, who was at once subdued and joyful on hearing the news. Strangely enough, Diana did seem to have sincere regrets about her great-aunt's death, but said she'd be right over, and would Ellie like to move in with Diana for the time being because although her little flat was a bit cramped, little Frank could easily go back to his father's. At this Ellie heard Frank yelling 'No!' in the background.

Ellie said, 'That's really nice of you, Diana, but I'll stay where I am for the time being.' Rose had brought in the morning's post, at which Ellie shuddered. Who was going to deal with it? Not Ellie. What about Aunt Drusilla's solicitor? Ellie couldn't remember the name, which was absurd, because she'd remembered it last night, hadn't she? Perhaps it would come to her in a minute.

Diana was still quacking away. 'I had meant to take little Frank out for the day to the zoo, but now of course I'll come over to help you instead.'

At this Frank could be heard yelling his disapproval. Diana told him to be quiet, but he didn't take any notice. The noise was horrible. Ellie had just discovered Miss Quicke's address book and started to leaf through it. She'd just remembered that Aunt Drusilla's solicitor had a foreign name. Gunnar something.

Another cup of tea materialized. The front doorbell rang, and Rose came in to say something about some people calling to see her, which Ellie couldn't quite catch, because she was still trying to deal with Diana while tracing her aunt's solicitor's number.

Ah, there it was. Gunnar something. Gunnar Brooks? He'd had a Swedish mother but a British father. Ellie finished the call to Diana and pressed buttons for Gunnar's home number. They'd met once at a dinner party in this very house, and Ellie had been impressed by him. He was massively built, probably hadn't been able to tie his shoelaces for years, but was highly intelligent and not only Aunt Drusilla's solicitor, but also an old friend.

Gunnar came on the phone at once, deep-voiced, slow-pacing his words, a man to be relied on. 'I've been expecting it. The end of an era. I shall miss her. I'm her sole executor, as it happens. We met some time ago, did we not?'

'We did. I'm so glad it's you, because you'll know what ought to be done about, oh, about everything. I'm thinking she may have left instructions about her funeral and so on?'

'Of course. Are you at the house now?'

'I am.' Ellie explained why.

'Well, well. Man proposes, but God disposes. All very suitable, since you own the place. May I suggest that you refer all business affairs to me for the time being? And don't sign anything.'

'Er, no. I mean, why . . . ?'

'All will be made clear in due course. If you have any trouble, any at all, then I'll send my young colleague over to deal with it for you. Understood? Now, may I call upon you this afternoon at four? No need to get out the Madeira, even though my dear old friend used to stock it specially for me. No, no. A cup of Lady Grey tea will suffice, and tell Rose not to bake anything specially. High cholesterol, you know.'

'Er, thank you.' It was clear to Ellie that he meant the opposite of what he'd said. Gunnar was to be entertained with a glass of Madeira and some home-made cake. She wondered where Aunt Drusilla had kept the Madeira. In the wine cabinet in the dining room, perhaps? Rose would know.

Ellie had forgotten that she had some other callers and they, tired of waiting, now entered the room. Police! To Ellie's dismay, one of them was the man she'd christened 'Ears' because of the way his stuck out. She'd had cause in the past to question his ability, and it was clear from his expression that he'd neither forgiven nor forgotten.

'Well, well,' he said, 'has Ellie been a naughty little girl, then?'

* * *

Toby didn't like travelling in the back of the car and expressed himself forcibly about it. Cleaning up sick was not a job that Mick enjoyed doing. He took the first turn off the motorway to give Toby a run, and when they got back into the car he wound the windows right down to get rid of the smell. The car was fit for nothing but the breakers' yard, without air conditioning or even power steering. Every time he got up speed, something in the back started to rattle.

The aunt hadn't been out of bed when he left, but he'd left her a note to say he'd be back in a few days. There was nothing she could do about it. She wouldn't report him to the police, not she.

And he'd miss her stupid party. Fancy her expecting him to hand round drinks and nibbly bits! Fat chance.

Only a couple of hours more and he'd be meeting up with some of the old crowd. He knew where the next fight was to be held and was going to enter Toby for an early round. He'd have to go slow, placing his bets, get some of his mates to help him, so's he could make a killing. Tich's dogs always went in with a good chance because he trained them so well, but they wouldn't know that this was one of Tich's dogs, would they?

CHAPTER FOURTEEN

Ellie half rose from her chair as the police entered, and then decided to sit still. 'I'm afraid I don't know your name.' Wasn't he supposed to show his badge and tell her his name before he said anything? And how dare he treat her like that?

It didn't matter what she said, he'd always take it wrongly. Now his nose blushed as red as his ears, because she'd put him in the wrong. 'DC Bottrill. And this is—'

'WPC Mills,' said the policewoman standing one pace to the rear.

Ellie smiled at her and got a smile in return. 'I remember you well. You were most helpful when we met some time ago.'

Ears Bottrill was not amused. 'You two weren't at school together, I take it? So let's get down to the nitty-gritty, shall we? This your new place, then? Flying high, aren't we?' He took a seat without being asked, crossing his legs, flapping open a notebook. His colleague sent an apologetic look towards Ellie and would have remained standing, but Ellie waved her to a seat, too.

Ears cleared his throat, his eyes on the cup of tea at Ellie's elbow. Did he mean he'd like one himself? Ellie decided she wouldn't offer him one, unless his manners improved. Midge strolled into the room, sniffed at the WPC's shoes and let her rub his head.

'This is my house, yes. So what can I do for you?' asked Ellie, her hand straying to the telephone book. So many people to ring still. Midge walked around Ears, giving him a wide berth. Midge had always been a good judge of character.

'A little matter of arson in the night. The fire investigation team were not at all happy with what they discovered when they went into your house. Your *old* house, I should say. So can you explain how you suddenly have two houses to your name?'

'Easily,' said Ellie. 'My husband inherited this house from his father, but allowed my aunt to live in it for life. When my husband died, he left the house to me, but naturally I didn't wish to turn my aunt out.'

'Very convenient to have this house to live in, if you were planning an insurance fraud at the other place.'

Ellie held on to her temper. 'I wasn't planning anything.'

'You must admit it was convenient that you weren't at home last night when the house went up in flames.'

'I thank God for it.'

'Or perhaps you'd very cleverly arranged it that way?'

'My aunt was dying and . . .' She could feel herself getting angry, and knew it wouldn't help matters if she lost her temper. She repeated, more softly, 'My aunt was dying. The doctor was calling every day. My aunt didn't want to go to hospital. She wanted to die in her bed. One of us sat with her, taking it in turns. Last night it was my turn.'

'With your cat!' Ears laughed. 'You actually remembered to take your cat with you! What a nerve! I almost admire it.' Stupidly, Ears reached out to stroke Midge's head.

Midge reacted as only he knew how. He doubled in size, arched his back and spat. A low growl started in his throat and ended in a screech.

'Midge!' said Ellie, shocked at this behaviour. She'd never known Midge react so strongly to anyone before, except of course in the car yesterday with Madam, but that had probably been because he hated being carted around in his basket. Ears retracted his hand, shaken. WPC Mills hid a smile.

Ellie pointed to the half-open door. 'Midge, out!' The cat deflated and marched out of the room, tail held high.

'Sorry about that,' said Ellie. She met the WPC's eye and tried not to giggle. 'So what were you saying? Oh, why did I bring Midge? It's lucky I did, isn't it, or he might have died. There was a mouse problem here, you see, and the housekeeper wanted to see if Midge could deal with it. Which he did. Now is that all, because I'm very busy this morning?'

'We've only just started. What time did you leave this house last night? One o'clock, say?'

'No, no. Some time after three, wasn't it? Rose came to wake me—'

'So you weren't watching by your aunt's bedside?'

'She died about, oh, about eleven? You'd have to ask the nurse. I expect she can tell you the exact time.'

'What nurse?'

'The agency nurse. They were there in shifts. I'll give you the address of the agency if you'd like to check.' WPC Mills had her notebook out, and took down the details.

Ears was not giving up. 'So you couldn't get away till your aunt died and the agency nurse let you out of her sight, right. Then what? You went off to bed like a good little girl, waited till all was quiet and then sneaked out of this house to carry out your little plan. Did you take a cab, or did you walk?'

Ellie blinked. 'I'm sorry, I'm not with you. Kate, my next-door neighbour, came to collect me but by that time the fire was out. About four, I think.'

'I put it to you that some time after midnight you went back to your old home to set the fire, knowing everything was well insured and that you had this place to move in to. You used one of your own spades to prise open the back door, set the fire with some sort of timer, and returned here to give yourself an alibi.'

'Why would I do that?' asked Ellie, too weary to be indignant. 'Or rather, in terms that even you can understand, if I were going to set fire to my old home, why didn't I make sure that I had taken some of my most precious possessions with me, and at least one change of clothes? My engagement ring, my pearls, a rather nice cameo brooch, my mother's art nouveau clock, photographs of my husband and my family. Souvenirs from holidays . . . oh!'

She put her hand over the locket she wore around her neck. At least she still had that. She sought for a handkerchief and didn't find one. She would not give in and cry in front of Ears, she would not.

She located her handbag, found a handkerchief and blew her nose. 'Look,' she said, holding up the bag. 'It's not even my good new handbag, but the one I use for shopping in the Avenue. Look at my sandals. I haven't a pair of shoes to my name, and these clothes I'm wearing have been lent to me by Rose, the housekeeper. If I'd wanted to commit arson, I'd have arranged things much better.'

'What would you have done?' asked the WPC. 'Just as a matter of interest.'

Ellie thought about it. 'I suppose that, with my aunt being so ill, I could have suggested a few days ago that I move in with her for a bit. I'd have cancelled the newspapers and the milk . . . I bet they've been delivered this morning, haven't they? You never thought of that, did you?'

'What I think is,' said Ears, getting to his feet, 'that you have committed a particularly nasty crime, and I'm on your trail. I'm not going to let you get away it, understand? I think you set fire to your own home because you needed the money from the insurance and—'

'I don't need the money. Ask my solicitor, ask anyone.'

'—you set up a very clumsy, unconvincing alibi to—'

Ellie felt her temper rise. 'Suppose you use the brains you were supposedly born with? And while we're on the subject, hasn't it occurred to you that if I didn't do it — and I certainly did not do it — then someone else did? Someone else went to my house last night, prised open the back door and set a fire. I don't know who or why, but I assume it was a burglary gone wrong. Is there anything much missing? I haven't that much, I know, but still . . . my bits and pieces of jewellery, that sort of thing. Have you looked?'

'I knew you'd try to throw suspicion somewhere else. You had a confederate, didn't you? To give you an alibi. Someone who knew exactly where you'd be last night.'

'No, I did not,' said Ellie, exhaustion taking over. 'I suppose it was an opportunist burglar, spotting that the house was empty. Kate usually draws the curtains and leaves a light on in my house when I'm away. Perhaps she forgot to do so last night.'

'No, the curtains were drawn, back and front. So it has to be someone who knew you were out. Let's get back to your confederate. Who did you advise that you'd be away from home, that the coast was clear?'

Ellie pressed her fingers to her temples. 'I have no confederate. I wouldn't ever have destroyed my own home. As for who might have known that I was going to be away last night, well, lots of people might have known, I suppose. Kate and Armand, who live next door. I told them and I told Roy and Felicity, that's my cousin and his wife. My aunt's nurses knew. Rose, the housekeeper. My aunt, of course. Oh, I don't know. Lots of people might have heard, but I assure you none of them would have the slightest interest in helping me torch my own house because they all knew how much it meant to me. Well, not the nurses, of course, because I only saw them once, but the others are family. Tell me, have you looked for fingerprints yet?'

'The wooden handle of a spade won't hold fingerprints.'

'Oh. Well, will the fire have destroyed fingerprints inside the house? I don't know about such things, but maybe the fire investigation team will be able to help you there.'

'We shall see,' said Ears, flapping his notebook shut and getting to his feet. She didn't think he'd made any notes at all in it, though WPC Mills had done so.

He said, 'Now suppose you come along with us to visit the scene of the crime. I'll be watching you all the time. If you can prove that something has been stolen, then I suppose it might help your case.'

'Is it safe to go into the house yet?' asked Ellie, thinking she didn't really want to see what had been done to her home.

'Yes, we've got the all-clear to go in.' He stalked out into the hall.

WPC Mills got to her feet, too. She kept her voice down so that he couldn't hear. 'I'm so sorry. Believe me, we'll do all we can to find the person responsible.'

Ellie felt tears threaten. 'I loved my little house, you know. I would never, ever have—'

'I know, but we have to ask these questions when it's a case of arson. Now we've got to check to see if anything's missing. Do you feel up to it?'

Ellie nodded. 'You're a good girl. Thank you. I ought to have offered you a cup of tea, but . . .' She waved her hands in the air, just as the phone rang. 'Can you wait till I answer this?'

'We'd rather not, if you don't mind. Let the messages pile up on the answerphone. Oh, and I must warn you, the papers might be ringing you for your story. Is there anyone who can take over here for a while?'

'My cousin Roy said he'd be over straight away, but he's not here yet.' Ellie shrugged. 'I suppose the sooner I come with you, the sooner I can get back. It's just that there are so many people . . . no, no. Let's go now, before anything else happens. I'll just tell Rose what's happening.'

The phone stopped ringing. And then started again.

* * *

Kate met them as they got out of the police car. In daylight Ellie's little house looked at once better and worse than she'd thought. The downstairs windows of the sitting room were missing, the woodwork rimmed with soot. The study window and the front door looked all right. Her bedroom window upstairs was blackened with streaks of soot but otherwise intact, as was the window of the little bedroom in which Frank often slept.

Workmen were already there, fitting boards over the damage.

Kate had her toddler clinging to her leg. 'Are you OK, Ellie? Baby's asleep. The firemen left a couple of hours ago, saying there's no danger of the fire starting up again. The workmen have boarded over the back door where the burglar broke in but otherwise it looks all right. The plants in the conservatory have taken a bit of a beating but some might be saved, I suppose.'

'How about my goldfish?' asked Ellie, thinking this was a silly thing to ask when so much else was wrong.

Kate pulled a face. 'Come in and see me when you've finished?' She glanced down at the toddler, and Ellie nodded, understanding. It wouldn't be right to take the little one into a scene of such devastation.

Ears was on the alert. 'How come your neighbour knows so much?'

'Kate's got my duplicate keys, and I've got hers,' said Ellie. 'We look after one another's houses when we're away. Which reminds me, Kate. You'd better take your keys back for the time being.'

The front door looked untouched. Presumably the firemen had got in through the broken windows, and exited via the front door without damaging it in any way. The hall was exactly as she'd left it the day before, only everything was covered with soot, including her secateurs on the hall table. As they entered, the grandmother clock chimed the hour. Indomitable clock, which continued to work despite all that had happened around it.

Ellie swiped her hand across her eyes. She would not cry! The stink was awful. She gagged. Would not give in. She must see the worst.

The door to the study was open, and some drawers in Frank's old secretaire had been pulled out and papers chucked around. Ellie hugged herself. 'The computer's been shifted to one side. Someone seems to have been looking for something. Money, perhaps? I don't keep any money in the house.' She poked around in the drawers and riffled through the papers on the desk. 'My passport's gone, and my chequebook. Luckily my insurance details were of no interest.' She picked them up, and then gritted her teeth for they were covered in a thin film of dirt.

'Passport, chequebook.' The WPC made notes. 'Have you got their details somewhere?'

Ellie found the security numbers on an insurance document and read them out. She led the way to the kitchen. Her little radio had been unplugged from the wall and left on its side on the kitchen table. Her breakfast things from the day before — was it only twenty-four hours ago? — were still in the washing-up bowl in the sink. There was a thin layer of soot overall, but it wasn't too bad. A good clean would do wonders, she told herself. She didn't open the fridge door, or the door of the freezer. Perhaps the contents would keep for a while.

The door to the conservatory was open and she went in, treading with care on the pretty floor tiles which had cracked and broken with the heat. The French windows into the living room had burst open and the fire had scorched all her precious plants. The lead tank which stood against the inner wall had melted so that the water had seeped out over the floor and drained away under the door leading to the garden. There were dead goldfish everywhere.

She swayed on her feet, but would not give in. 'They tell me fish don't feel pain.' She remembered her aunt wondering if animals were allowed in heaven. Cats, maybe. Goldfish? Probably not. A pity, that.

'Are you all right?' The policewoman took hold of Ellie's arm to steady her.

'In a minute,' said Ellie. 'Give me a minute. I do love . . . I did love my plants. Building the conservatory was the only big change I made to this house after my husband died. I used to sit here a lot, looking out over the garden. I had most of my meals here. It was such a happy place.'

'Yes, yes.' The policewoman pressed Ellie's arm. 'I can see how pretty it must have been. You can rebuild, you know.'

Ellie sniffed. 'Right. Now the sitting room. I expect that's the worst.'

She took a couple of steps in through the shattered doors and stopped. Even though the front windows had been boarded over, sufficient light came through from the wrecked conservatory to show her the extent of the desolation. Everything was black, and nothing was the shape it was supposed to be. The floor was a sheet of smelly black water. The mirror over the mantelpiece didn't reflect anything anymore. The three-piece suite had been reduced to its frames and to mounds of sooty flakes.

Ellie steadied herself, setting her feet a little apart. Trying to make sense of what she was seeing. 'There was an art nouveau clock on the mantelpiece. It was my mother's, almost the only thing of value that she left me. In the cabinet over there . . . well, it doesn't look much like a cabinet now, but that's what it was . . . some crystal ware of my mother's, and some nice bits of china. I can't see them. Oh, perhaps those shards on the floor may be the china. Glass melts, doesn't it? But what about the clock? I didn't have any other antiques or anything else worth stealing, except the grandmother clock in the hall and the secretaire in the study, and presumably they were too big for him to carry away under his arm.'

She backed out of the room, wondering if she were going to faint until she realized that if she did, she'd fall on that stinking, dirty floor, and there was no way she was going to allow herself to do that.

'Upstairs?' she said, leading the way. The banister was dirty with soot. She tried not to touch the wall. Every room was going to have to be redecorated. Putting this right was going to take weeks, if not months.

She'd left the door open to the small bedroom where little Frank slept. The bright curtains and bed linen were filthy. Likewise his computer and his toys. She opened his clothes cupboard and found the clothes looking fairly clean but stinking of fire.

The guest room. No one had slept there for a while. Stink and dirt, but nothing seemed to have been touched, except . . . 'There was a digital clock here on the bedside table. It's of no great value, but it's gone.'

The bathroom . . . nothing amiss, except the dirt.

Her bedroom. She stifled a cry. There was the same layer of soot, but the flames hadn't reached this room. Every drawer in her dressing table had been pulled out, everything taken out of the wardrobe, and the contents dumped on the floor. The box in which she kept her bits and pieces of jewellery was gaping, empty, on the bed.

'My engagement ring's gone, and my mother's pearls. A couple of other nice rings.' She wrung her hands. 'My good watch that I only wear in the evenings. A cameo brooch, some Victorian stuff that my aunt gave me years ago that belonged to Frank's mother.'

'Sentimental value only, I assume?' said Ears, being sarcastic.

Ellie said, 'Some of it was quite good. Kate had the best bits valued. She saw to all my insurance for me, so I suppose it was insured, but . . .' She stopped, fighting for control. 'I think I'd better sit down for a minute.'

The WPC twitched back the duvet on Ellie's bed so that she could sit on a patch of clean sheet. 'Shall I get you a drink of water?'

'*Is* there any water?' asked Ellie, aiming for humour and missing. 'I thought it had been turned off. I'll be all right in a minute.'

'You don't look all right,' said the WPC. 'Shall I fetch your friend from next door?'

'She's got a toddler and a baby to look after, and she was up most of the night, too. Her husband might be there. No, he won't be. It's Saturday morning, isn't it? He'll be umpiring some game or other. At the high school.'

'Details of the jewellery that's missing?' demanded Ears.

Ellie stared at him and through him. 'You might be able to get some fingerprints off stuff in here? At least you must admit that I was burgled before the house was torched. Everything on the floor here is covered with soot, so my clothes must have been turned out of the drawers and cupboards before the fire was set, right?'

'So you say.' He wasn't prepared to admit it.

'I'll get Forensics to give this room a going over,' said the WPC, accessing her mobile. 'It won't take long.'

'Meanwhile,' said Ellie, 'I can't retrieve any of my possessions?'

'This is a crime scene,' said Ears. 'I suppose you thought your confederate would leave your stuff alone. Well, tough!'

'Someone,' said Ellie, pleasantly, 'ought to have taught you to respect your elders when you were a child. They ought also to have reminded you that I'm innocent until proven guilty. That is the law, by the way. Which appears not to have made any impression on your infantile brain.'

He gasped, turned purple, tried to think of a retort and failed. 'I'll get you yet,' he said. He turned on his heel and thumped off down the stairs.

WPC Mills stifled laughter. 'Oh, Mrs Quicke, you shouldn't, really!'

'How could he take offence at what I just said?' asked Ellie, blandly. 'Surely it was the truth, the whole truth, and nothing but the truth?'

'He could make things difficult for you.'

'Let him try. I have a good solicitor and I've done nothing wrong. Now, my dear, I'm going to take a change of underclothes and a couple of bits of clothing that will need washing but will see me through the next couple of days. I promise not to touch anything that might have taken a fingerprint. Is that all right by you?'

Ears called to his colleague to come along; they hadn't got all day. The WPC hesitated. 'He'll have my guts for garters if I leave you alone at a crime scene. Look, I'll wait on the landing while you get some clothes together, but do try not to touch your cupboards or the jewellery box — anything that might have taken a fingerprint, right? Forensics should be here soon.'

She went out of the room. Ellie looked at the devastation around her and felt rather faint. She told herself she was going to survive, of course she was. She sent up an arrow prayer, *Lord, help me to get through this. Lord, thank you for taking me out of the house last night. Lord, I am grateful, really. Just . . . in need of support.*

She set about picking up one or two articles of clothing and stowing them in one of the suitcases which she kept on a shelf above the airing cupboard. The burglar hadn't touched that, thank goodness. Everything felt gritty. She opened the window to get the air circulating.

Dear Lord, this comes of placing too much store on my possessions. I am grieving for them almost more than I'm grieving for my aunt, and that's not right, I know. But, just for a little while, please bear with me? I feel as if I've been bereaved twice over. First my home, then my little treasures, some of the few things that I have from my parents and my husband. Forgive me for being such a cry-baby when I know I ought to be praising you for bringing me through this business in one piece.

Turning back into the room, she was shocked to see her reflection, dustily, in the mirror. She thought, I'm turning into an old lady. I'm turning into my mother. She began to laugh. She laughed until she wept. Eventually she went into the bathroom to clean herself up. Luckily there was still some water left in the tank. Probably not enough for a bath, though. The WPC asked if she were all right, and she said, 'Of course.' Though of course she wasn't.

Then she settled down on the clean part of the bed and rang the insurance people and the bank. The insurance people were helpful but the bank transferred her to a voice from India, which wasn't much help when she couldn't remember who the last cheque she'd sent off had been made out to, or for exactly how much. Ah well, press on. Who was next on her list?

The WPC came in. 'Are you finished? Forensics have arrived and will want to come in here in a minute. Here's the number of the station, in case you haven't got it. I'll give them your phone number here — oh, that'll be out of order, won't it? Have you got a mobile phone number that I can give them?'

Ellie scribbled it down for her, and told herself to look forward, not back. This would end, sometime.

* * *

Mick was not enjoying himself. In fact, he didn't want to admit it, but he was getting the heebies. He'd met up with some of his old gang, but they'd all formed new alliances, were talking about events he knew nothing about. Only the presence of Toby got him any respect.

He'd found someone who'd take the passport and chequebook off him. He'd thought it would be easy to get rid of the jewellery and the clock too, but it turned out that the man he needed wasn't around that weekend.

The really bad news was that Tich had managed to get bail and was to join them that evening, when he'd entered one of his dogs for a fight. Even if Mick managed to keep out of sight, the moment Tich clapped eyes on Toby in the ring, he'd know it was one of his and want him back.

What was Mick to do? He wasn't about to give Toby up, not he. He'd got fond of the dog. Who'd looked after him all this time? He had. He deserved to keep him. But perhaps not to put him into the ring. Perhaps it might be best if Tich didn't see him, this time round. Which meant getting back in that tin heap of a car and returning to the aunt. He couldn't believe his bad luck!

CHAPTER FIFTEEN

Ellie arrived back at the big house in a state of fatigue which was not lifted by the sight of her reception committee.

What a morning it had been. Back at her own little house she'd watched the Forensics man use his brushes and what looked like graphite powder to lift some prints. He seemed to think he'd got some viable evidence, which was good news for a change. Then she'd gone next door to Kate's for a bowl of soup and a good wash. Kate suggested that it might be an opportunity for Ellie to get rid of some of her old clothes and buy herself a new wardrobe. As for the things she really wanted to keep, why not drop them into the dry-cleaner's? The bill would be heavy, but it would be worth it. Ellie agreed. They both agreed it was a pity about Ellie's shoes, but they probably ought to be thrown away.

There was one thing Ellie was determined not to leave behind. When Armand returned from his umpiring they wiped the worst of the dirt off the grandmother clock in the hall, manoeuvred it up to the road and into a minicab.

Ellie said, 'I know exactly where to put it in the big house. Later on I'll get professional removers to shift Frank's secretaire back there as well. It came from the big house originally, and now it must go back.'

Kate had a frown which made her face look heavy. 'You've got me worried. It sounds as if you're not coming back here to live.'

Ellie said, 'I don't know what's going to happen, I really don't. All I know is that I've lost many precious things, and that this house is not going to be habitable for ages. I want to make sure some things are safe.'

Kate embraced Ellie. 'Of course you do. I'll ring you this evening, shall I? See how you're getting on.'

Ellie got into the cab and waved goodbye, realizing that Kate had stumbled on the truth. Ellie was indeed moving, mentally at least, away to the big house.

Only, when she got there, she was faced with a different set of demands on her patience. Even as the cab driver helped her transfer herself and her belongings into the hall, she was met by little Frank, who shouted out, 'Pooh, you stink!' He ran back into the sitting room, crying, 'She's here, and she stinks!'

'That's a nice welcome,' said Ellie, under her breath. In spite of the good wash she'd had at Kate's, she knew her clothes stank of the fire, but she'd hoped for a short rest before she had to face any of her relatives. It was not to be. Even as Diana and Roy jostled one another in the doorway from the sitting room, Rose opened the door from the kitchen quarters and came to greet her.

'There you are!' said Roy. 'Ellie, we have to talk.'

Ellie ignored him to hand Rose her bags of clothing, 'My dear, can you put all this stuff in the washing machine for me?'

'Of course I can. There's plenty of hot water if you'd like a bath.' Rose rolled her eyes, meaning, Forget your guests and look after yourself for once.

Ellie tried to act on the hint. 'That would be heaven. Thanks, Rose. Roy, Diana. Lovely to see you, but I must have a shower and change before I can think straight. Is that Felicity with you, too? Lovely to see you, too, Felicity. Oh, and Stewart, too? Any more for any more? No, don't answer that. I'm too tired to make sense. Give me half an hour and I'll be with you again.'

'Yes, but Ellie . . .' That was Roy.

Ellie started to pull herself up the stairs, ignoring them all.

'Mother, I need to talk to you urgently. Shall I come up and sit with you while you have a bath?'

'Certainly not,' said Ellie, pausing on the landing. 'And Rose — don't forget that Gunnar's arriving at four and would like—'

'Madeira and a Victoria sponge,' said Rose. 'Understood.'

'Yes, but Ellie . . .' That was Felicity, with little Mel over her shoulder.

'Tough titties,' said Ellie, going down the corridor to her bedroom and shutting the door firmly behind her. She shucked off her clothes and her shoes as she made her way into the bathroom and, remembering how Aunt Drusilla had kept everyone at bay, turned the lock on the door.

* * *

Rose had laid out some fresh clothes for her, including a couple of white blouses, another black skirt and a heavy-weight black wool cardigan. Judging by the length of the skirt, these things had come from Felicity. Thank you, Felicity.

Ellie couldn't bear to put her grubby sandals on again, but wore her own bedroom slippers, which luckily were not too fluffy to wear around the house. She towelled her hair dry and brushed it roughly into shape. Then took a deep breath, closed her eyes, and said out loud, *Lord, put the right words in my mouth, because I don't think this is going to be easy.*

She went down the stairs slowly, aware of discordant voices in the sitting room. Instead of joining her loved ones, Ellie went into the kitchen to find Rose. Ellie said, 'Are you all right, Rose?' even as Rose said, 'Was it very bad?'

Ellie gave Rose a hug. 'I'll survive. You're a star.'

Rose blew her nose. 'I keep telling myself things are going to get better, and then I find myself in the weeps again.

Silly of me. Sitting beside her poor dear body that she'd left behind last night, I told her she'd given me the best years of my life, bringing me here and giving me such a lovely home, because home it was, never mind that she paid me a good salary, and I'm going to remember that all my life.'

'She knew how you felt about it, Rose, and she told me she'd never been so well cared for in her whole life, as well. No one ever troubled to think of her as a human being till you came, and I think it's entirely due to you that she became, well, much more human herself in her last few years. You made a mountain of difference to her.'

'You did, too. She was always saying that.' The pinger on the oven went off, and Rose gave a little scream. 'My cake!' Scrambling to get it out, Rose said, 'The phone's been ringing non-stop, so Mr Roy has put it on answerphone for the time being and killed the bell sound, if you know what I mean. Thomas rang. He'd heard about her poor dear self dying, bless her, and he's been trying to ring you on your mobile, but you're always engaged, he says, and so I told him about the fire and he was that shocked. I said you'd ring him back as soon as you could, right?'

Ellie remembered how wonderful it used to be to tell Thomas her troubles and let him put them in perspective for her, but she couldn't do that now, not when he was leaving the parish. She wished, how she wished, that he wasn't going. But there, she'd had her chance to spend the rest of her life with him, and muffed it.

She closed the kitchen door, spent a moment adjusting herself to face the others, pushing the memory of her burned-out house to the back of her mind. Angry faces turned to her as she entered the sitting room. The air seemed to splinter with accusations. Little Frank ran across the room and jumped at her so that she staggered, trying to hold him in her arms. He was red-faced, had been crying. Roy's face was red, too. Diana looked white and drawn. Felicity was weeping, trying to feed Mel with a bottle. Stewart was staring out into the garden, his back turned to the others.

Ellie said, 'Frank, dear, I'll have to put you down. There, now. Let's sit here, shall we, and you can tell me what this is all about?' She collapsed into her aunt's high-backed chair, drawing him on to her knee. He was getting too heavy for her, but it seemed he needed the contact today, and perhaps she did, too.

'She said we were going to Chessington to the zoo, and now she says we're not, and not to bother her. It's not fair!'

'Things happen,' said Ellie, stroking his head. Poor little boy, so unsure of himself, so unsettled by recent events. Ellie remembered, with a start, the death of the woman in the park, and how that had affected so many people. She'd been meaning to do something about that, but . . . oh dear, God did dispose, didn't he? Frank's little world had been unsettled by the first death, and now his great-great-aunt had died too. It was no wonder he was failing to cope.

Roy reached out a hand to Ellie. 'Thank the Lord you've come. Just in time. My mother must have a Christian funeral. You do agree, don't you?' Felicity wept silently in her corner.

Diana folded her arms at him. 'Great-Aunt was never one to waste money, nor was she one to get religious when she was dying. I've told the funeral directors we want a no-frills cremation at Breakspear, as soon as possible.'

Stewart's head jerked back, and he muttered something about wanting the best for his old employer.

Diana was relentless, very sure of herself. 'You think you know better than her own flesh and blood?'

Stewart winced, but managed to say firmly enough that he thought Miss Quicke had been going to church quite a lot since he'd known her, and that perhaps they ought to ask Thomas what she'd have liked.

'As if it were up to him!' said Diana, dismissive of her ex-husband's ideas as usual.

'I agree with Stewart,' said Roy. 'We should ask Thomas. I'm all for a church service and I know Felicity is, as well. So let's take a vote on it, shall we?'

Ellie tried to reduce the heat in the atmosphere. 'It's not a question of what we want, but of what my aunt would have wanted. She's left full instructions as to her funeral arrangements with her solicitor and I suggest we abide by them.' Everyone looked relieved at this. Even Stewart relaxed.

Ellie said, 'Now, Frank, suppose you run out to the kitchen and ask Rose if she can give us a cup of tea in a little while? Maybe she'll find you a biscuit or two as well.'

He went eagerly enough. Ellie stood up to shake out her skirt. 'Felicity, I believe I have to thank you for these clothes. It was good of you. Thanks.' She looked around for Midge but couldn't see him. Midge didn't like Diana and would no doubt have made himself scarce when she entered the house.

'Could we talk a minute?' said Roy, steering Ellie out of the sitting room and into the conservatory. Ellie exclaimed how hot it was in there and went about opening windows. 'Yes, what is it, Roy? I'm listening.'

'First, I'm sorry to hear about your house, that's a terrible thing and of course I'll help in whatever way I can to get it habitable again.'

Ellie nodded. He was a good boy, Roy.

'The thing is, I don't know exactly how to put it, but my mother's death just at this moment, it's, well, it's bad timing, to say the least. Not that I wasn't fond of her, you know that I am. Was. Am. I wish she were back here right now, telling me off, putting me straight, always there with good advice, you know what I mean?'

Yes, he was a good boy, but he needed a hand twitching the reins now and again, to make him run straight. 'You're in a fix because . . . ?'

'That's just it.' He was relieved she was so quick on the uptake. 'I have to sign this contract to develop a warehouse in the Docklands, turn it into luxury apartments. It's a big job, prestigious development, you know the kind of thing. Good profit margins, sure to succeed. My mother was going to back me, not that I needed her money behind me, exactly, though they did say they wanted me to put some money down to secure the deal. Now without her signature—'

'Can't Felicity help you out?'

'Well, of course she would, normally. But that accountant of hers, that Kate person, has told her that she can't spare the capital at the moment, all tied up in other directions, you know how it is?'

Ellie didn't like the way this conversation was going. 'I don't have the sort of money you need, Roy.'

'You could put this house up as security? That sounds awful, but—'

'How did you know that I own it?'

'My mother told me, ages ago. She said you didn't want it known, and to keep the information to myself, so of course I did. But now . . . ?'

'With my own house a burned-out shell?'

He reddened. 'Yes, I know. It's such bad timing. But you could move in with us for the time being. Felicity would love to have you, I could make sure your house was done up properly, and it would solve all our problems. And of course if you came in on this project, you'd get an excellent return on your money.'

He was a good boy, thought Ellie, but naive. She remembered Gunnar telling her not to sign anything and wondered if he'd heard about this latest caper. It was true that Roy's career as an architect and developer had been ever onwards and upwards, but Ellie had always considered his success was more than half due to Miss Quicke's making the decisions about which of his ventures she would back, and which leave on one side. It sounded to Ellie — although she might be mistaken — as if Miss Quicke had not been totally sold on this one.

'Your mother might have left you enough money to carry the cost yourself,' she said. 'Let's see what's in her will, shall we?'

He shook his head. 'She always told me not to expect anything from her, and I think she meant it, although . . . do you think she might have done? No, she probably left it all to a cats' home, knowing her. Which would be sucks to Diana . . .' He looked uncomfortable. 'I didn't mean—'

'Yes, you did,' said Ellie, trying to suppress a smile. 'I understand where you're at, Roy, and I will give the matter some thought but I think on the whole that I'd rather like to live in this house—'

'And sell your old one?' This was from Diana, butting in as usual. 'It's a good opportunity to develop the site properly. The insurance money would cover the cost of putting it right, and house prices are still rising so you'd get a good price for it, which would release enough capital to set you up in a small flat somewhere.'

'Thank you both for your kind thoughts,' said Ellie, 'but I'm not doing anything about selling either house for the time being. Diana, how did you know that I owned this house, too?'

Diana grimaced. 'Well, you didn't tell me, that's for sure. No, something you said about Great-Aunt only renting the place made me wonder, so I looked it up on the Internet. I didn't say anything before because I knew you'd never turn her out, but now, well, why not cash in?'

'That's enough,' said Ellie, as the front doorbell rang. Hopefully, this would be Gunnar. She opened the door, and found not only Gunnar, but also Thomas on the doorstep. For a moment, meeting Thomas's warm and anxious smile, she was tempted to throw herself at him, let him cradle and cuddle her and tell her that he loved her and . . .

Really! She was no better than half a dozen other spinsters and widows of the parish who'd had designs on him ever since he arrived.

'We met on the doorstep,' said Thomas, 'but as it happens we've known one another for years.'

'From Cambridge days, to be exact,' said Gunnar, who was always exact.

'Come on in, both of you. Just in time for tea.'

'I do hope you didn't go to any trouble for me,' said Gunnar, his voice so deep that it was more of a rumble than an ordinary bass.

'I smell baking,' said Thomas, putting his arm around Ellie, and giving her a hug which almost reduced her to tears again. 'How are you coping, my dear?'

'Not too well.' Her voice cracked but she held on to her smile. 'Go on in, do. The clan has gathered and is waiting impatiently for decisions to be handed down from on high.'

Gunnar inclined his head. 'We shall do our best to oblige.' Really, he ought not to be eating cake of any kind, with his weight problem. Thomas looked a mere stripling beside him.

Ellie ushered them into the sitting room at the same time as little Frank catapulted himself from the kitchens and made a dive for the big chair.

'Does everyone know Gunnar Brooks?' Apparently everyone did. Even Felicity and Stewart. Felicity had popped little Mel into her car seat and was rocking her to sleep.

'Come and sit with me, Granny.' Frank had jam around his mouth, and a biscuit in either hand. She obliged, hoping he wouldn't spread jam all over her clean blouse, but resigned to the fact that he probably would.

Gunnar took his stand before the empty fireplace and cleared his throat. He put his hands behind his back and Ellie, over-tired, allowed herself to fancy that in the old days he'd probably have gone in for a tailcoat, and put his hands under that. How her brain did run on, so. Tailcoats would have been his father's style, not his.

'We're all ears,' said Roy.

'Great-Aunt wouldn't have wanted any fuss, would she?' That was Diana. 'So I've taken the liberty of arranging a no-frills ceremony at the crematorium in a week's time.'

Gunnar's eyebrows quivered. He had substantial eyebrows and if he'd been a schoolmaster, he would have cowed a class full of awkward teenagers by twitching them at his charges. Ellie sneaked a glance at Thomas, only to see him covering an amused smile with one hand. He caught her eye, she suppressed a grin, and then looked at the floor. How good it was to share a sense of humour with someone, and how sad that this delightful contact must end.

Gunnar took a sheaf of papers from his breast pocket and rattled them open. 'Miss Quicke was a lady who knew her own mind. Her instructions were quite clear. She said, and I quote: "My body is not to be put on general view for everyone to gawp at. Thomas will officiate at the funeral service at his church, which I have been attending for some years. I append a list of the hymns I wish to be played. Roy and Gunnar — myself — will provide whatever readings seem good to them, but I must ask that there be no modern poetry. The order of service will be settled with Thomas, and Ellie will arrange for it to be printed in silver on good white paper.

'"Following the service in church, there will be a cremation at Breakspear Crematorium, to be attended by immediate members of the family only. No flowers by request, except that Rose may arrange a small spray to go on the coffin. Following the cremation there will be a substantial repast at my house, which Rose will not cook all by herself, but which she will order from Waitrose to be delivered on the morning of the funeral, and which will be served by waitresses provided by Maria's agency.

'"I wish my executor — in conjunction with my lettings manager, Stewart — to advise my business contacts here and in the city of my death, so that they may attend if they wish to do so. Ellie will be responsible for inviting members of the congregation at church to attend. The cost of this open house will be borne by the estate."'

Diana punched the air. 'Told you so. Cremation.'

Gunnar waggled his eyebrows at her, and she fell silent. 'I continue. "There will be no silly business of naming anything after me, no trees are to be planted in my memory, no plaques put up anywhere with my name on. I live as I die, alone."' He refolded the sheets and tucked them away. 'Her will has been lodged with me. I am her sole executor. I will read the will to the immediate family and to Miss Quicke's housekeeper when the repast of baked meats has been cleared away after the funeral. I think that's all.'

There was an uneasy silence. Ellie could see that Roy and Diana were dying to ask for details about the will but didn't quite dare.

It was Stewart who raised his hand, as if he were indeed in class. 'Could you tell me, sir, what is to happen in the meantime with regard to Miss Quicke's estate? I've been acting manager for the lettings and sales for some time, and I assume that her heirs will be looking to appoint someone of their own, but what would you like me to do till then?'

Gunnar held up one large hand, thumb and second finger in a circle. 'Miss Quicke was quite clear. She wished you to continue as you are for the time being.'

Diana was leaping ahead. 'Her business empire? Her portfolio of stocks and shares?'

Gunnar turned his eyes on her, and she fell silent. Ellie wasn't surprised at this; Gunnar had very pale blue eyes with heavy lids.

A tinge of colour came into Diana's face, and she said in a chastened tone, 'I suppose we have to wait till the will is read, and then wait for probate. It will all take for ever.'

Gunnar inclined his head. Yes, it would. He turned to Ellie, 'Now, dear lady, if you would be so kind as to ring that bell on the table beside you, I fancy it is time for some refreshment.'

Ellie disentangled an arm from around Frank and did as she was bid, suppressing a giggle as she thought how neatly she had fallen into sitting in her aunt's chair and continuing her little ways. Ah well.

Frank gave a little wriggle and announced to the company, 'I like this house. When it's mine, I shall have Rose bake me a different cake every day of the week.'

Ellie could feel shockwaves wash around the room. Even Gunnar looked taken aback. It was obviously up to Ellie to say something. 'Well, my love, if you grow up to be a successful businessman and earn an enormous amount of money, I daresay you'll be able to afford a house like this some day. In the meantime, do you think you could go out into the garden and find Midge?'

He slid off her lap. 'Rose says he's catching mice for her. I want to see him do that.'

Luckily at that point Rose entered with a silver tray upon which reposed a hand-cut wine glass containing Madeira, and a huge slice of Victoria sponge on a hand-painted plate. She handed this to Gunnar, spotted Thomas, said she'd one for him, too, and asked Stewart to help her in with the trolley, which he was delighted to do.

Thomas broke what promised to be a silence full of unspoken, difficult thoughts. 'Well, Gunnar, if you can let me have the list of hymns that Miss Quicke wanted? Roy, Ellie; are there any particular poems or readings you'd like in the service? Diana, I don't know whether you attend church, but—'

'I am certainly not going to be a hypocrite and pretend to be a churchgoer for this. Naturally, I shall attend the ceremony, as her closest legitimate relative—' and here she shot a glance of pure poison at Roy — 'but I beg that you do not try to sit me in the same pew as those who only made up to her for what they could get out of it.'

Roy looked shaken. Ellie felt sorry for him, because he really was not a fortune hunter at heart.

She said, 'Shall I pour out?'

* * *

The day drew to a close as any day must, go the minutes as slowly as they might. Little Frank reported that he hadn't been able to find Midge, and why wasn't there a swing or a climbing frame for him to play with, and could he have a go on his great-great-aunt's computer? No, he could not. Then he wanted to stay the night with Ellie, so that he could explore every room in the big house. Ellie didn't feel up to taking care of him so was happy to recall that he was supposed to be spending the weekend with his mother.

Unfortunately, Diana said she'd work to do, so he was born off, protesting, by his father, who was clearly anxious about his future, but refrained from talking about it. A nice man, and trustworthy. Ellie hoped very much that her aunt's heirs would keep him on.

She avoided talking to Thomas, but he did manage to snatch a few minutes with her before he left. 'Are you all right, my dear? I went round by the house. Horrible! Kate said you were being remarkably brave, and of course that's expected of Ellie Quicke, but even the strongest have times when they break down and weep.'

Almost, then, she did break down and weep. Somehow she managed to withdraw her hand from his, reminding herself that he was only being professional when he was sympathetic. Soon he'd be gone and sooner or later she was going to have to come to terms with the gap he was going to leave in her life. So she said she was coping all right, but would be glad when things settled down a bit.

She even remembered to ask after Corinne's bereaved family, and to tell him about poor dear Mae, who'd also been attacked by the dog. Thomas had no good news to impart on either front. He suggested they might have lunch or supper together soon, but she shook her head, saying she couldn't make any plans just at the moment. He understood, of course.

Gunnar understood, too. Those pale bright eyes of his seemed to see everything. He said he'd send over that young rapscallion Mark Hadley from his practice first thing on Monday, to collect any correspondence and deal with business matters for her, the order of service, and so on. Was that agreeable to Ellie? Yes, after a fashion, it was. She'd not been particularly impressed with young Mark when they'd met on an earlier occasion, but perhaps he could be trusted to deal with this and that.

She was exhausted by the time everyone had gone. She drifted through the big rooms, telling herself that all this was hers now, to do what she liked with. She could sell, or divide the house into flats, or just keep it as it was. She couldn't convince herself that one lone woman needed all these rooms, but the peace and quiet, the high ceilings, the space was soothing to someone who'd been through so much lately. Once or twice she stopped and listened for traffic noises, but there were none. The house was set back from the road behind a semicircular drive. The garden behind it was enclosed by high walls with climbers growing on trellis above them.

The lawn was neat and green. There was a garden seat in the shade, but no water feature, not that she'd had a pool in her old garden, but she'd very much enjoyed the fish swimming in the cistern in her conservatory. She shut off the thought of her poor goldfish dying. It hurt. Everything hurt. She turned her mind away from the memory with an effort.

She'd never viewed this house as hers before. In the past, she'd always thought of it as her aunt's, even when Roy was revamping and updating it. She hadn't had anything to do with the redecoration.

She walked through the upstairs rooms in the dusk, fancying in her over-tired state, that she could hear echoes of all the people who had lived in it over the years. Upstairs only two bedrooms, her aunt's and her own, were furnished. Two more had been painted magnolia and the furniture piled higgledy-piggledy in the centre, covered with dust sheets. A third bathroom looked clean but was staringly white — walls, tiles, everything. Too white, too bright.

Downstairs the sitting room and dining room had been redecorated to Aunt Drusilla's taste, but the morning room which Rose despised so much, the study, and what had once been a spacious library, had been left in much the same condition. Magnolia paint and piled up furniture, boxes and boxes and boxes of old books which would probably never be read again. What on earth use did she have for so many rooms?

It was getting dark. She walked out into the garden in search of Midge and spotted him asleep on the roof of the conservatory. He condescended to jump down and wind himself around her ankles, purring. It seemed that Midge liked it here and wasn't at all intimidated by the space. Ellie thought he'd probably investigated every room in the house already. Even the attic. And yes, she remembered that there was indeed an attic. She'd spotted the unobtrusive stair that led up to it, but hadn't bothered to explore. It was all just too much.

Ellie stood in the softly fading light, trying not to think about anything much, wondering if she had the energy to make it to church on the morrow, dreading the thought of all the answerphone messages that still had to be listened to. Trying to calm down. Trying to pray and not succeeding, except for saying over and over, *Lord, in your mercy, hear my prayer.*

Which seemed to work quite well, for she went to bed feeling reasonably calm and slept almost at once.

* * *

Mick was livid. He'd thought his connections were pretty sound, but someone had talked and Tich had come after him, demanding his dog back. Had Tich really thought Mick would let Toby go so easily? In your dreams, mate.

He pointed the car back down the motorway. Tich didn't know where he was staying down south. Tich would probably go to Mick's place and pull it apart till his mum told him about the aunt. Probably.

But not this weekend. Nah, Tich wouldn't want to miss the fight they'd got set up in that barn, way back of beyond. So, it was safe to go back to the aunt for a few days.

It would be best for him to move on, though. He'd have to get some more cash, fast. He smiled. He knew just where he could get that.

CHAPTER SIXTEEN

Ellie got up early on Sunday morning, made herself a cuppa in the kitchen before Rose could get there, and took it into the sitting room, opening all the curtains and the windows. One of the windows stuck; she must have Neil take a look at it. The early morning sun struck glints from Midge's fur as he walked along the ridge tiles atop the conservatory. She thought about watering the plants in the conservatory but didn't because they were Rose's pride and joy, and Ellie wasn't going to interfere with Rose's pleasures.

She sat down to attend to the messages on the answerphone and sort through yesterday's post. Various journalists had called with pleas for information; there would be obituaries in several newspapers. Aunt Drusilla had been a formidable presence in the world of finance. Ellie made notes of names and phone numbers, meaning to pass them on to Gunnar to deal with.

There were two messages from Thomas on the answerphone. He'd sounded anxious. Dear, dear Thomas. Oh dear. She tried not to think about him, switching her mind away with an effort.

Rose brought in some breakfast for her, which she ate while making notes. There was a call from Kate, also anxious, saying there'd been people calling at Ellie's old house about the insurance, the rebuilding and so on. Kate was giving them Miss Quicke's phone number and hoped it was the right thing to do.

So yes, insurance people; builders looking for work; neighbours hoping she was all right . . . she must remember to return the blanket someone had lent her. Where was it, anyway? Perhaps she'd left it at Kate's? Yes, she was sure she had.

The phone rang. It was Roy, worried for her, worried for the future of his next project. Had she given any consideration to backing him? No, she hadn't. She remembered he'd said Kate had persuaded Felicity to veto it. Kate had been something in the city before she'd settled down to having babies, and Kate was the very safe pair of hands that now looked after the wealth Felicity had inherited from her first husband. If Kate thought the project dicey, then it probably was.

Ellie phoned Kate, hoping she'd be up and about, which she was.

'Oh, that,' said Kate. 'No, I think it's probably a good investment for someone, but Felicity doesn't have that much money free at the moment. Besides which, Miss Quicke was in two minds about going into it herself, because she wanted more control.'

'She liked to keep her hand on the financial reins. Yes, that's rather what I thought. Although I'd like to help Roy, I don't think even selling this house would be enough to do the trick, would it?'

'No, it wouldn't. Besides, doing the financial thing is not exactly your bent, is it? Forgive me; I was ungracious to you yesterday, but I've had time to think and even though I don't want to lose you as a next-door neighbour, I believe you might enjoy living in that big house.'

Ellie wasn't so sure about that. 'There is one other person who might help Roy on this . . . ?'

'Are you thinking what I'm thinking? Felicity's father?'

There was silence while both women thought this through. Mr Talbot was a multi-billionaire, a soft-voiced power behind a number of city thrones. He'd long been divorced from Felicity's mother and had lost touch with his daughter since his ex-wife — a difficult woman — had schemed to keep them apart. Only recently had father and daughter begun to see one another for the occasional meal.

Kate was dubious. 'In view of everything that's happened in the past, I'm not sure Felicity would want to ask him for anything.'

'No, but you could. He knows all about you and trusts you. You could ask his opinion of the project, couldn't you? If he thought it was feasible, he could either find someone to go into partnership with Roy or do it himself. Right?'

'What a sneaky woman you are, Ellie Quicke. Remind me to tell you some day how much I enjoy being friends with you. Yes, I'll do it. Tomorrow. I'm not missing out on church. The kids love going, and it gives Armand a chance to show off as the devoted father of two lovely children. See you there?'

'I'll try.' But even as Ellie put the phone down, it rang again.

This time it was Diana. 'Mother, it is you, isn't it? I've had the greatest idea. Why don't little Frank and I move in with you? Of course we'll be very well off when we inherit and probate is granted, but in the meantime you've got all that space, and he'd love it.'

'No!' Ellie slammed the phone down. She was shaking. She'd answered without thinking but now she found she was clinging to the peace and quiet of this big house by her fingernails. If Diana were to move in . . . no, a thousand times, no!

The phone rang again. It would be Diana, furious at being cut off. Ellie let it ring this time. She even got out of her chair and tried to make out the time on the clock sitting on the mantelpiece. Her own grandmother clock was being cleaned up for her by Rose and the plan was to put it on the landing upstairs where she could hear the chimes during the night.

Was that really the time? She was going to be late for church, if she didn't get a move on. For some reason or for none she wanted to cry. She discovered that she really did not want to go to church today, to see everyone being sorry for her, and dressed as she was in other people's clothes plus . . . her bedroom slippers!

It was all wrong, of course. She ought to be going to church to have fellowship with her friends, listen to the word of God, learn more about him. Sing in the choir? No, she couldn't do that today. And — oh, no! — wasn't she down to help on the coffee rota? Probably. Was it the first Sunday in the month, or the second?

Her mind refused to work on the problem.

Rose came in to remove the breakfast tray. 'What's the matter, Ellie? As if I need to ask. Back to bed with you, this minute.'

'No, no! It's just church, bedroom slippers, I can't face it.'

'Is that all? Well, it won't do you any harm to miss church for once, although I daresay Thomas will be round wondering where you are, the moment he realizes. Now you dry your eyes and find your handbag and check that you've got your cards with you, and call for a cab and tell them to take you up to the Brent Cross shops, and get yourself another wardrobe, starting with three or four pairs of shoes, that's the ticket. I'd come with you like a shot, but I'm down on the coffee rota, and I'll make your excuses all round.'

'But I don't want to shop on a Sunday.'

'This,' said Rose, firmly, 'is an emergency. Make a list in the cab. Shoes first. Then something for the funeral and make it black for once, though I know you don't like wearing black, but you need never wear it again after. And don't worry about locking up here, for I'll do it for you.'

Ellie tried to stop crying and failed. 'I ought to be going out and about, asking about that savage dog that killed Corinne, and seeing to her poor boys and checking on poor

Mae who nearly got savaged by the dog, too, and answering the phone and—'

Rose picked up Ellie's breakfast tray. 'I was never so shocked as when Thomas told me about Corinne and I'll ask around about the dog at church, never you mind.'

Ellie tried to control her voice. 'Diana thinks it would be a good idea if she moved in here. You won't let her, will you?'

'Over my dead body! Anyway, she can't get in without the extra key, and I'll put the dead bolt on before I leave for church.'

* * *

It had been years since Ellie had missed going to church on a Sunday. She felt really guilty about that, but as soon as it got past the hour when she ought to have been in the vestry, getting ready to sing in the choir, she began to enjoy herself. She believed that if the first thing you wanted to buy happened to be just right, then the day went on like that. If the first thing you wanted was out of stock or in the wrong colour, the whole day would be a disaster. For once, everything went right.

She bought shoes, three pairs. Then some new, very expensive underwear that she told herself she'd keep for best. Then a fine wool black suit, with a silky cream top to go underneath it, and a wisp of a hat which was more of an apology for a hat than a proper hat that covered the head. She bought a summer dress in her favourite cornflower-blue, a couple of summer skirts and some T-shirts that had sleeves down to the elbow and showed off her pretty bosom.

She changed into this and tried that on. She told herself not to look at the total of what she'd bought. She had lunch in Fenwick's and bought a long-sleeved blouse in a becoming pink, and a swishy dark blue evening skirt that would do for almost any formal occasion. Oh, and two handbags.

She phoned Rose to say she was on her way home in a cab to unload but if there were nothing vitally important happening, she'd take the cab on to her old house as there were one or two things she'd thought about that needed attention, like getting Kate to take the stuff from the fridge and freezer.

'Enjoy yourself,' said Rose. 'I'll hold the fort.'

Rose was on the doorstep when Ellie got to the big house, ready to take in all her packages. Ellie told herself not to feel guilty that she'd bought so much and went on to the old house.

Did it look better or worse than she remembered it? She let herself in and noted that the stink had abated a bit, but not much. The insurance people would meet her here tomorrow, and if the police agreed she could start getting things cleared up after that. She tried the landline phone and to her surprise it still worked, though the answerphone was dead. She phoned Kate to ask if she'd like the food in the house, and Kate said she'd be round in a minute.

Ellie went out through the back door and down into the garden. Here everything was as she'd left it. The Albertine rose was still not blooming well; the love-in-a-mist seedlings were rampaging around the sundial. There was no Midge, of course. Two lads walked along the alleyway at the bottom of the garden and she waved to them as she always did. But this time, instead of continuing on their way, they stopped to have a short confab, and walked through the garden gate up the path towards her.

She knew them both well. Tod lived just down the road and had often dropped in on her for tea in the old days before he grew up and went to high school. She also knew his best friend, who was the son of the local Methodist minister. Unlike his father, the boy didn't talk a lot. Nice boys, both of them.

Tod had grown tall and his voice had broken. 'We're dead sorry about the fire—' his companion nodded — 'and we were just so pleased you weren't here. Or Midge.'

'Thank you, boys. I appreciate it.'

Tod said, 'The thing is, we didn't know whether to say anything or not, but I heard you were asking about a strange dog.'

'How did you hear that?'

'I heard it after church today. Someone, a friend of yours doing coffee, the one they call Rose, was asking everyone if they knew about a strange dog because we all knew about Corinne being attacked by one and dying. It's not the sort of thing you expect to happen around here. We were all shocked, weren't we?' Tod looked at his friend for support and got a vigorous nod, but no verbal help.

'Well,' said Tod, 'we haven't seen any strange dog and I didn't think anything of it until she started asking and *he*—' indicating his companion — 'said what about the new lad who came to youth club the other night? And I thought it *might* be, but it was just hearsay and we couldn't take that to the police. Then we spotted you today, and we thought we might as well say.'

Ellie followed this as best she could. 'Rose was at church this morning, and you heard her asking if anyone knew about the dog that attacked Corinne? You remembered that there was someone new at the youth club, and he's got a dog that might fit the description?'

Both lads nodded. 'There's a couple of lads, not really our sort, but they hang around at youth club nowadays because their leader — if you can call him that — he got an ASBO and was sent up north to get him out of the way. There's not much harm in them,' said Tod, judiciously, 'but they can be a bit of a nuisance at youth club. Showing off, smoking in corners, that sort of thing. Only, when they saw this new lad come in, they — what would you say? — they sort of shrank into themselves. He knew them, sure, and they knew him, but they didn't want to know, see. This new lad started throwing his weight about and I was going to, well, reason with him, till one of his friends hissed at me that I'd better watch my step because Mick owned a savage dog and wasn't above setting it on people.'

'Ah. That fits.'

The boys both nodded. 'Maybe it does, but it's all hearsay. We don't *know* that the dog exists, though we're pretty sure he does. It takes a bit to frighten those two friends of his. I didn't have to speak to Mick myself because one of the youth club leaders came up and told him off, and we forgot about it till your friend Rose spoke about it, and she said that you were looking into it, too. Then we thought you might be interested.'

'Any name, apart from Mick? Any idea where he's from?'

The two boys exchanged glances. 'He's not from around here. He was signed in by some older woman that's never been to the youth club before. We think we've seen her around in the Avenue, but we're not sure where. We thought we might ask the woman who takes the register, if you were interested.'

Tod's friend gave him a nudge, and Tod added, 'Oh, the only other thing, Mick boasted about his aunt having a four-by-four. If that's any help.'

Ellie froze. Could it possibly be *Madam* who'd brought the lad to the club? Oh, surely not. She didn't have any children of that age. Ellie tried to remember what she did know of her. Two grown-up children, gone through university? 'What age was this Mick?'

'Fifteen, maybe sixteen. Small for his age, maybe, but mean with it. It's the right one?'

Ellie gave them an uncertain smile. 'I don't think it can be. Except . . . no, it can't be. The woman I'm thinking of . . . no, no! But, if you could ask the organizer . . . ? I wouldn't wish to point the police in the direction of someone who's totally innocent.' Except that there had been someone in the back of the car with Madam the other day, and that someone would have heard about Ellie being out of the house that night.

Tod said, 'We'll ask and give you a ring, shall we? We're so sorry about . . .' He nodded towards the house and left with his friend. Ellie called after them not to ring her here, but to try her aunt's place, Miss Quicke, the number's in the phone book. She hoped they'd heard her, but couldn't be sure.

* * *

With Kate's help, Ellie cleared out the fridge and freezer, collected a box of family photographs and other odds and ends, and made it back to the big house at teatime . . . only to find her cab followed into the drive by a plain clothes police car.

Ears got out, followed by a tight-lipped WPC Mills.

Now what? thought Ellie, who'd been feeling better able to cope until that moment.

'A few more questions, if we may,' said Ears, looking forward to it.

'Oh, very well. I suppose you'd better come in.' Ellie dumped her things in the porch and got out her key. It turned in the lock, but the door didn't open. Just like the other night. Whatever was the matter with it? She tried her key again and it turned, but still the door didn't open. And yes, there were definitely two keyholes in the massive door now, instead of just the one.

'Trying to burgle your own house?' Ears thought this hilarious.

Ellie set her teeth and rang the doorbell. Surely Rose must be in? She'd have got back from church by lunchtime. Perhaps she was in the garden and hadn't heard the bell? Ellie leaned on the bell again, and at long last she heard a key turn in the lock inside, and the door opened.

'Silly me, I forgot to give you one of the new keys, didn't I?' said Rose. 'It's a new security precaution Miss Quicke had put in a couple of weeks back.' To the police, 'So what do you want now?'

Ellie pulled her belongings inside the house. 'Rose, you said something about giving me another key the other night, but forgot?'

Rose let them all into the hall, closed the front door and locked it behind her, taking the key out of the lock and returning it to her pocket. 'I was thinking that that Diana might come around and try to get in while you were out, so I double-locked the door just in case. No one gets in or out without this second key in future, and the only people who're going to have second keys are me and Ellie, apart from Miss

Quicke, God rest her soul and bless her, and I've got her bunch of keys safely locked up where no one can find them.'

Ellie held out her bunch of keys for the police to see. 'See these? One latch key to this door, and no second key. No key to the back door, either. Rose has been double-locking the door at nights. I didn't have a second key. So I couldn't have left this house the night my aunt died, even I'd wanted to. Or got back in again if I'd managed somehow to get out. Now are you satisfied?'

WPC Mills grinned, happy that Ellie was exonerated. Ears looked as if he'd swallowed something the wrong way.

Ellie said, 'Well, if that's all . . . ? I look forward to hearing something positive from Forensics. Oh, and by the way, I might have a lead for you on another matter. The case of the killer dog. A stranger turned up at the church youth club on Friday night who is supposed to have a savage dog in tow. It might be worth looking into.'

She wouldn't tell them about Madam. It was too far-fetched, to think of Mrs Goss with a teenage thug.

'Not our case,' said Ears, dismissing the very idea.

Ellie looked at WPC Mills to see if she'd taken the hint on board, which she had. In Ellie's opinion, the policewoman had twice the brains of her superior officer. Now she nodded her understanding of what Ellie had said, but didn't speak. Fair enough. The hint had been registered somewhere and might bear fruit in due course.

Rose saw the police out, closed and relocked the front door. 'Now I want to see everything you've bought, but would you like to eat first? Oh, and Thomas came round, very worried he was about you, but I said a little retail therapy would work wonders, even if it was on a Sunday, and he agreed that sometimes strong measures are called for and said would you ring him when you were able. The phone's been ringing off and on all day, but I left it alone, thinking it better for you to deal with it on a full stomach as they say. So, bath first, or food?'

* * *

On Monday morning came young Mark Hadley, freshly shaven and tickety-boo from Gunnar's office. Ellie hadn't thought much of him when she'd called on him to help her a while back, but either Gunnar had given him a lecture or he'd sobered up, and he turned out to be very helpful. He scooped up all the post and manned the relentlessly ringing phone. Enquiries from the press, enquiries from Miss Quicke's business associates, enquiries about the funeral; all these Mark dealt with in exemplary fashion. Ellie and Rose set him up in the dining room, which Miss Quicke had been accustomed to use as her office, and left him to it.

Funeral arrangements fell into place. The order of service was settled by telephone with Thomas and went off to the printers. The organist was advised of the hymns to be played. Distant relatives and friends rang asking if they could be put up for the funeral, and Mark booked them into hotels nearby. It was going to be a big do.

Ellie was glad that Rose had made her buy a good black outfit.

Mark Hadley also fielded calls from the family. Ellie told him to say she was out for the day on business but would ring them back when she could.

With Rose, Ellie worked out roughly what they needed by way of food and drink for the reception and went off to order it from the nearest Waitrose. Rose wanted to do some shopping in the Avenue on the way back, so Ellie took the cab on to her old house to meet the insurance adjuster.

He was there already, a thin, grey man with cold eyes. 'Arson and burglary?' he asked. 'A break-in, yes, that's clear. Much taken?'

She gave him the list of everything she could remember, and he nodded. 'You're properly covered, you'll be pleased to know. The fire didn't spread beyond the living room and conservatory and structurally the house seems sound, though we'd like to have a surveyor look it over, just to make sure. I'll get him round as soon as possible. Let us have at least two quotes for everything that needs doing, we'll advise you which to take and then you can get moving. Replace the jewellery and the clock as soon as you like. I imagine you've reported your passport and chequebook stolen?'

'Yes, that's been done. Now, if the surveyor gives the go ahead, do you think I can get away with a good clean around in the kitchen and upstairs?'

He shook his head. 'You might, but all the electrics will have to be checked and by the look of it will have to be renewed. We'd advise you to take any furniture out of the house that you want to keep, send it to the restorers. Bin the rest.'

'It's going to take months. If only I'd replaced the padlock on the tool shed that day!'

'If it's any consolation, if a thief really wants to get in and isn't disturbed, there's no way you can keep him out. You might think of putting a high fence around your garden, growing roses up it, that deters them because of the thorns. They don't want to risk getting scratched. DNA, you know.'

Ellie saw him leave, checked that Kate was out — her morning at the toddlers' club? — and decided to have an early lunch at the Italian restaurant she used to patronize with Thomas, in the days when they saw so much of one another. Don't think about Thomas.

She turned her mind away from him with an effort. Think about savage dogs, and poor Corinne and her children. Think about . . . think about the boy waiter whose mother had done some cleaning at a house where there was a troublesome dog. What was his name? She couldn't remember. Maybe had never heard it.

The boy wasn't there. His place had been taken by a buxom lass with brightly blonded hair and a sullen look. Ellie chose a salad and asked after the boy. The waitress said she didn't know nothing about no waiter and did Ellie want chips with it? No chips, but perhaps she could have a word with the manager?

'What have I done now?' the girl demanded.

'Nothing,' said Ellie. 'The boy was going to do something for me, that's all.'

The girl flounced off. She really did flounce. Her bottom wobbled, her stomach — rather too much of it on show between cropped top and low-cut jeans — also wobbled. Oh dear. Ellie made herself think about something else. Her new clothes, for instance. Did her new black skirt need turning up at the hem, just a trifle? Was there time to do it? Probably not. Rose was getting young Neil to put cat flaps into the conservatory today, so that Midge could get in from the garden, and then into the house from the conservatory. Rose didn't like to think of Midge's steeplejack adventures, and he probably wouldn't use the cat flaps, but there . . . if it pleased Rose, it should be done.

The manager came. A dumpy man, Middle Eastern in origin. He knew Ellie by sight, was none too happy that she should be enquiring about the boy. 'He no good, that boy. Nervy, nervy. Drops things. I can't afford him dropping things.'

'I understand. But could you give me his address, do you think? He told me his mother did cleaning jobs, and I wanted to speak to her about it.'

The manager snorted. 'I hear she just as bad; nervy, nervy. I can't afford to be nervy, can I?'

'No, indeed.' Ellie tried to be soothing. 'You run this place beautifully. But perhaps his mother might be all right at my place, which is very quiet. What was his name again?'

He shrugged. 'If that is all, fine. His name is Barry. Barry Smadgy, Barry Patchy. Who can remember these silly names?' Ellie tried not to smile as his own name was probably something she'd find difficult to remember. He hit his head to get his memory working. 'They're in a council place, opposite the swimming pool, the other side of the park. Number six, I think.' He yelled back into the kitchen. 'Was it number six that the idiot lives in? Number eight? I suppose he'll be at home, watching the telly. Not much good for anything else, that boy.'

Ellie didn't place too much reliance on having been given the right number, but ate her salad and had a cup of coffee, trying not to jump every time the door opened and another customer came in, hoping it wouldn't be Thomas, not knowing what to say to him, if he did come in. But he didn't.

She tried to turn her mind away from Thomas and it went back to her dear dead husband. What would he have said if he could see her now, tracking down criminals, living in his aunt's house, fancying herself in love with the vicar? Now they were back to Thomas again. In love with Thomas, indeed! Of course she wasn't. She loved him, of course. Like a brother. Like a dear friend. But not . . . not that way. She told herself.

She called for the bill.

She took the bus from the Avenue to the swimming pool and began to knock on doors. Anything was better than going back to the turmoil that had enveloped the big house.

* * *

Mick was furious. The old banger wouldn't be pushed over fifty, and he couldn't afford to draw attention to himself, not having any driving licence or insurance or anything. So he'd had to abandon the motorway and take to the old main roads. Then there'd been trouble with the radiator boiling over. There was a leak somewhere . . . but where? He'd kept filling up with water but when it got dark, he'd had to stop and spend the night in the car. In the morning he remembered something about a general fix-it liquid that you could pour into the radiator and it sealed leaks. He'd stopped at the next garage, bought some and put it in. The garage attendant had given him a funny look, asked if he were sure he was old enough to be driving. Mick said of course he was and showed his newly acquired student ID. Well, he was old enough to drive. Almost.

Every few hours he'd turned off the main road on to a quiet country lane, put Toby on a lead and taken him for a run. Toby had not been himself, hating the journey. Mick didn't think much of it, either. But what else could he do? He couldn't go back north, and the aunt did at least give him house room.

Once back in London he'd soon get something going, find himself some more lads to follow him around, sell the jewellery he'd picked up on the last job, get some dosh together. First thing, he'd raid that big house with the two old women in it. One of them was dying, the other too old to offer any resistance. Yes, that's what he'd do. That night.

CHAPTER SEVENTEEN

Nobody knew anything about a Barry Patchy at numbers six and eight. Nor at number ten. Ellie began to wonder if he even lived in the neighbourhood. The development was well kept, comprising some maisonettes and some small, terraced houses. Ellie went on knocking and eventually a black woman came to the door of number twelve, nursing a teething, grizzling infant.

'Barry?' she said. 'Barry Patchett? You mean the one where his mother's in the clinic weeks at a time? The one the Social's always visiting?'

'I expect I do. His mother does cleaning jobs, doesn't she?'

'Not that she's up to much, I shouldn't think, but there, it takes all sorts, don't it?' She shifted her child from one hip to the other. What Ellie could see of the woman's own house was beautifully clean. 'If you want my opinion, I shouldn't think she's up to cleaning her own kitchen sink at the moment, but you could always try. Number sixteen.'

Number sixteen it was. Barry himself came to the door, bringing with him a sour, defeated smell. This house was not clean, nor was he, particularly. He'd been smoking and yes, he'd been watching television and had left it on when he answered the door.

Ellie said, 'May I come in? You promised to ring me, remember? About the dog?' He should have had 'Defeated by Life' tattooed across his forehead. She wanted to take him by the shoulders and shake some energy into him, but there you are, it takes all sorts, as his neighbour had said.

'Mum isn't up to it,' he said, not letting her in. 'She was took bad, been bad ever since. Might have to go back in for a bit.'

'I'm sorry to hear it because she was doing so well, wasn't she? What happened?'

'She were that worried about the dog she couldn't sleep, so she turned up late to clean and got such an earful she got the shakes and when she gets the shakes she can't do nothing. The first I knew, she were back here in a cab and she won't go back there, so you needn't come round asking for her.'

'I'm not. At least, yes, I was concerned about her because of the dog. It was the dog that caused your mother to be ill again?'

'That, and the woman wanting her to work extra, some big party she was throwing. She told my mother she were shirking and she ought to be reported to the Social.'

If Ellie interpreted that correctly, the woman had said that his mother ought to be reported to the social services because she was on benefits and should tell them if she got a job. 'I'm only interested in the dog. Would you give me the name of the woman who is letting her dog cause trouble? It would make your mother feel so much better if I could stop it, wouldn't it?'

He screwed up his face, pulling out a cigarette, lighting up, thinking. 'Dunno her name. Mrs something.'

'Yes, of course,' said Ellie, sitting on impatience. 'Can't you ask your mother?'

He shook his head. 'She won't come to the door while she's like this. Tell you what, I've seen the bit of paper somewhere with the telephone number on it, the one where she wrote it down when she first saw the advert in the newsagent's.' He yelled into the house, 'Mum, where you left your handbag?'

A muffled voice replied something, and he vanished only to return in a minute with a scruffy tote bag, which he rifled through, eventually pulling out a scrap of paper on which a shopping list had been written. In one corner was a telephone number. 'There.' He stabbed at it with a yellowed finger. 'That do you?'

'Thank you very much,' said Ellie. She didn't recognize the number, but she wasn't good with numbers and didn't expect to. She crossed the road to the bus stop, thinking that she'd ring the number herself and find out who it was who owned the dog, but as she switched her mobile on, she saw that voice messages had piled up for her there.

In the bus, she tried to listen to her messages. Diana, of course. Roy, of course. Both wanting her to ring them urgently. Felicity, wondering if Ellie needed some more clothes and was the size all right of the ones she'd lent her already, and hoping that Ellie might have time to drop in for a cuppa if it were convenient. Ellie diagnosed this as Felicity wanting to be sure that she'd been right to refuse her husband the financial backing he needed. Felicity could be very unsure of herself at times.

Stewart had also rung; he was man enough not to mention his own anxieties about the job, but wondered if he or Maria could help Ellie get her own house back to normal in any way. 'Just say the word, Ellie, and we'll descend on you and get it cleaned up, stuff thrown out, whatever you want. Just let me know, right?'

Stewart was a good lad.

Thomas had also phoned, but sighed and not left a message, except to ask her to ring back. Thomas was . . . something else.

She would *not* cry.

She got off the bus in the Avenue and walked through the back streets to the big house. Rose let her in, saying that Neil had come to fit the cat flaps and done that but Midge had refused to use them although she'd shown him how, and Gunnar's young lad was still on the phone in the dining room, she'd fed him while he worked, he seemed to be pulling his weight. Oh, and Midge had moved into the big bedroom as soon as the cleaners left, and was asleep on Miss Quicke's chair in the window, if you please, and was that all right with Ellie?

'Yes, of course. I have to make some calls myself.' Ellie went into the sitting room, and since Mark was still on the landline, used her mobile to get through to the number Barry had given her.

A recorded message. 'This is the Goss residence. Neither of us are available to take your call at the moment, so please leave a message after the tone.'

Ellie shut off her phone, sitting quite still. Sitting very, very still. Was it true? Could the high and mighty Madam Goss actually be harbouring a killer dog? Surely not. Yet Tod and his mate had said that the woman who'd taken Mick to the youth club had been driving a 4x4, and that they'd recognized her as a local.

But Madam? No! Madam hadn't any children at home, and she certainly wasn't the sort to go in for a large dog. Or any kind of dog, come to think of it.

What to do?

Leave it alone? Yes, but . . .

After some hesitation, Ellie looked up the number of the charity shop in the Avenue where she and Rose had worked for so many years. Her old friend Anita answered the phone.

'Anita, it's Ellie. Is Mrs Goss there?'

Ellie heard Madam say, 'Who is it, Anita? Someone for me? Oh, I'll take it . . . This is Mrs Goss speaking.'

'Ellie Quicke here. May I ask if you have a teenage boy and a dog staying with you at the moment?'

'What? What was that? Why do you ask? What business is it of yours, anyway?'

'So you do? I wonder if we could meet somewhere — not at your house — when you finish at the shop this afternoon?'

'What on earth for?' Madam was angry, but also anxious. Ellie could hear it in her voice.

'I'm trying to give you the benefit of the doubt. I really don't think you can have any idea what that dog's been up to. Shall we say four o'clock at the Sunflower Café?'

'No, I can't possibly, I have a committee meeting, and then I'm due at the . . . oh, nobody you'd know, but I can't possibly cancel. It's out of the question. Anyway, they're not with me at the moment. Really, Ellie, when you rang I thought you'd come to your senses and were prepared to give us some of your time now that you're a lady of leisure.' The spite spilled through the telephone line into Ellie's ears, and she felt herself tighten up in response.

Ellie said, 'Do you know where they are?'

'No, I don't, and I'd like to know what makes you think you can—'

'Four o'clock, Sunflower Café, right?'

Ellie put the phone down over Madam's objections and held out her hands, palm downwards. Yes, she was shaking. It had taken some courage to stand up to the woman who'd made her life a misery for so long, even if all that was in the past. But she'd done it. Good for you, Ellie.

She picked up the phone again, to ring Felicity. No, more urgent still, she must ring the police and find out if they had dismissed their suspicions that she'd committed arson. Then, and only then, could she begin to sort out the mess at her old house.

Mark Hadley put his head around the door. 'Free for a minute? I've got a long list of things to clear with you. Is that all right?'

* * *

Madam was late, of course. Ellie pulled out the notes of things to do that she'd been making, ticking some items off, and adding others.

The police. Tick. They'd told her to go ahead and do what she liked with the house. So they no longer considered her a criminal? Good.

Stewart. Tick. He'd meet her at the old house at nine tomorrow and work out how to proceed. He could get Frank's secretaire moved to the big house, get a furniture restorer to advise what she was to keep, organize a house clearance man to take what was still saleable, and order a skip to remove what couldn't be salvaged.

Diana. Tick, sort of. She was to meet Diana at her estate agency and have supper with her after work tomorrow. Diana was manning the office today and couldn't leave it, but desperately wanted to talk. Not something Ellie was looking forward to. Diana was a ticking time bomb, making plans for a future in which she and her son would inherit the earth. Ellie remembered her aunt saying that Diana would get what she deserved. In Aunt Drusilla's terms that might mean inheriting a fortune, of course; but it might also mean a slap in the face, or being cut off with the proverbial shilling or whatever was the equivalent nowadays. Ellie wasn't sure how to damp down Diana's enthusiasm, or what words to say to her if her daughter's dreams of infinite wealth failed to materialize.

Felicity. Tick. Ellie had phoned Felicity and assured her that Roy would still love her even if she couldn't back his latest plan with money, and that Kate had an idea about someone who might be helpful in that direction. Once reassured of that, Felicity was full of her new friend Caroline, and how they were going to have a picnic in the park with their babies one day soon — when the dog had been dealt with.

Roy. Tick. She'd spoken to Roy and advised him to hold off signing anything for a while, as there was a possible new partner on the horizon. Actually, Kate had tried to speak to Felicity's father that morning but he was out of the country, back at the weekend. Kate would speak to him then.

Ellie sighed, worrying about Roy. Of course he *said* that he didn't expect or want anything under his mother's will, but she could see that he really both expected and wanted a substantial inheritance. He kept saying that it would make sense, wouldn't it, for his mother to have left him enough to go on developing properties in a big way? After all, she'd had so much fun doing it with him, hadn't she?

Well, of course she had, but she'd also kept tight control of the finances and had had no opinion of her son's ability in that respect. Ellie rather doubted that Miss Quicke would have left Roy much beyond her good wishes. How to explain that to a man who was born an optimist and had never saved pennies in his life?

Both Diana and Roy had asked Ellie how she thought Miss Quicke might have left her money, and to both she'd replied, truthfully, that she thought it would go to some charitable concern or trust. Neither liked the thought of this.

Mark Hadley, Gunnar's young colleague. Tick. Mark was doing better than she'd expected. He was going to get the death registered that afternoon and the arrangements for the funeral service were more or less in place. She didn't want to have to read at the funeral service, but Roy would. Together with Thomas and Stewart, Mark seemed to have contacted everybody who should be contacted, and he had dealt with the press for her.

Thomas. No tick. She was avoiding him for the time being. It hurt to think about him, so she tried not to.

Add: Maria had agreed to supply waitresses for the reception after the funeral and people to clean up afterwards. Should this be in the dining room of the big house, or in the sitting room as well? Discuss with Rose and Maria.

Add: little Frank. Diana wanted him to come to the funeral, but Ellie really didn't think this suitable. Stewart didn't think so, either. What to do?

'Busy as ever, I see.' A grating voice, a faint whiff of expensive perfume. Madam took a seat beside Ellie and pronounced herself dissatisfied with the venue. 'A bit cramped here, isn't it?'

'I didn't want to take you away from the shop for too long,' said Ellie, who had deliberately chosen a public place in which to meet, in case Madam turned nasty. 'And since my house was burned out, I'd business in the area.'

'What? Really? How sad.' She didn't mean it. She picked up the menu, which also met with disfavour. She sniffed. 'Cottage pie and chips, liver and bacon and chips. Don't they have anything wholesome to eat?'

'They have salads. I'm having a croissant and coffee,' said Ellie, almost enjoying herself. 'I had an early lunch.'

Madam gave the waitress her order. 'Lemon tea, with a couple of slices of real lemon.'

'No lemon today,' said the waitress.

'Very well. I'll have an espresso coffee.' Turning to Ellie with raised eyebrows, Madam said, 'I hope what you have to say justifies taking me away from the shop.'

'You have — or have had — a young lad staying with you, who brought his dog along.'

'No secret. My brother's boy, from his first marriage. His mother is having a difficult time, so asked if I'd have him for a little while. He brought his dog, yes. I don't let the dog in the house, naturally. Not that that's any business of yours.'

'What sort of dog is it?'

'I really have no idea. I do not care for dogs.'

'Large. Brown and white. A pit bull, or a pit bull cross. Ring a bell?'

Madam shrugged.

Ellie persevered. 'A dog answering to that description, a strange dog whom nobody has seen around here before, was responsible for a savage attack on a young mother in the park last Wednesday. The woman died. Two days later, last Friday, a boy with a dog attacked Mae in a street near your house. Again, the description matches.'

Madam swatted away a non-existent fly. 'There must be plenty of boys looking after dogs around here.'

'Not really, no. The dog-walkers in the park don't recognize his description, and they should know. Two other people have given me leads to your house.'

'Are you suggesting that I would harbour a criminal?'

Ellie wanted to say 'Yes', but didn't. 'I don't think you knew anything about it. I'm sure you find it hard to believe that your nephew could be responsible, but it sounds as if his dog is out of control.'

'What nonsense!' But she'd gone very pale. The waitress served Ellie her croissant and coffee and departed, saying that the espresso would be along in a jiff.

Mrs Goss said, 'Do you honestly expect me to sit here and listen to this . . . this slander?'

'You said that the boy had gone, that you didn't know where he was.'

'He took off with my son's old car on Saturday morning, before I was up. I don't know where he went.'

Ellie poured sugar into her coffee. 'I suppose he's gone back to his mother's. Well, if he's disappeared all we have to do is inform the police, who will keep a look out for him in his old haunts. It will be a great relief to everyone around here to know that he's gone.'

Madam half closed her eyes. 'As he's no longer here, couldn't we keep this between ourselves?'

'The police must be told.'

'Oh, of course. But nobody else needs to know, do they? I mean, they'll pick him up in Leeds at his mother's, and charge him there. It won't even get into the local papers here, with luck. Waitress, I'm still waiting for my espresso.'

Ellie sat back in her chair, to survey Madam. 'This can't be brushed under the carpet. A woman died, and her family is devastated. One of her children may have to be taken into care, with all that that means for his future. Mae was mugged, and at her age that's not something to be taken lightly. Of course people will have to know.'

'You want me to beg?'

Ellie looked away from the humiliation in her old boss's face. 'No, please. This is not right.'

'You want me to buy you a present? A cruise, perhaps? Of course we'll say no more about your working in the shop again.'

Ellie felt herself redden. 'Please, stop. I don't want anything, that's not what . . . can't you see that this has got to come out? Oh, not your part in it, because I'm sure you knew nothing, at least, I hope you didn't—'

'Certainly not!' Now it was Madam's turn to go red.

'But the police have to know, they have to find him and stop him. The dog will have to be destroyed. If your nephew can prove he didn't know what the animal could do, I'm sure they'll treat him leniently. Although there is the mugging, of course.'

Madam found it hard to plead for mercy. 'But everyone will know! All our friends, the people I know on committees, my husband when he comes back next week, my golf partners. I'll die of shame.'

'No, of course you won't,' said Ellie, feeling pity for a woman who had never extended sympathy to anyone herself. 'Now, let's think how this can be done. Suppose you go to the police, tell them that you've only just heard that there might be a connection. If you report it yourself, then you'll be the innocent bystander doing her duty by the law. How does that sound?'

The woman looked out of the window at the busy street. She nodded.

Ellie wondered why Madam was not meeting her eye. She experienced a moment of doubt. Had she missed something? Was the woman lying to her? But why should she? No, no.

'Look,' said Madam, taking a deep breath, 'I'm taking this very seriously. Don't think I'm not. But what you don't know is, that my sister-in-law is not at all well. She's not exactly . . . well, he married her when they were both very young, and it wasn't to be expected that it would last, she's gone her own way, and so has he.'

'Your brother doesn't have anything to do with the boy? Is that what you're trying to say?'

'He emigrated to Canada years ago, remarried, has four children of his own now. He hasn't seen the boy since he was a toddler, though he kept up his payments, of course he did. Between you and me, my sister-in-law is not quite, well, not exactly . . . if you see what I mean?'

'You mean she doesn't run to a four-by-four?' Ellie tried not to let her tone become acid.

Madam changed colour. 'You're making me sound . . . well . . . no, I suppose that is it. She's had various partners since she walked out on my brother, been in and out, drying out, then getting back into the club scene again. So no, we don't normally communicate. Different lifestyles. I didn't really want to take Mick in, but she pleaded with me, she needed to know he was safe for a while, since her doctor wanted her to go into hospital for tests, probably cancer, reading between the lines. Mick's been mixing with a bad crowd, and her latest partner had walked out on her as they all do. So I said I'd have him for a fortnight. The thing is, I need a day's grace. I need to phone her in the hospital, to warn her that he's probably on his way back, might even be there by now. It's the least I can do. Then tomorrow morning I'll go to the police.'

Ellie found this a reasonable solution. 'Do you want me to come with you?'

'No need. I know the chief constable socially, and I'm sure he'll look after me.'

Ellie sighed, thinking of all the difficult times she'd had with lower echelons of the police. Ah well, some people had all the luck.

'I must get back,' said Madam. 'Please don't come into the shop again. All this has upset me terribly. I wish I hadn't got to go to this function tonight, but I suppose I must. Keep the flag flying, and all that.' She picked up her bag and left, just as the waitress brought her espresso.

'Something wrong?' asked the waitress.

Ellie pushed aside her own empty plate. 'I don't think she's feeling very well. Let me have her bill and I'll pay for us both.'

* * *

It was late when the aunt got back from her evening function. Mick had been longer than he'd intended on the road, what with having such a wreck of a car to drive and having to make so many stops to suit Toby. She'd already gone out when he returned, so he helped himself to food from the fridge and was lounging on the settee with his feet up watching the telly, when he heard her car draw up. He didn't bother to move until she rushed in, all shiny evening dress, glittering with diamonds, and gave him such a slap around his head that he felt his neck snap.

'So you're back, are you? How dare you drag me into your sordid little crimes!'

He said, 'What did you do that for?'

She was in a hard, cold rage. She slapped him again. He tried to back out of range of her fists, drawing his knees up to his chest, pulling his arms over his head. She took hold of his arm, and swung him off the settee on to the floor. He hadn't realized she was so strong. He yelled with fury, but she kicked him with her pointed shoes, once, twice . . . and then stood back, arms akimbo, out of breath.

'You evil little toad! I should never have listened to your mother, never let you within a mile of this place! Prison is too good for you!'

Seeing that her fury was at least temporarily spent, he uncurled and backed away, holding on to his neck. 'What's got into you?'

'Murder, that's what!' She thrust her head forward, hands on hips. 'I agreed to give you a second chance, introduce you to some decent people, feed you and give you pocket money. But it seems I've brought a spawn of Satan into my life. As for that dog! If I'd known, I'd have banned it, never allowed it anywhere near me.'

'What murder?' he asked, still holding his neck.

'You murdered some woman in the park by setting the dog on her, right?'

'I didn't murder no one.'

'The dog did, and you're responsible. Not content with that, you also set the dog on one of the people who help to run my shop and robbed her. Did you think I'd never get to hear about it? I had to hear it from Ellie Quicke, of all people! The humiliation! Didn't you think about the inconvenience to me, when you knocked Mae out? What else have you been up to!' She took him by the shoulders and shook him.

'Nothing!'

She slapped him again, hard. He couldn't believe that this was happening to him. His mother hadn't lifted a finger to him for years, hadn't dared. And this . . . bitch . . . he simply couldn't believe it. He felt blood begin to seep down his face. One of her rings must have cut him. She lifted her hand again and he could see by the wild look in her eye that she meant to give him a proper old beating.

'Nothing much,' he mumbled, his mouth thickening from where her fist had caught him. 'I picked up a few things from the house where you gave that old woman a lift, that's all.'

She paused, hand upraised. Her eyes sharpened. 'Mrs Quicke's house? You burgled that? Was it you set it on fire?'

He thought she looked almost pleased, so hastened to explain. 'She wasn't very nice to you, so I thought you wouldn't mind. Dunno nothing about a fire. I had a ciggie while I was there . . .' He shrugged. 'Might of set a fire going, I suppose. Do you want to see what I got? Just trinkets and an old clock. Nothing much.'

She let her hand drop, turning away, thinking. 'It might help if I could give it back. Where is it?'

'Upstairs in my room.'

It didn't look as if she were going to attack him again, so he straightened his clothes, rolled his shoulders, and used the hem of his T-shirt to pat blood from his mouth. She hadn't heard about the bike and the satnav, evidently. Nor the chequebook and passport. He'd keep that to himself.

She poured herself a drink, but didn't offer him one. 'I suppose it could be worse. If I give back the jewellery, tell them I knew nothing, they'll believe me. But the dog. I'm not sure . . .' She tapped her teeth with the rim of her glass. 'He'll have to be destroyed.'

What? No, he'd never allow that!

She made up her mind, reached for her handbag. 'I'm giving you a day's start. Take my son's car again, if you wish. I'll give you some money, enough to get well away from here. I promised I wouldn't go to the police until tomorrow morning. I got a day's grace by saying I've got to break the news to your mother first. I said she was in hospital with cancer . . .'

Mick grinned. His mother was 'away', all right. With the fairies. Drink, not cancer. The aunt could put a good lie together when she tried.

'. . . So let's see how much money I can spare.'

'The dog goes with me,' said Mick.

'Don't be ridiculous!' She turned her back on him, which was a mistake. He picked up the heavy cut-glass dish which she liked to keep filled with peanuts, and hit her on the side of the head with it. She dropped her handbag, hands clawing the air. He hit her again, and again. Till she didn't move any more.

That would learn her. There was a lot of blood everywhere. Well, her cleaner could deal with that. He picked up her evening bag, and the keys to her 4x4 fell out. Well, why shouldn't he take that? He wasn't going to get anywhere with her son's battered old hulk. What else? Credit cards, of course. A wad of notes, but not as many as he would need. He took the lot. Bending over her body, he removed her diamond bracelet, her earrings and her watch.

Even now, she hadn't supplied him with enough cash to keep him for long. The jewellery he could sell tomorrow, but maybe not in London. Maybe he ought to be thinking of getting back up north, not too near home so that Tich could find him, but far enough from London to avoid the police picking him up.

He checked to see if the aunt's watch was keeping good time and it was. Nigh on twelve. He checked on his aunt. She had a pulse still, but he didn't want her raising the alarm too quickly. He hit her once more, to make sure she stayed out for a while.

He'd got a lot of blood on him. Bother. Better have a shower and change before he left. And while he was at it, he'd go through her jewellery box, too.

He was thinking hard. He'd plenty of time to get away, but there was one more job he could pull off before he went. He'd pay that nosy parker busybody woman a visit at the big house. It was only a few doors from here. Easy pickings.

That sort thought that if they put good locks on the front door, they were invulnerable, but he knew better. A back door often offered an easy way in, or a side window. With Toby at his side, no one would dare get in his way.

CHAPTER EIGHTEEN

The kitchen clock ticked on while Ellie and Rose sat at the table holding empty mugs of cocoa, putting the world to rights. In theory they were waiting for Midge to make an appearance before going up to bed, but in reality both were almost too tired to move.

'It's getting late.' Ellie yawned. 'That's a comfortable bed.'

'Finished?' Rose took Ellie's mug for the dishwasher. 'Would you like to move into the big bedroom? It's been cleaned and readied up nicely, with some brand-new linen that we bought in John Lewis's some time back. She said then that she thought you'd like it.'

Ellie shook her head. 'Wouldn't feel right. Rose, what am I going to do with this house? It's far too big for just me but the thought of sharing it with Diana gives me the shivers.'

'You didn't think of getting married again?'

Ellie knew Rose was referring to Thomas, and felt the usual pang of dismay and loss which mention of his name gave her nowadays. 'Chance would be a fine thing.' She tried to make a joke of it, pushing herself upright, yawning again.

'How many times has he asked you?'

Ellie forced a smile. 'Never, my dear.'

Rose slapped some breakfast things on to the table. 'I meant, how many times has he wanted to ask you and you've put him off?'

'How would I know?' Ellie aimed for a light tone, and knew she'd missed. 'No sign of Midge? He'll find his own way in, I suppose. Goodnight, Rose. Sleep well.'

'God bless.'

Rose checked that the front door was double-locked while Ellie took the front stairs, dragging herself up by the banister. There was still no sign of Midge. She went along the corridor to her own dear room, had a quick shower and dropped into bed. She'd left her door and her bedroom window open a little way in case Midge decided to come in, and a light breeze was perhaps making the room a little too cool.

She humped herself under the duvet. To her pleasure she heard Midge plop down into the room and jump up on to the bed. He started to give himself a good wash, and then froze. So did Ellie.

The sound of glass breaking? She knew that sound, a sound that every householder dreads. It might be nothing worse than a window swinging wide in the breeze, or a stone thrown up from the street. Or a football from lads playing where they ought not to be. But the breeze wasn't strong enough to stir the curtains, never mind slam a window shut; she was on the far side of the road from the street, and what boys in their right mind would be playing football at this hour of the night?

Besides which, it had sounded curiously muffled. Perhaps the noise had come from next door? But the houses here were all detached. Mrs Goss's house was only three doors away.

Ellie thought about that and sat up in bed. She looked at Midge, who had suspended his grooming with one hind leg pointing to the ceiling. Midge was staring at the door. Midge thought there was something wrong. So did Ellie.

A nasty thought. If the boy Mick had been in the back of Madam's car on Friday evening, then he'd have known not only that her little house was empty, but also where she'd been going. Three doors away from his aunt.

Madam had said Mick had gone and she didn't know where he was. Looking back on that conversation, Ellie wasn't a hundred per cent convinced that Madam had told the truth. Madam had asked for twenty-four hours before she went to the police. Suppose Mick was really still at his aunt's?

Ellie got out of bed, found her handbag and fingered her mobile phone.

No, no. She couldn't ring the police on the off-chance that someone might have tried to break into the house. Definitely not. Except that Midge had lowered his hind leg and was preparing to jump off the bed. Of course, he might be going to find some other place to sleep tonight. He did do that, sometimes.

Another thought struck; if some glass had been broken somewhere in this big house, then perhaps Rose had heard it, too. If she had, then Ellie would certainly phone for the police. Rose's quarters were on the far side of the landing. Perhaps Ellie could just check on Rose, see if she were all right?

On the other hand, she could go back to bed and pretend she hadn't heard anything. Midge was in stalking mode, making for the bedroom door, putting his paws down deliberately, one by one. Was he growling? Oh dear.

Ellie put on her slippers and dressing gown, and looked around for a weapon. She told herself she was being unnecessarily alarmist, but could see nothing in her bedroom to help her fend off a burglar especially — and here she had to take a firm hold of her courage — if the burglar had a savage dog in tow.

For a moment she wavered. She could lock herself in her bathroom and be safe. She could remember only too vividly the crunch of the dog as it bit into the back of her leg, all those years ago. Would she ever be able to forget it? But could she leave Rose defenceless and alone, if there really were a burglar in the house?

How long did she stand there, paralyzed by fear? Midge eased the door further open with his paw and disappeared. He was a lot braver than she.

She could hear nothing amiss. She had imagined the crash of breaking glass. She could go back to bed with a clear conscience. Or move out on to the landing and listen for untoward noises in the night.

There was a moon and it threw bright oblongs of light across the landing. Her throat was dry. Could she hear movement on the ground floor? Yes, she could. Also a light was bobbing around in the sitting room. Now came the clink of objects being removed. In her mind's eye, she checked over the valuable contents of the room below. The clock on the mantelpiece? Some pieces of silver?

She would ring the police now, but first she must put a locked door between her and the burglar. The door of her own bedroom had no lock on it, but she knew that her aunt's bathroom did.

The cleaners had been at work in the master bedroom. It smelt fresh, free of medications. The bars of moonlight made the room appear even larger than usual. Patches of ghostly light gleamed from the old-fashioned silver-backed hairbrushes on the dressing table, and from the silver handle of her aunt's walking stick, which had been left propped up against Miss Quicke's high-backed chair.

A walking stick wasn't much defence against a large, savage dog, of course. In her imagination, the dog would take the stick and worry at it, perhaps snap it in two. But it was something for her to hold on to.

Where was Midge? Oh dear, what was he up to?

First things first. She held her mobile phone up to the moonlight to locate the emergency number. The landing light went on, bright, too bright, and someone screamed. Ellie tore out of her aunt's room to see Rose standing in the doorway to her quarters, with one hand on the light switch, and the other holding an old-fashioned poker. So Rose had been disturbed, too?

A low growl drew her horrified eyes downwards. Up the stairs came a youngish lad, towed by a large, brown and white dog, a pit bull, with red lights in his eyes. The dog was straining at his lead, his claws clicking on the bare stairs, his eyes fixed on Rose.

The lad had a large torch in his left hand and a bulging satchel over his shoulder. 'Kill, Toby. Kill!' He let go of the dog's lead.

Ellie screamed. Both dog and intruder turned to look her way. The dog wavered, not knowing which target to choose.

Rose screamed again, but Ellie was closer.

The dog changed direction, launched himself at her. Ellie dropped her phone, putting both hands around the stick in an effort to fend off the monster.

She couldn't run, there was no time, and anyway, he could run faster.

She was trapped.

In slow motion she saw the dog taking the last few stairs, gathering itself together to leap at her, and in her ears she could hear the echo and reecho as she and Rose screamed together.

From nowhere came an alien cat, twice as large as Midge, with claws out, a yowl distending its throat, defending its territory. The dog, taken aback, lost concentration, wavered for a moment.

'Kill!' screamed the lad, halfway up the stairs.

The dog leaped for Ellie's throat, but his momentary hesitation was fatal, for his leap did not take him as high as intended.

Ellie had been holding the stick out before her with some idea of using it to keep the dog at arm's length.

The end of the stick entered the dog's open mouth. Ellie felt the shock right up her arms and shoulders. It threw her back against the wall as the impetus of the dog's leap forced him on and on.

Ellie could feel the monster's breath, hear the sounds of agony he made, the cough, the attempt to dislodge the impediment in his throat.

She held on to the stick with both hands, that sturdy stick which had been Aunt Drusilla's helpmeet for so many years.

The dog squirmed and flailed around, but could not release itself, wrenching to the right, and then to the left, shuddering. Ellie lost her hold on the stick and in his dying throes, the dog turned back on itself, and toppled back down the staircase, that slippery wide wooden staircase, colliding with his master and taking him down, too, bumping down with him.

Rose was still screaming. So, she discovered, was Ellie. And crying, too.

The lad finally came to rest with his head on the floor and the dog pinning him to the ground. He was howling with pain because the dog had landed full on him. There was blood and flecks of foam everywhere.

Ellie closed her eyes and slid to the ground.

Rose went on screaming. Even after she'd stopped, the house seemed to echo with her screams.

'Help me!' cried the boy, trying to get out from under the dog's still writhing body.

Ellie groped for her phone, found it and rang for the police and an ambulance.

* * *

In his fall, the dog had broken Mick's pelvis. The dog lived until a police marksman was called to put it out of its misery. The satchel Mick had been carrying over his shoulder contained, among other items, Ellie's jewellery and clock, the key to Mrs Goss's Range Rover, her credit cards and her jewellery.

Mrs Goss was still alive when they got to her, but died that morning. Later that day the boy Tod rang Ellie to say that it was a Mrs Goss who had signed Mick into the youth club.

During their investigation, the police discovered that Mick had climbed over the high gate that led to the kitchen quarters at the back of the big old house and then unbolted the gate to let the dog through. Once in the back garden, he'd smashed in a window to the disused morning room directly below the room in which Ellie slept.

Rose had been disturbed by the sound of the bolts being withdrawn on the gate, which lay under her own bedroom at the side of the house. Mick had got it wrong, twice.

Mick wept, not for himself, but for the loss of Toby. He only left hospital in a wheelchair. His destination, a young offenders' institution.

* * *

After the funeral, Ellie found herself acting as hostess for the reception, which was held, naturally, in the house in which Miss Quicke had been born and in which she had died.

Ellie tried to have a word with everybody, with the people who came from church, and with all the tradespeople Miss Quicke had patronized. There was also a well-dressed contingent from the city, who tended to congregate in the dining room nearest the food and drink. Tycoon to decorator, they responded well to being asked about themselves.

Roy held sway in one room and Diana in the other. Both glittered with excitement, and were of little assistance when it came to looking after the guests.

Ellie's head ached with trying to retain all the information she was given, but she felt it was worth the effort. Miss Quicke might have been a tartar in her lifetime but she'd also been something of a Midas figure, turning everything she touched to gold. Stories of her acerbic wit were being handed around as freely as the glasses of wine.

Kate was there, dressed in her city gear instead of sloppy suburban wear. Kate knew a lot of these people, and Ellie was pleased to see that she was treated with respect. Kate had left the children with her husband, who'd taken the day off school to look after them.

Felicity was also there, having entrusted baby Mel to her new friend Caroline for the morning. 'I've never been parted from her for so many hours before. I do hope Gunnar isn't going to take for ever to read the will when everyone's gone.'

Gunnar was holding court in front of the fireplace, as usual. He seemed to gravitate towards fireplaces, and however large and imposing they happened to be, he dominated them. Perhaps, thought Ellie, he should be painted in oils, standing in front of a marble fireplace, with a glass of Madeira in his hand, and only crumbs on his plate to show where he'd done justice to the buffet. Maria's waitresses circulated, keeping everyone well fed. The hubbub proclaimed that everyone was having a good time, which was just as Miss Quicke would have wanted it.

Thomas had been there, but had left early for some reason. Ellie had tried to avoid him, but he'd cornered her in the sitting room to say that he was on his way to visit Mae, who was still pretty shaken and afraid to leave her house, but that there was some good news as Leona had decided to apply for her murdered sister's flat and keep the boy in with her family. He didn't ask when he could see Ellie again, and she didn't suggest it herself, even though it was on the tip of her tongue to do so.

Rose was there. Rose wasn't supposed to be working, but somehow whenever there was a problem — a shortage of milk for the coffee, a sausage roll slipping on to the floor — Rose was there, dealing with it.

Stewart was doing his bit, too, talking to every one of Miss Quicke's contacts in her housing empire, never drawing attention to himself but saying and doing the right thing. He must be anxious about his job, but he didn't allow his anxiety to interfere with good manners.

Eventually Ellie found herself in the hall bidding goodbye to everyone; to the city folk, to the builders and decorators and plumbers and electricians that Miss Quicke had used in her lifetime, and to the people who'd only come to know the old lady in later years through church.

It was only then, talking to her old friend, the doyenne of the flower arranging classes, the massive Mrs Dawes, that

Ellie learned that the news about Thomas leaving was already out. '. . . Though we hope he won't go far, because we've got used to him sorting things out around here. Of course we know that when a vicar leaves, it's traditional that he moves out of the parish but luckily, leaving the parish doesn't mean he'll be leaving the neighbourhood.'

Ellie looked her surprise, and Mrs Dawes gave her a knowing smile. 'The parish boundary, my dear Ellie, stops short at the Avenue. Your aunt ought by rights to have attended the church down by the river, but there, she was always one to go her own way, and attending a church in a different parish was no barrier to one of her calibre. We shall miss her.'

'Yes, indeed,' said Ellie, her mind whirling. Did this mean what she thought it meant? Had Mrs Dawes been hinting that Ellie and Thomas could . . . ? She couldn't follow this thought through, while so much else was going on around her.

As the front door closed on the last of the guests Gunnar led Miss Quicke's family and friends to the sitting room, which the waitresses were in the process of clearing, and said it was time to talk business. The waitresses faded away, carrying the last of the food with them.

Stewart seated himself at the back of the room, only his tightly clenched hands betraying his fear for the future. Rose hovered till Gunnar waved her to a small chair to one side. Diana took the carved high-backed chair by the window, spreading her hands over its arms as if to claim it for herself. Felicity and Roy seated themselves on the settee, Felicity patting her husband's knee and Roy swallowing, firming his jaw.

Ellie found herself in her aunt's old chair, and surprise! Little Frank appeared at her side, and scrambled on to her knee. 'Mummy says I'm not going back to my old school and I've told all my friends there that I won't be seeing them again because I'm going to be so rich that I'm only going to be playing with boys who live in big houses in future. Mummy says I'm going to a really good school next term, where they play rugby and not soccer, and we're going to Disneyland next week!'

Ellie blinked. What dream was this? Was Diana thinking of sending him to a private school, costing maybe twenty thousand a year? And Disneyland? Paris or Florida? Either way, what about Diana's job? Or . . . sinking feeling . . . was Diana thinking of giving up her job? Was she so sure of a large inheritance?

Gunnar wafted yet another glass of Madeira under his nose before suggesting that they all settle down, as he didn't intend to read through the whole twenty pages of the will, but would summarize. Young Mark Hadley appeared at his side, opening a briefcase from which he extracted a number of envelopes.

Without looking at him, Gunnar held out his left hand in Mark Hadley's direction, and an envelope was duly placed in it.

'Before I begin, I should explain that I am Miss Quicke's sole executor, having known her for many years,' said Gunnar. 'During that time she made various wills leaving her estate to charity but of recent years she decided to make some provision for those of her family and friends close to her. To each of you now present, she has written a note explaining the reason for her decision, but she asked me to read them aloud so that everyone could hear what was in them. Is that clear?'

Everyone nodded.

Gunnar opened the first envelope and read out the note within.

'The first note is to Stewart, to whom she has left £20,000 . . .'

There was a ripple of surprise, which Gunnar quickly hushed. Stewart's mouth dropped open. He hadn't been expecting this. '"To Stewart. You have been a good and faithful servant. I give you £20,000 to spend as you wish, and a good reference if you decide to look for another job. I cannot control the future, but if my wishes are worth anything, I trust you will continue to be employed." Understood, Stewart?'

Stewart nodded, cleared his throat, and accepted the envelope. His eyes were shiny. Diana remarked, 'He'll be looking for another job if I have anything to do with it.'

Gunnar raised his eyebrows and extended his hand, into which Mark placed a second envelope. '"To my dear friend and housekeeper, Rose. You have made all the difference in the world to my last few years. Besides the flat and your annuity already gifted, I leave you £20,000 in the faint hope that you will spend it on yourself and not on your family. Either way, it is yours to do what you wish with."'

'All that?' gasped Diana. 'Well!'

'I might add,' said Gunnar, 'that if any of you challenges an item in the will, your own share will be forfeit. Also,' and here he smoothed out a smile, 'I insisted on her including a clause to the effect that if any one of you refuses their inheritance, the whole lot goes to the People's Dispensary for Sick Animals. All of it. Is that clear? Rose, my dear, no need to weep.'

Rose wiped across her eyelids with her palms. 'I'm crying for myself, who've lost a good friend.'

'Humph!' said Diana, but said no more.

'Little Frank,' said Gunnar, opening another envelope. 'Well, my lad, I'm not sure that you're going to understand this till you grow up, but may I say that your great-great-aunt considered what she should do for you most carefully. "Little Frank, I am leaving you £200 to spend on toys, but nothing else, in trust or otherwise—"'

Diana half rose from her chair, exclaiming, '*What?*'

'"—because I believe that everyone should have to earn their living, as I had to earn mine. Your loving great-great-aunt."'

'What does that mean?' asked Frank, frowning. 'I am going to be rich, aren't I?'

'It's all right, Frank,' said his mother, agitated. 'It means my share will be all the bigger.'

Gunnar handed Frank the envelope, which he refused to take, turning his face into Ellie's jacket. Gunnar shrugged, and opened another envelope. '"To my dear son Roy, you have brought great joy into my life since you came to find me. My giving you up for adoption was my loss, and your gain. You have a beautiful wife, a lovely child and a flair for your profession. These should be more than enough to bring you happiness so I will not burden you with great wealth as well, because you are not best fitted to deal with it. Instead, I leave you the freehold of Minster Court, with the recommendation that you never sell any of the flats, but consider them as providing you with a stable income."'

Gunnar lowered the paper. 'I believe there are twenty-four flats in that block, which bring in a sizeable income per annum, particularly if they are well managed, as they have been under Stewart's eye.'

'I see,' said Roy, letting out a long breath, and trying to disguise his disappointment. 'I think I understand. Felicity, she's right, of course. Finance is not my thing. I didn't really expect her to leave me anything. She was a very wise woman.'

Felicity kissed his cheek and he put his arm around her, smiling bravely.

Diana stood up and punched the air. 'So it's all mine! Yes!'

Gunnar gave a little cough, holding out his hand for another envelope. 'I haven't finished yet. "To my great-niece Diana. I leave you the sum of £50,000 in the hope that you will learn before it is too late that blood is thicker than water."'

'*What?*' Diana couldn't take it in. 'If I don't get the money, then who does? You mean she's left it all to charity? I don't understand!'

'Not so,' said Gunnar, opening the last envelope. 'To my dear niece Ellie Quicke, who is my residual legatee, I leave my love and my deep respect."'

'And that's it?' Diana was open-mouthed. '*My mother gets everything?*'

'Surely not,' said Ellie, even as Gunnar handed her that one last envelope. 'There must be some mistake. I don't want it. I never wanted it. She *knew* I didn't want it.'

Gunnar inclined his head. 'That is why. She suggested various options you might like to follow, such as—'

'Giving it to me?' said Diana, feverishly holding out her hands.

'Such as turning your inheritance over to the charitable trust you established when you inherited some money from your husband some years ago. In which case, the number of trustees may need to be expanded to deal with the extra work. Your aunt had one or two names to suggest of people who might be useful to you in this respect. You will need someone with a business head to deal with the portfolio, for instance, but we will speak more about that at a later date.'

'No, no!' said Ellie. 'I can't, I won't accept it!'

'I'm afraid you must,' said Gunnar. 'You remember I told you there was a clause in the will saying that if one of you doesn't accept his or her inheritance, then you all lose out to charity?'

There was a considerable silence before Stewart began to laugh. He stood up, clapping his hands. 'I accept. It couldn't happen to a nicer person than you, Mother-in-Law.'

Rose was smiling. 'I accept, too. Anyone like a cuppa?'

Roy also stood, his arm about Felicity. 'I accept. Ellie, my mother was wiser than all of us. I thoroughly approve of her choice.'

Gunnar said, 'Well, Diana? Do you and your son accept what's been left to you? Or agree to forego your £50,000?'

'I can't bear it!' Diana strode about the room, wrenching at her hands. 'Fifty thousand! A pittance.'

'It's enough for a trip to Disneyland and a couple of years of private schooling,' said Gunnar.

'I don't understand,' said Frank. 'What's happening? Aren't I going to be rich?'

Diana held on to her head with both hands. 'Fifty thousand! I must have a new car, and then I suppose we could afford to employ someone else in the office . . .'

Frank slid off Ellie's lap. 'I *am* going to play with rich boys, aren't I?'

She brushed him aside. 'No, no. That's all out of the question, now.'

He reached up to her. 'But we are going to Disneyland? You promised!'

'Another time, perhaps. This has changed everything. I'd better ring the office, tell them what's happened.'

All the colour left Frank's face. He didn't weep, but burst out with words formed in months and years of frustration. 'You're always breaking your promises. You keep on saying we'll do something, and then we don't! You said we could go to Alton Towers, and then we didn't! I've told everyone I'm going to a better school and I'm going to Disney, and now you say I'm not! You're always letting me down. I hate you!'

He ran out of the room, leaving everyone in a state of suspended animation. For once Diana had run out of excuses. She looked shocked.

Stewart said quietly, but meaning it, 'Diana, he's right. Half the time you arrange to have him at weekends, and cancel at the last minute. He doesn't know whether he's coming or going. You always put your own convenience first.'

'I have to earn a living for both of us.'

'I'm still paying for his maintenance, he lives with us from Monday to Friday, so that excuse doesn't wash.'

'He's my son. I love him.'

'Prove it. Go after him now. Reassure him. He's one very hurt little boy.'

'I . . . what would I say?' Her hands twisted. Was she really upset? How much did she really love her son?

Ellie began to pray, *Lord, have pity on her. Give her the right words to say. Don't let her lose Frank. He's the only good thing in her life.*

Stewart put his arm around her and urged her towards the door. Perhaps this was the first time he'd touched her since she walked out on him years ago, but Stewart had grown a lot since then. Like Roy, he'd found happiness in a second marriage and like Roy, his masculinity had been confirmed by the production of other children.

'Go to him,' said Stewart. 'Give him a cuddle. Try to explain how difficult things are for you, but say — and you must mean it — that in future it's going to be different, that when you make a promise to him in future, it will be kept.

Because if you don't, I swear to you I'll ask the courts to give him to me for good.'

She was actually in tears. 'I don't want to lose him. He's all I've got.' She took a couple of paces towards the door, hesitated, and then marched out.

Everyone in the room let out a sigh of relief.

'Well done, Stewart,' said Roy, helping Felicity to her feet. 'That poor little tyke. One minute he's a prince, and the next he's a pauper. Come along, Felicity, I know you're anxious to retrieve Mel. My turn to bath her tonight.' He bent down to kiss Ellie's cheek. 'Congratulations, Ellie. As Stewart said, it couldn't have happened to a nicer person.'

Felicity also kissed Ellie, murmuring that she would be in touch on the morrow. Rose went to let them out, saying she wanted to see if the cleaners had put everything to rights and she'd be making a cuppa if anyone wanted it. Stewart said he'd wait in the hall since Diana and Frank were having a heart to heart in the conservatory, and he didn't want to disturb them.

Mark Hadley shut up his briefcase, and said he'd drive Gunnar back when he was ready. Gunnar took Ellie's hand, and kissed it. Only Gunnar could do that without making it look theatrical.

'Dear lady, when you've got over the shock, I suggest we set up a meeting to discuss the future. You will keep Stewart on, I suppose? Yes? Good, good. Now, where am I supposed to be now, Mark?'

'Back to the office, and then you have a committee meeting at eight.'

'So I have. You see, Ellie, everyone needs someone to look after them. Even my dear Drusilla did, at times. Ring me any time you experience a difficulty.'

He wafted himself away and Ellie sat on, trying to work out if she felt more stunned or frightened. Or did she, perhaps, feel a little excited? Yes, there was a thread of excitement there.

She heard Stewart in the hall, talking to Diana, telling Frank he could sit in the front of the car going back, but that he must put his seat belt on and not fiddle with the air conditioning. The front door opened and shut.

Rose brought in a small tray containing a pot of tea for one, and a plate of digestive biscuits. Just what Ellie needed.

'Rose, you're going to stay on, aren't you?'

'For as long as you need me, and I'll cook for just as long as he doesn't want to get in the kitchen. He's looked at the oven and says he likes cooking on gas. He said he's not going to have much time in future, but he'd like to keep his hand in.'

So Rose was pushing her towards Thomas, as well. Ellie said, 'Get along with you,' but laughed.

When Rose had gone, Ellie picked up the phone and got through to Thomas. He answered straight away. 'Thomas, where are you?'

'Sitting on the bench outside the church. It's my day off, remember? At least, it ought to have been.'

'Would you like to come over? There's something I want to ask you.'

He clicked the phone off. For a moment she wondered if he was playing hard to get. But no, not Thomas.

She went upstairs and got out of her black clothes, putting on one of the pretty summer dresses and the new sandals she'd bought the previous weekend. She brushed her hair out, pulled a face at herself, told herself not to get too excited. He might not want to play the game she had in mind. She hoped she was doing the right thing. She sent up an arrow prayer, *Lord, please tell me the right words to use.*

She was descending the stairs when he arrived and rang the bell. She let him in, calling out to Rose that it was 'only' Thomas.

'Well?' he asked, keeping his hands by his side.

She put her hand over the locket he'd given her at Christmas. 'Would you like to give me a photo of yourself to put in my locket?'

His grin was as wide as the ocean. 'Anything else?'

'Will you marry me?'

'I thought you'd never ask.'

The next few minutes were highly satisfactory.

Finally she extricated herself long enough to tow him into the sitting room, where they made themselves comfortable on the settee.

Thomas put his arm around her. 'Am I marrying a billionairess, or a comparatively wealthy widow?'

'Oh, that. Aunt Drusilla did leave me her money, but it's going to be tied up so tightly that neither you nor I will be able to squander it on trifles. It will all go into the trust, and I'm to get some businesspeople to look after it, and we'll have to go cap in hand if we want to spend more than you earn. Gunnar will help me sort it out.'

'Good. I'm not marrying you for your money, and I don't want to sit on your trust or influence you in any way. You do know that, don't you?' He was good at this kissing lark. It was surprising how well her curves fitted into his.

'Ground rules,' she said, trying to be sensible. 'You don't want me to be your secretary or assistant in your new job, do you?'

'Perish the thought. You are such a busy woman, I'll probably have to fight my way through your family and friends to snatch a meal with you now and then.'

She suppressed a giggle. 'It's not as bad as that, surely.'

'It's every bit as bad as that.'

'You're one to talk. By the way, have you any idea where we should live?'

He was guarded. 'Much as I liked your old house, it was perhaps a trifle on the small side.'

'And currently uninhabitable. I was thinking that I might make it over to Diana to put right and live in. It would be much nicer for little Frank to visit her there, and she could then sell her flat, which would help her finances. That is, if you agree?'

'It's nothing to do with me. So, where do you suggest we live?'

He was teasing her. He knew as well as she where they would end up. 'I suppose we could live here, if you like. I've just heard that it's outside the parish, so that wouldn't be a problem. I don't know how many rooms you'd need for your work, but the morning room and the study here are neither of them being used at the moment. I suggest that you take the morning room for your magazine work, and I use the study for my charity affairs. Then there's the library, which you might like to keep as your den.'

'Exactly what your aunt suggested.'

'She knew?'

'Did you ever try keeping anything from your aunt? Of course she knew. She also suggested that — with the exception of Rose, who thoroughly approves, by the way — we keep our engagement quiet. I propose that the day after I leave the parish we get married quietly and go away on honeymoon, returning as an old married couple. Would you like to keep your own name? Ellie Quicke. Why not?'

She liked the idea. 'Do I have to promise to obey?'

He rolled his eyes. 'You never have yet, and although I firmly believe in miracles, I don't expect this to be one of them. You are one very independent, capable woman, Ellie Quicke.'

She was astonished. 'Gracious, am I?'

'Yes, you are.'

She couldn't think how he'd come by such an extraordinary idea of her character, but decided to let it pass. After all, he was the wisest person she knew so perhaps, in time, she'd become the strong person he thought she was. As her mother had always said, never reject a compliment.

Now, what should she wear to get married in?

THE END

THE JOFFE BOOKS STORY

We began in 2014 when Jasper agreed to publish his mum's much-rejected romance novel and it became a bestseller.

Since then we've grown into the largest independent publisher in the UK. We're extremely proud to publish some of the very best writers in the world, including Joy Ellis, Faith Martin, Caro Ramsay, Helen Forrester, Simon Brett and Robert Goddard. Everyone at Joffe Books loves reading and we never forget that it all begins with the magic of an author telling a story.

We are proud to publish talented first-time authors, as well as established writers whose books we love introducing to a new generation of readers.

We won Trade Publisher of the Year at the Independent Publishing Awards in 2023. We have been shortlisted for Independent Publisher of the Year at the British Book Awards for the last four years, and were shortlisted for the Diversity and Inclusivity Award at the 2022 Independent Publishing Awards. In 2023 we were shortlisted for Publisher of the Year at the RNA Industry Awards.

We built this company with your help, and we love to hear from you, so please email us about absolutely anything bookish at feedback@joffebooks.com

If you want to receive free books every Friday and hear about all our new releases, join our mailing list: www.joffebooks.com/contact

And when you tell your friends about us, just remember: it's pronounced Joffe as in coffee or toffee!

ALSO BY VERONICA HELEY

THE ELLIE QUICKE MYSTERIES

Book 1: MURDER AT THE ALTAR
Book 2: MURDER BY POISON PEN
Book 3: MURDER OF INNOCENCE
Book 4: MURDER BY ACCIDENT
Book 5: MURDER IN THE GARDEN
Book 6: MURDER BY COMMITTEE
Book 7: MURDER BY BICYCLE
Book 8: MURDER OF IDENTITY
Book 9: MURDER IN THE PARK

THE BEA ABBOT AGENCY MYSTERIES

Book 1: A FALSE CHARITY
Book 2: A FALSE PICTURE
Book 3: A FALSE STEP
Book 4: A FALSE PRETENCE
Book 5: FALSE MONEY
Book 6: A FALSE REPORT
Book 7: A FALSE ALARM
Book 8: A FALSE DIAMOND
Book 9: A FALSE IMPRESSION
Book 10: A FALSE WALL
Book 11: A FALSE FIRE
Book 12: A FALSE PRIDE
Book 13: A FALSE ACCOUNT
Book 14: A FALSE CONCLUSION
Book 15: A FALSE FACE

Printed in Great Britain
by Amazon

39482030R00148